"Holt fills the pages with lovers' angst, loving embraces, and plenty of conflict to ensure that the road to happily ever after isn't smooth . . . Holt truly has another winner on her hands . . . [an] utterly romantic story of love in the most unexpected of places."

—*Fallen Angel Reviews*

"An entertaining read. The pages are filled with deceit, debauchery, romance, heartache, and lust . . . the characters are interesting with a lot of depth to them."

—*Joyfully Reviewed*

"The passion . . . is hot enough to singe the fingers . . . a pleasing tale."

—*Romance Reviews Today*

"Captures the reader from the first scene . . . Holt weaves this erotic romance like a master . . . an enjoyable afternoon read."

—*Romance Divas*

"A delightful historical with a slight twist."

—*Midwest Book Review*

FURTHER THAN PASSION

"Fantastic . . . a keeper . . . Holt has finely tuned the art of delving into secret fantasies and drawing out what women want. In this deliciously sensual story, she keeps readers glued to the pages by infusing every one with plenty of sizzle. Very sensual."

—*Romantic Times* (starred review)

MORE THAN SEDUCTION

"Fantastic . . . a keeper . . . Holt demonstrates why she's a grand mistress at keeping sensuality at a high boil in her latest and most tempting romance. She adds depth to this sensual tale with her mature characters, a touch of poignancy, and a strong plot. Holt truly understands what readers crave."

—*Romantic Times*

"Hang onto your hats! Cheryl Holt gives you hot romance with characters you love and admire in all her books, but I think she outdid herself with her latest book. To me it's her best work yet. It's a winning story you can't read fast enough. Excellent, stirring, steamy, and so darn good you just about melt in a puddle of desire if you aren't careful. Cheryl Holt is magnificent once again. I wonder what she will do next? I can hardly wait!"

—*Reader to Reader Reviews*

"*More Than Seduction* is another winner for Cheryl Holt. This book pulls you in and you won't be able to put it down. The sexual tension is extreme and the love scenes are blazing hot. This is definitely a keeper."

—*The Romance Studio*

"An enticing story, rich with sensuality . . . a tantalizing read."

—*Romance Reviews Today*

"A tempting treat."

—*Romance Junkies*

DEEPER THAN DESIRE

"Just about the best writer of erotic romance that we've got."
—*Statesman Journal* (Salem, Oregon)

"Sexy, titillating love story . . . add some suspense, abductions, a mad villain, and an exciting climax and you have all you need in an erotic romance."
—*Romantic Times*

"A jewel . . . intriguing, compelling, and passionate."
—*Old Book Barn Gazette*

"The thing that I like best about Cheryl Holt's writing is that she makes her characters come alive as their stories unfold. You get mad, glad, sad, and sexy as the devil while reading her glorious books that not only are well-written erotic stories but have substance and a good storyline concerning the characters' lives that make them human and realistic. Now this is a writer to watch because she is going places. Ms. Holt delivers stories that you love reading. They are hot and spicy . . . filled with compelling characters that set your heart to racing with her imaginative and titillating storytelling."
—ReaderToReader.com

"An intricate tapestry of intriguing characters."
—Romancereaderatheart.com

"Romance fans will enjoy this erotic tale of forbidden love that feels and is right. Holt turns up the heat with this superior historical."
—TheBestReviews.com

SECRET FANTASY

CHERYL HOLT

St. Martin's Paperbacks

This is a work of fiction. All of the characters, organizations, and events portrayed in this novel are either products of the author's imagination or are used fictitiously.

SECRET FANTASY

Copyright © 2007 by Cheryl Holt.

Cover photo © Shirley Green

ISBN: 0-312-94254-0
EAN: 978-0-312-94254-0

Printed in the United States of America

St. Martin's Paperbacks edition / March 2007

St. Martin's Paperbacks are published by St. Martin's Press, 175 Fifth Avenue, New York, NY 10010.

10 9 8 7 6 5 4 3 2 1

CHAPTER ONE

Rural Sussex, England, 1812 . . .

Y ou have a visitor."

"Who?"

Margaret Gray removed her bonnet and hung it on the hook by the door. She'd spent the day at the school she'd started in an abandoned cottage at the edge of the property. After walking home in the bright May sunshine, she blinked several times, her vision adjusting to the dim foyer.

"I don't know who it is," her cousin, sixteen-year-old Penelope Gray, sneered.

"Is it a man or a woman?"

"A man."

At relaying the peculiar and somewhat frightening news Penelope was rippling with a cruel curiosity, eager to view Margaret's reaction, so Margaret concealed any piqued interest. After suffering through years of Penelope's malicious gossip and petty slights, Margaret was an expert at pretending not to care what the horrid child said or did.

Margaret frowned. "Why would he wish to see me?"

"I was eavesdropping. I heard he's a suitor, and he's considering marrying you. He's come to discuss it with Lavinia!"

Lavinia was Penelope's mother, but there was little affection between the two, and Penelope referred to her mother by her Christian name. They had a tempestuous relationship that resembled battling siblings, and Margaret had spent her entire life caught between them as they fought like cats trapped in a sack.

"He's investigating a marriage to *me*?" At the ludicrous idea Margaret scoffed. "You can't be serious."

"You think I'm lying?"

"No. You had to have misunderstood."

"Hah! The butler specifically said the man plans to meet *Miss Gray*."

Margaret's alarm calmed significantly. "Penelope *Gray*, he's here to meet *you*."

Penelope gasped. "Me!"

"Yes, you. Why would you automatically assume the butler meant me?"

"Lavinia would never contemplate a match without mentioning it to me."

"Wouldn't she?"

"No, she wouldn't, Miss Know-It-All." She turned toward the small mirror hanging behind her and primped her perfect curls. "Besides, you're aware that I'm off to London for the Season. I'm to find my husband in town—after I've made all the other girls green with envy."

"Maybe Lavinia decided to save her money and cut to the chase. She continually harangues about the cost. Perhaps she's skipped the middle part of the process and jumped straight to the end."

"She wouldn't do it without telling me!" Penelope insisted.

Staving off a full-blown argument, Margaret held up a hand. "Fine. I'm sure you're correct."

"Of course, I am. I'm always right."

"Yes, you are."

"You're just jealous that I'm going to London and not you."

"Absolutely."

"You hate it that I'm rich, and you're not," Penelope charged.

"I'm completely devastated by the fact."

"You're poor, and you're old."

"I am. I am. I'm twenty-five and positively decrepit. I haven't two farthings to rub together." In a dramatic gesture, Margaret laid a wrist on her forehead. "Oh, woe is me!"

Penelope glowered, trying to discern if Margaret was being sarcastic, and Margaret struggled to keep from laughing. She'd sat through hundreds of conversations about Penelope's debut, and she was sick of the calculating. Penelope's departure for London was six weeks away, and in the interim, the prospects for incessant marital plotting were maddening.

"You can joke all you want," Penelope sniped. "Let's see who marries first, shall we?"

"There's no doubt it will be you and that you'll be fabulously happy."

Margaret had no illusions. Though she would love to have a home and family of her own, it would never happen. She was an orphan who'd come to live with her uncle Horatio when she was only six. After his death, her aunt Lavinia had allowed her to stay on, but as Lavinia constantly stated, Margaret subsisted on Lavinia's charity.

Marriage would never be a possibility.

Penelope spun to go, cackling like a witch as she stomped out, declaring, "You and your suitor will have a lot in common. He's old, too, and ugly as a crone. And he's a murderer!"

Margaret sighed.

With her blond hair and blue eyes, her petite height and rounded figure, Penelope was very fetching, but it was sad that so much spite could be contained in such a pretty package. She could be charming and gay, but also ruthless and intolerable. In many ways, she was Lavinia's twin.

Margaret was tired of both women, and she would give anything to move away and start over in a new place. She wished fairy tales were real, that she could swallow a magic potion and be altered into a different person with a different life.

Her mind racing, she walked to the servants' stairs and tiptoed to her room. She was certain that Penelope had been lying about a gentleman caller, but what if Lavinia had actually approached someone?

The notion—of Lavinia selecting Margaret's spouse—was disturbing.

Lavinia kept hinting that they were broke, that after Penelope's *entrée* into Society, there'd be nothing left. For months, she'd been slyly commenting about how she was weary of supporting Margaret, and Margaret had ignored the remarks, but what if Lavinia had been serious? What if she demanded that Margaret wed?

Still, Margaret yearned to marry, so she wouldn't

summarily discount any suggestion from Lavinia. Even if the man was elderly and unattractive, as Penelope claimed, he might be kind and courteous. Most important, as her husband, he would take her away from Gray's Manor, and she would be the mistress of her own home.

Her heart pounding with excitement and trepidation, she went into the dressing room to wash. If Lavinia sent for her, she wanted to look her best.

Evaluating herself in the mirror, she stripped down to chemise and petticoat. She pulled the combs from her hair, and the lengthy mass swooshed down. It was a thick, rich auburn, her eyes a vibrant green, and in a world where everyone was pale and fair, she was a definite oddity.

She was slender, neither tall nor short, and her face had arched brows, a pert nose, and a generous mouth, but after enduring nearly two decades of Lavinia's criticisms, she'd accepted that she was very average. When she noticed herself pining for it to be otherwise—that she be a great beauty with dozens of swains, instead of a lonely, ordinary woman with foibles and flaws—she chuckled at her whimsy.

What was she doing, bared to her undergarments and moping in front of the mirror? She couldn't change who she was.

She proceeded to the washstand, swished a cloth, and was swabbing it across her arms when a male voice murmured, "Very nice."

Scowling, she froze, trying to be sure that she'd really heard a man speak, that it wasn't her imagination.

"Turn around," he said. "Let me see all of you."

There was someone in the room with her! She was

about to whip around and challenge him when she remembered that she was practically naked. She glared over her shoulder, ready to chastise, but she was so stunned that she was speechless.

The man loitering in the threshold was incredibly handsome. He was a few years older than herself, probably thirty or so, and he was tall and muscular, his chest broad, his waist narrow, his legs ridiculously long. His hair was dark, almost black, and his eyes were a shrewd, piercing blue, the color she envisioned the Mediterranean to be.

Obviously, he'd been traveling. His jacket was dusty, his boots scuffed, his hair windblown. He smelled like sweat and horses and another scent that was more subtle, that she suspected was his very essence.

"Who are you," she questioned, "and why are you in my room?"

"Funny," he replied, "but I could have sworn it was *my* room—at least that's what a footman told me a few minutes ago. So I might ask the same: Why are you in here?"

"I am bathing."

"And *I* am watching you."

Margaret was frantic, but secretly thrilled, too. He had to be the mysterious guest Penelope had mentioned, but he was too charismatic, too dynamic, too . . . too . . . everything. He was like a prince in a storybook, like a statue in a museum.

Lavinia didn't have a humane bone in her body, so he couldn't be the man she'd invited to Gray's Manor. She would never have done something so wonderful.

Margaret's dressing room was connected to the adjoining bedchamber, but no one was ever housed there.

Visitors were lodged in the other wing, closer to Lavinia and Penelope.

Who had located him next to Margaret? And why?

Was Lavinia hoping to have Margaret ruined? Was she planning to burst in and *discover* Margaret in a compromising situation? Lavinia must have felt the need to force an encounter, but in light of the man's godlike countenance, why would Lavinia presume that Margaret would hesitate?

What was wrong with him? Was he deranged? Was he a wife-beater? Penelope had said he was a murderer. Whom had he killed? His prior wives?

"You've made a horrible mistake," she advised. "Get out at once."

"I don't think so."

"I must confer with the housekeeper to have you moved. I can't do it while you're standing there."

"Can't you?"

"No."

"Lavinia insisted you were very friendly. Why be shy?"

He was amused by her predicament, and she yearned to strangle him. "I'm not decent—as you can plainly see—and if you were any sort of gentleman, you'd do as I've requested."

"There's the rub," he responded. "I'm not a gentleman and never have been."

He took a step toward her, then another, and she wanted to retreat, but she was trapped in the corner. Short of knocking him down, she couldn't escape.

"Aah!" she shrieked, spinning toward the wall. "Will you go away?"

"No."

He kept coming till he was directly behind her, and she panicked, not certain of what he meant to do. She didn't sense any menace or threat, so she wasn't afraid for her physical safety, but she'd had scant dealings with men, so she couldn't figure out what he intended.

Without warning, he snuggled himself to her backside, his hands on her waist, and the scandalous contact was so marvelous that she worried she might faint. She hadn't known that a man's touch would be so hot, so strong. She actually shivered—not with outrage or shock as she ought, but with complete and utter delight.

"Are you mad?" she sputtered.

"I've frequently heard people say that I am."

So . . . that was why Lavinia had chosen him. He was demented. Lavinia was about to pawn her off on a lunatic!

She elbowed him in the ribs, but the paltry blow had no effect.

"Get out of here before someone stumbles in and sees us."

"I don't care if we're caught. We wouldn't have to make any decisions; they'd be made for us."

His fingers were lean and crafty, and he was caressing them in slow circles, stroking down her flanks, then up again. The motion was so hypnotic that she could scarcely keep from purring like a kitten.

"You smell good," he said.

"Release me this second!"

"No." He was riffling through her hair, assessing weight and texture. "This auburn is such an interesting color. I was so sure you'd be blond."

"I'm sorry to disappoint you."

"You haven't—yet."

"I will eventually."

"I'm positive you're correct." He was resigned, sounding as if he'd been let down so often that he expected the worst from everyone.

He bent down and kissed her shoulder, his teeth nipping at her nape and sending goose bumps down her arms and legs. The soft feel of his mouth on her bare skin was too arousing to be believed. Forgetting her dishabille, she wiggled away and whirled to face him, and he towered over her, his huge, masculine form taking up so much space that she was dizzy and off balance.

"What are you doing?" she demanded.

"Making love to you. Can't you tell?"

She was a sheltered spinster, for pity's sake. How was she supposed to know? "No, I can't *tell*."

"Then I must be out of practice."

Amusement flickered in his expression. He was having great fun at her expense, and she'd had enough of his boorish behavior.

"Get out!" Trying to look stern, she gestured to the door.

"Not quite yet."

"You can't stay in here. Are you deaf?"

"You're very pretty."

To the best of her recollection, no one had ever told her she was pretty before, so she was flabbergasted. It rocked her view of the world where she'd always considered herself middling and—at times—inferior in every way.

He continued to scrutinize her, as if devouring every inch, his blue, blue eyes not missing a single detail.

"Yes, very pretty," he repeated, "but older than I anticipated."

"Older!" she grumbled, hating to be denigrated because of her advanced age. "You are the most rude person I've ever met."

As if she hadn't spoken, he added, "Of course, your maturity might be an advantage. And I can see that you'll enjoy marital romping, which is another benefit, because I'll insist on a lot of it."

"Romping?"

"We're going to lump along just fine. I'm glad Lavinia persuaded me to visit."

He reached out with his finger, and he laid it on her chin, then traced it down her neck and bosom, till he arrived at the lace on the edge of her chemise. For a crazed instant, she thought he would slip under the fabric to fondle her breast, but he didn't.

He dropped his hand and stepped away. Swiftly, his demeanor changed, the seductive lover vanishing. Feet clicking together, he bowed and said, "Miss Gray, I presume?"

"Yes."

"Jordan Prescott, Viscount Romsey, at your service."

"Viscount . . . Romsey?"

"Yes." He leaned nearer and whispered, "But when we're in the throes of passion, you may call me Jordan."

She shoved him away, rattled by how his warm breath tickled her ear. "Your penchant for discourtesy is astounding."

"That's true, but you're no shrinking violet, yourself."

He strolled out, stopping for a last glance at her. He narrowed his focus, evaluating her as if he didn't understand what he was witnessing.

"I'm so amazed," he muttered.

"By what?"

"By Lavinia's opinion that we'd suit. She's right. For once."

He left, the door shutting behind him, and she collapsed onto a chair.

What had just occurred? What did it mean? What did he want?

He'd confirmed—as Penelope had contended—that he'd come to explore a marriage, but it couldn't be. Lavinia never proceeded without having plotted her own gain. If Margaret were to wed the Viscount, what profit could there be to Lavinia?

Margaret paced, trying to make sense of the situation. Her body was in a state of feminine agitation, her mind awhirl and careening between hope and dread.

Jordan Prescott was a gift too spectacular to imagine, a reward too unlikely to be granted, and she had to learn what was really transpiring.

Desperate for answers, she tugged on her clothes, pinned up her hair, and went to find her aunt.

CHAPTER TWO

M argaret rushed down the hall to Lavinia's suite, and since the door was open, she entered without knocking. The outer parlor was empty, but voices emanated from Lavinia's private boudoir.

"What did you think, darling?" Lavinia cooed.

"She was extremely intriguing."

"Didn't I tell you she would be?"

"Yes, but I didn't believe you."

Lavinia and Lord Romsey! Sequestered in Lavinia's bedchamber!

Margaret tiptoed over and peeked through the crack in the door. It was wrong to eavesdrop, but the rest of her life was at stake, so she refused to feel guilty.

Romsey was lounged on a sofa, sipping a brandy and looking bored. He'd removed his coat and rolled back the sleeves of his shirt, which made the tawdry scene unbearably intimate. But then, as she'd already gleaned, he wasn't a stickler for proprieties. With him, any outrageous conduct seemed likely.

Lavinia popped into sight and perched a shapely hip on the arm of the sofa. At age thirty-four, she was still a great beauty, with long blond hair and big blue eyes, a curvaceous figure and flawless features, but her appearance couldn't mask her temper and selfishness.

She was dressed in a flimsy nightgown that barely covered anything that ought to be covered. The neckline plunged dramatically so that much of her bosom was revealed, and her nipples were visible, the dark centers poking at the sheer fabric.

On witnessing the garment Margaret stifled a gasp. Obviously, there was more going on between the couple than Margaret could have imagined.

"What do you mean," Lavinia asked him, "that you didn't believe me?"

"You have no common sense, so I didn't expect what you'd told me about Miss Gray to be true."

Lavinia pursed her lips in an unbecoming pout, which she quickly smoothed away. "Don't be nasty."

"I'm not being *nasty*. I'm simply being candid."

"I said I was sorry about what happened in London."

"I'm sure you were."

They knew each other? From London? Margaret's curiosity spiraled.

"When I crawled into your bed," Lavinia was justifying, "how could I have guessed that you'd bring another woman home with you?"

Lavinia had been in his bed? The admission was the most shocking thing Margaret had ever heard.

"How could you have *guessed,* indeed!" Romsey scoffed. "Why would my mistress of two years be with me?"

"I hadn't planned on creating a scene."

"I disagree. I'm positive it's what you absolutely intended." He toyed with his drink, his loathing of her blatant and impossible to hide. "You never explained what you wanted that night."

"I *wanted* to discuss the marriage."

"You couldn't do it in a letter?"

"At the time, I thought it would be better if we talked it over—personally."

"I'll just bet you did."

Lavinia's voice was unusually sultry, and she trailed a flirtatious finger down his chest, making it clear that she liked him very much, and Margaret wasn't surprised. Lavinia was fascinated by the aristocracy and had always bemoaned the fact that she'd married a rich brewer instead of holding out for a man with a title.

"We can chat about a wedding now," she said, "unless there's another topic that's captivated you." She leaned forward, the front of her nightgown perilously low, giving him an unimpeded view of her breasts.

He wasn't impressed, and he shrugged. "Let's stick with Miss Gray. What should I know about her?"

His indifference incensed Lavinia, and she'd had enough. She stood and stared down at him.

"You're being an ass."

"Yes, I am."

"Go away. I'm sick of you."

She waved toward the door, and when he didn't move, she turned to stomp out. Margaret cowered, terrified that discovery was imminent, and she couldn't defend her spying on them.

Luckily, Lord Romsey saved her by grabbing Lavinia's wrist and drawing her back to the couch. He didn't tug very hard, but Lavinia collapsed down onto him and giggled like a schoolgirl.

"Convince me to offer for her," he urged.

"You know you want to."

"Do I?"

Lavinia was sprawled across him, their chests, loins, and legs pressed together. He was stroking her bottom, rubbing in slow circles, when he'd only recently caressed Margaret in much the same way.

The man was a dog!

"She's young," Lavinia was saying.

"But mature."

"Oh, *very* mature," Lavinia concurred. "She's been too sheltered, though."

"I realize that."

"But that could be a benefit for you."

"I was pondering the very same."

"You could teach her what you'd like her to do. You could make her practice till she gets it right."

"Practice makes perfect," he snickered.

"She'd be too inexperienced to refuse or complain. Isn't that every husband's fantasy?"

"Not mine. I'd rather have a woman who knows what she's doing."

"Liar," Lavinia chided. "You can't fool me. You men all think with your cocks, and you like to plant them between a fresh pair of virginal thighs."

"Too true."

They both chuckled, and Margaret frowned. The statement had a hidden meaning she didn't understand. She felt as if they were speaking in a foreign language.

"I put you in the room next to hers," Lavinia said. "In

case you decide to be swept away by passion, there'll be nothing to prevent you."

"Are you suggesting I sneak in and ravage her?"

"I wouldn't mind—so long as you wed her afterward."

He shuddered in mock horror. "You're cold, Lavinia."

"Why? I aim to ensnare you. I'm happy to do whatever will accomplish my goal."

"Even if it involves an innocent's ruination?"

"Every female has to spread her legs sooner or later. It's not much of a loss for her, but a gain of everything for me."

"That being?"

"A *close* alliance with your family."

"Have you a speck of remorse about any of this?"

"No."

"I'm astounded." He toasted her with his glass. "You're even more of a mercenary than I supposed."

"Why? Merely because I insist on a Grand Match for her?"

"No. Because you'll stop at nothing to get what you want."

"Precisely. Don't you forget it."

"I won't. I shall be completely on guard throughout my visit."

Margaret was furious. They were bartering over her as if she were a prized cow. In light of Lavinia's enthrallment with the nobility, her motives weren't surprising, but Margaret was disgusted by Romsey's blasé approval of violence to coerce Margaret into an untenable union.

How could either of them presume she'd blithely walk down the path they'd engineered? The moment she left Lavinia's boudoir, her initial order of business would be to have a new lock nailed to her door.

"And if I elect to force the matter," Romsey asked, "and I creep into her bed, what should I teach her first?"

Lavinia cocked a brow. "I know what you like. I've heard all about you."

"Have you?"

"Yes."

"Why don't you show me? Let me see if you've heard correctly."

She climbed onto his lap, her knees on the sofa cushion, her thighs draped over his. As they conversed, she was sliding the straps of her nightgown down her arms so that her breasts were bared, the nipples jutting out, and they were directly in his face. Almost reluctantly, he clasped the two mounds and petted the tips with his thumbs.

Margaret was mesmerized. She hadn't known that adults carried on so decadently. She felt as if she'd opened a portal to a secret world, and she couldn't keep herself from watching.

Lavinia purred, arching her back as she riffled her fingers through his lush, dark hair, and she wore a satisfied smile, as if she'd finally enticed him into behaving as she'd wanted all along.

She kissed him on the lips, the embrace going on and on, though Romsey appeared loathe to participate. As it became more heated, her hands were everywhere, touching and exploring, and oddly, Margaret's own anatomy was affected by the spectacle. Her own nipples came to life, growing rigid and poking at her corset. Blood pounded in her veins, her womb shifted and stirred.

Lavinia slipped to the side, and Margaret was desperate to see more, but the sofa blocked the view so she couldn't figure out what Lavinia was doing. It seemed that Lavinia was unbuttoning his trousers, but why would she? And why would Romsey let her?

The encounter was the strangest Margaret had ever witnessed. Lavinia was smug and preening, on fire with lust, but Romsey was impassive and aloof and had scarcely moved. How could one of them be so vain and inflated, while the other was so impervious?

Lavinia glanced up and smirked. "Are you ready, darling? Shall I escort you to paradise?"

"Would it be worth my while?"

"Of course," she declared. "I'm renowned for my prowess."

He was skeptical. "Are you?"

"Definitely."

Lavinia waited, on a precipice of anticipation, as Romsey studied her with no visible emotion. Ultimately, he shook his head.

"I doubt you could impress me, Vinnie"—he used a nickname for Lavinia that Margaret hadn't heard before—"so I believe I'll decline."

"You can't be serious!" Rage mottled Lavinia's cheeks, and she climbed to her feet.

"Oh, but I am. I really don't like you enough to have you go down on me, and considering my offensive habits, that's saying a great deal."

"You are a beast!" she fumed. "I don't know why I put up with you!"

"Maybe because you're eager to have a viscount in the family?"

"I don't want one this badly. You lesser nobles are a penny a dozen."

"Yes, but don't forget my dear father. He won't live forever. Someday, I'll be an earl."

"Bully for you." She yanked at her nightgown and tugged on a robe, pulling the belt tight and hiding what she'd been so keen for him to behold only minutes earlier.

He stood and walked away from the sofa so that Margaret couldn't see him, but Lavinia was bristling with malice. He was humored, and he laughed at her.

"Face it, Vinnie," he taunted. "You're a trollop. You always have been, and you always will be."

"Get out of here!" she bellowed. "And next time you need someone to suck you off, you can beg the house-maids. I'm sure any one of them will be happy to oblige you."

"I'm sure they will."

Margaret recognized it as her cue to sneak away. She hadn't ascertained why Romsey wished to marry her, and she didn't care why. He was a distasteful fiend, and she'd never agree.

Her eye was still pressed to the crack in the door, her hand on the knob, when abruptly, it was jerked open. She lost her balance and stumbled into the room.

Lord Romsey chuckled. "Hello, Miss Gray. How kind of you to join us. We were just talking about you."

With how he was grinning, he had to have been aware of her presence. When had he realized it? She was mortified, and she flushed with shame.

Lavinia whipped around, and she was more irate than Margaret had ever seen her. She stormed over, her anger so evident that Margaret worried Lavinia might strike her when she never had prior.

"Margaret!" she seethed. "What are you doing?"

"I . . . I . . ."

"Margaret?" Romsey gasped and frowned. "Your name is Margaret?"

"Yes," Margaret mumbled.

"You're not Penelope?"

"No, why?"

He was horrified. He assessed her for a charged moment; then he muttered an epithet and stomped across the room to stare out the window.

Lavinia leaned in until she and Margaret were toe-to-toe. Lavinia was only an inch or two taller, but she was so livid that she seemed much bigger. Margaret could detect the tiny age lines around her eyes, the creases around her mouth that she concealed with creams and powders.

"You were eavesdropping," Lavinia accused.

"No, I wasn't," Margaret lied. "I was searching for you. I was about to knock. Penelope said we had a visitor, and I was . . . was . . ."

Romsey butted in. "She's been loitering there and listening to us, practically the whole time."

"You knew, and you didn't tell me?" Lavinia hissed at him.

"She amuses me. I take it she's not your daughter."

"No, she's not my daughter," Lavinia spat. "Why would you presume something so ludicrous?"

Suddenly, she grabbed a fistful of Margaret's hair and wrenched hard enough to make Margaret wince. With her other hand, she seized Margaret's wrist, her nails digging deep, breaking the skin.

"Ow!" Margaret was stunned by the attack and wrestling to free herself.

"Jesus, Lavinia!" Romsey barked. "Are you mad?"

As if to intervene, he rushed over, but before he could assist, Lavinia warned, "You didn't see anything."

"No, I didn't," Margaret agreed.

"You didn't hear anything."

"No."

"If you whisper a word of this to Penelope, I'll kill you, do you understand me?"

"Yes, Lavinia, I understand."

"Get out!"

She pushed Margaret, and Margaret lurched away just as Romsey had reached out to separate them. Margaret glanced over, their gazes locking. He had the decency to appear apologetic, but his paltry concern provided no solace whatsoever.

Margaret had never been more humiliated in her entire life. Praying that she never saw the despicable man again as long as she lived, she turned and ran.

CHAPTER THREE

This is my darling daughter, Miss Penelope Gray."

"Hello, Miss Gray."

"Hello, Lord Romsey."

Jordan forced a smile at the pretty adolescent girl, but he was having trouble exhibiting any courtesy. His fury at Lavinia was palpable, the moment extremely awkward. An uncomfortable silence ensued.

"As I explained, Penelope"—Lavinia was desperate to smooth things over—"Lord Romsey has come specifically to meet you. Isn't that marvelous?"

"Oh, absolutely grand." Penelope's lack of enthusiasm was galling. "Your name is familiar to me. How would I know of it?"

"His father is the Earl of Kettering," Lavinia announced, before Jordan could say a word.

Penelope nodded. "It's more than that, though, isn't it? I've heard of you. Aren't you notorious?"

"Penelope!" Lavinia scolded. "Where are your manners?"

"It's all right, Lavinia," Jordan insisted. He was used

to snide comments, and his answer was to confront them directly. He didn't give two figs what others thought. "We might as well have it out in the open, so that there are no misunderstandings."

Lavinia bristled. "That may be, but I won't permit her to be rude to you."

"I'm not a child, Mother," Penelope sniped.

"You're acting like one."

"What did you do?" Penelope pressed. "I remember that it was something horrid."

In the bland fashion he'd adopted in telling the tale, he said, "Everyone assumes that I killed my older brother so that I could become the heir."

"Did you?" Penelope had the audacity to inquire.

"What do you think?"

Penelope studied him, then shrugged. "I haven't the faintest idea. You certainly appear as if you could be violent."

Jordan laughed. He had to give her credit. Most people were more circumspect. He liked that she was overtly offensive, rather than tittering about him behind his back.

He couldn't claim that he'd loved his dead brother, James, but he'd never wished him ill, either. James had committed suicide, so it had seemed only natural to cover up the true cause. Jordan had acceded to his father's demand for secrecy, circulating a false account of a hunting accident, but neither of them had peered down the road to envision the whispers their furtive deed would generate.

Jordan had been branded a murderer, but he never defended himself against the slander. Others could believe what they wanted about that awful day. He would never dignify their suspicions with a response. If he owed James anything, he owed him privacy as to the details of his squalid death, but it definitely made bridal hunting a chore.

"Lord Romsey was in the army," Lavinia clarified with a great deal of exasperation, "which is the reason for his rough edge. He's a decorated war hero. He's only recently returned to England."

"So what?" Penelope replied. "That doesn't mean he didn't murder his brother."

"For God's sake," Lavinia snapped, "shut up!"

"He asked my opinion!" Penelope complained.

"But he didn't really want it!" Lavinia struggled for calm. "He's going to stay with us for the next month. He's eager to get to know you better."

"Wonderful." Penelope looked as if she were chewing on shards of glass. "May I be excused?"

"Yes," Lavinia said, but an angry glare passed between them. "We'll talk later."

"I can't wait."

Penelope's sarcasm was impossible to conceal, but she made a suitable curtsy and departed, leaving him and Lavinia to fidget in the quiet until her footsteps faded on the stairs. He sighed, cursing his father, cursing his plight, and sick over the fact that Penelope was every bit as young and snotty as he'd predicted she'd be.

She wasn't the first rich girl to cross his path, but she was a prime example of why women shouldn't be allowed to have their own money. It elevated their sense of worth, imbuing them with a superiority they seldom deserved.

"Don't pay any attention to her," Lavinia counseled.

"I didn't."

She waved away Penelope's sour demeanor as if it

were a fetid odor; then she went to the sideboard and poured herself a brandy.

"Would you like one?" she offered.

"No, thank you."

"Do you mind if I indulge?" She chuckled in a sultry, affected way that never ceased to annoy him. "It's a vice, I'm afraid."

"Go ahead."

She sipped away as he gazed out the window into the garden, contemplating the manicured flowers, the trimmed hedges, the thick woods beyond.

He was worried about poor Miss Gray—the other *Miss Gray* whom he'd mistaken for Penelope. How was she faring? What had happened to her?

Lavinia's attack, carried out earlier in her boudoir, had been so unexpected that he hadn't been able to stop it, and he felt completely responsible for the hideous situation.

He wasn't sure when Miss Gray had arrived outside Lavinia's door, but once he'd realized she was there, he'd been curious to discover if she'd dare to watch, so he'd kept on much longer than he should have.

From the moment he'd entered his dressing room and espied her washing, he'd been intrigued. There was just something about her that he liked very much. As he was wife hunting, and in dire need of an heiress as fast as one could be found and bound, he'd been thrilled to have stumbled upon someone so fine.

But he should have known it wouldn't be that easy. Nothing ever was, and with his having met Penelope, he was even more revolted by his pathetic circumstances. When he'd joined the army, he'd owned property and had had hoards of cash in the bank, but due to the shenanigans of his father, he was broke. Who could have imagined that—while Jordan was off, serving his King—the disgraceful spendthrift and scoundrel, Charles Prescott, Earl of Kettering, could have convinced the bankers to transfer it all to him?

While Jordan was soldiering on the Continent, his father had squandered every acre and penny, so that now, Jordan had to chase after the Penelope Grays of the world. With Margaret Gray's identity revealed, he felt cheated, as if Fate had dangled a fantastic prize in front of him, then snatched it away.

He spun and stared at Lavinia. "Penelope didn't seem all that excited."

"I didn't tell her you were coming."

"Why not?"

"She didn't need to know."

"Isn't she aware that you've been discussing her marriage with me?"

"No."

"Why not apprise her?"

"She thinks she's about to have a Season in London," Lavinia explained.

"Not if she marries me. I loathe the city, so we'll rarely be in town."

"Don't fret over it. If you decide you want her, just say so."

"Penelope's view may be a tad different than yours," he warned.

"So? If she puts up a fuss, we'll simply have you ruin her. Then, she won't have any choice in the matter."

He whirled toward the window, reflecting on Penelope, on Margaret Gray.

"How is Miss Gray—the other Miss Gray—related to you?"

"She's Horatio's niece."

"Horatio is your late husband?"

"Yes."

"Has she lived here long?" he queried.

"Fifteen or twenty years."

"She's an orphan?"

"Horatio took her in when she was a child."

"So you've been a sort of mother to her?" Perish the thought! Her maternal instincts left much to be desired.

"No. I have scarcely any bond with her, at all."

"Really?"

"Yes, really," she said coldly. "What do I look like? A nanny for every stray urchin who strolls by?"

"No, hardly that," he murmured.

He started out, but at the last second, he peered over at her. He'd intentionally kept plenty of space between them so he couldn't reach over and throttle her.

"If you assault anyone again while I'm here, I'll leave, and you and your daughter can choke on all her money."

She merely smirked and finished her drink. "We'll see, Jordan. We'll see how badly you want it."

"Yes, we will."

He walked into the hall, continuing till he located an exit onto the rear verandah, and he descended into the garden and proceeded down the path to the woods.

He'd inquired after Margaret Gray, and a footman had advised that she was out for the afternoon, but would be returning shortly, and he was determined to speak with her. He had to ascertain that she was all right, that there were no lingering effects from Lavinia's vile conduct.

If he had another, more personal reason for wanting to see her, he wouldn't mull his motives. He was a man on a mission—that being his need to immediately wed an heiress—so he had no business seeking her out. Still, he couldn't be dissuaded. The unusual female had gotten under his skin, and he couldn't be easily shed of her.

Supposedly, she ran a school for the neighborhood children, and she earned an income by instructing them to read and write. He was bothered and fascinated by the peculiar report.

A working woman! A schoolteacher! Gad, to what was the world coming? When a gently bred female such as Miss Gray had to work for a living, it seemed as if the very fabric of British society was beginning to unravel.

He'd just rounded a bend when she approached. She was wearing a modest green dress, and a fetching straw bonnet with a matching ribbon. Her auburn hair was tucked into a tidy chignon, though several strands had escaped, giving her a rumpled air that he found much too appealing.

On his observing her, his heart did a little flip-flop, which was disturbing. He didn't want to like her, but apparently, he did, and he was sufficiently experienced in male and female relations to grasp how attractions could arise in the strangest places.

He stopped and waited for her to notice him, and when she finally did, she frowned so viciously that he almost felt sorry he'd forced the encounter. Almost.

She studied the surrounding forest, clearly pondering whether she should abandon the path and tromp through the briars rather than talk to him. The realization pricked at his pride, and he marched toward her, coming closer and closer, eager to learn precisely how near he could get before she panicked.

She didn't move, though, not a muscle. She wasn't afraid of him, and after so many years of nervous paramours and quaking debutantes, her brave disdain was a welcomed relief.

They were toe-to-toe, and sparks erupted, the very atmosphere charged with energy due to her proximity. The oddest sensation of . . . of . . . joy rushed through him. There was no other way to describe his delight.

"Hello, Margaret," he said.

"It's Miss Gray to you."

"I don't think I ought to call you *Miss Gray*. I'm apt to confuse you with the other Miss Gray in residence."

"It's Miss Gray to you," she repeated.

He reached out and toyed with a lock of her hair, but she batted his hand away.

"What do you want?" she asked.

"I had to see you."

"Well, now you have. Good-bye."

She tried to shift around him, but he shifted, too, so that she couldn't. She went in the other direction, and he followed. They kept at it, going side to side on the narrow trail, until she growled in frustration.

"Let me pass."

"No."

"You are either the most discourteous person I've ever met or the biggest ass. Which is it?"

"I am both."

"So we're in complete accord. Farewell. If I'm very lucky—which I haven't been so far—I won't bump into you ever again."

"Is that really what you're hoping?"

"Absolutely."

"Women generally love me," he said. "Aren't you the least bit smitten?"

"I'm adding vanity to your list of foul traits."

"Did you know I'm scheduled to visit Gray's Manor for a full month?"

"No, and I must tell you that it's the worst news I've heard in my entire life."

"Do you hate all men? Or is it just me?"

"It's just you."

He laughed, and he couldn't recollect when he'd last had so much fun. After such a lengthy and miserable marital search, her pithy, insulting banter was so refreshing.

"You're very pretty," he declared.

"And *you* are deranged."

"But I like you better without any clothes on."

"I can't believe you have the temerity to mention such an appalling incident."

"I was particularly thrilled when you dabbed that washcloth between your breasts."

"Each time you open your mouth," she scolded, "you say something more outrageous."

"And I don't even care."

"Were you raised in a cave?"

"No, I was raised by my father, which is about the same thing."

"Is he a beast, too?"

"Yes. Are you acquainted with him?"

"No, thank goodness."

"If you ever meet him, you'll understand why I'm so unpleasant."

"Are you blaming your base character on heredity?"

"It's easier than claiming I prefer to be a boor on purpose."

"Yes, it is." She stepped away. "It's been most enlightening to chat with you. Now if you'll excuse me . . ."

"I don't."

She scowled. "What?"

"I don't excuse you."

He clasped her wrist and pushed back the sleeve of her dress. Lavinia had pinched her very hard, had dug in with her nails before he'd been speedy enough to intervene, and he'd been wondering if there'd be marks.

There were.

"I'm sorry," he murmured as he traced a finger over the raw spot.

"Why would you be sorry?"

"It was my fault. I was teasing you, when I know Lavinia's temper, but I never expected that she'd assault you." He tried for a smile, but couldn't quite manage it. "I apologize."

"Accepted."

Suddenly, the encounter grew intimate, and he was on the verge of spilling his pitiful saga so that she would comprehend why he was such a dreadful lout. He yearned to speak of his widowed father, Charles, how Charles lied and cheated and ruined everything he touched. Jordan's boyhood had been one awful drama after the next, and he'd attempted to escape by purchasing a commission in the army, but he'd survived only to face penury and bankruptcy.

He didn't care if his father starved in the poorhouse, and he didn't *want* to care if the properties were lost, the farms idle, the fields fallow. He didn't want to worry about the hundreds of employees who'd worked for his family for generations. Most of all, he didn't want to fret over the plight of his numerous and much younger half siblings, sired during his father's many marriages and peccadilloes.

Who would see to their welfare? Not Charles, that was for damned sure. And if Charles wouldn't do it, who would?

They were all depending on Jordan, and how could he refuse to assist? Especially the children. Someone had to be in charge and make the right choices, even if it meant marrying a spoiled adolescent simply to get her fortune so he could buy them all some shoes.

He bit his tongue, declining to let the humiliating remarks spill out. Usually, he was so tough, content to handle every problem alone, but for some ridiculous reason, he wanted to lean on Margaret Gray.

She sensed his distress, and their gazes locked, the intimacy stronger than ever, the interlude stretching to infinity.

"I like you," he finally admitted. "I don't know why; I just do."

"Well, I don't like you. How could you trifle with my aunt—while you're hoping to marry my cousin? And I was watching you! Have you no standard of decency?"

"It's fairly low."

"Can you truly switch from mother to daughter in the blink of an eye?"

He blushed. "What can I say?"

"You're wicked in a realm beyond my limited experience."

"I don't suppose you have any money, do you?"

"Not a penny."

"That's too bad."

"Why?"

"If you were rich, I'd ask you to marry me."

She grinned and shook her head. "You are impossible."

He stroked his thumb across her bottom lip, relishing how warm it was, how soft. "What you saw me doing in Lavinia's bedchamber, that's not the kind of man I am."

It was a huge falsehood, but he felt compelled to utter it. He couldn't explain why, but he wanted to garner her esteem, to erase the contemptible opinion he'd generated.

"Hah!" she scoffed. "It's precisely the sort of man you are. You shouldn't ever lie to me. I can tell when you are."

He shrugged. "It was worth a shot."

"You're a viscount. Why don't you have any money of your own?"

"My father stole it and spent it—while I was away in the army."

"How terribly uncouth of him."

"I thought so."

"Will you marry Penelope?"

"Most likely."

"You'll always regret it."

"I'm certain you're correct."

"I am. I've known her a long time. She insists you're a murderer, which is a peculiar footing upon which to commence a marriage."

He frowned, hating that she'd already heard the stories. "Do you think I'm a killer?"

She scrutinized him. "No. You're a roué and a scapegrace, though."

Her response gave him an inane burst of pleasure. "People say that I killed my older brother for his title."

"*People* are absurd."

"Is it hard for you to reside with Lavinia and Penelope?"

"It just *is*," she said. "It's my life."

"I'd change it for you if I could."

She was humored by the statement. "And how would you do that?"

"I'd take you away; I'd make you happy."

"No, you wouldn't. I'm positive you'd make me miserable."

"You're wrong."

He took her wrist again, and he tugged her closer. She was wary, but she didn't resist, so he slipped an arm around her waist, her body pressed to his, and he bent down and kissed her.

In the history of kisses, it was exceedingly chaste, but he reveled in the sweetness. Her lashes fluttered shut, and her warm breath coursed across his cheek. It was heaven, being with her, and he lingered until she drew away.

She studied him, her green eyes digging deep, taking his measure.

"You shouldn't have done that," she said.

"Probably not."

"Why are you pestering me, Lord Romsey? What is it you want?"

What did he want? He hadn't a clue. "I don't know."

"Leave me be. Please. Propose to Penelope, marry her, then go away. Keep me out of it."

"I can't."

She sighed. "I don't care to suffer your attentions."

"It's not up to you. It will never be up to you."

"I won't be bullied."

"I wish you'd call me Jordan—at least when we're alone."

"I can't."

"Why do you detest me so much?" Since he'd behaved like an ass from the very beginning, it was a silly question, but he needed her to answer it.

"I thought you were planning to marry *me*." She chuckled, though not with mirth. "Were you aware of what happened? When you first arrived, Penelope misunderstood, and she told me that's why you'd come. For a few minutes there, I actually assumed . . . well . . ."

She was too embarrassed to finish. Her gaze was troubled and filled with hurt, and he rippled with mortification and no small amount of shame.

"I didn't realize that," he muttered. "I'm sorry."

She rested her palm on his cheek. "I recognize that it was foolish, but I was hoping Penelope's story was true, that someone finally wanted me, and I'm glad she was mistaken. But I'll always wonder what might have been, you know?"

"Yes, I know."

She walked around him and proceeded down the path, and he didn't try to stop her. He watched till the woods swallowed her up, and as she disappeared, an unnerving quiet descended. Even the birds ceased their chirping, as if they couldn't bear to see her go.

He felt as if he'd relinquished something precious, as if bliss had been within his grasp, but he'd frittered it away.

He shook off the bizarre sentiment and followed her
to the house, braced to socialize with Penelope, to find
some reason to enjoy her company no matter how difficult it proved to be.

CHAPTER FOUR

L avinia lounged on the daybed in her boudoir and glared at Penelope. "You'll do as I say, and you'll be glad about it."

"I won't," Penelope had the audacity to reply. "I'll have the London debut you promised me, or I won't have anything. You and your precious Lord Romsey can go hang."

"He's the most eligible bachelor in the realm. If he settles on you, we can skip the London folderol. When your engagement is announced, the entire world will be agog."

"He's a poverty-stricken murderer and maniac," Penelope argued. "Everybody knows it, and now, you're foisting him off on me as if he's a Grand Catch, and you order me to be happy about it. Well, I won't be, I tell you. I won't pretend."

Lavinia unfolded from the couch, and she stalked over until they were nose-to-nose. "He's a heartbeat away from being an earl. I thought you yearned to be a countess."

"I do."

"Then what—precisely—is your problem? And please be very clear, because you are trying my patience."

"He's not an earl—yet. His father is only fifty-four. The old codger might live another two or three decades! Then where would I be?"

"You'll be next in line to assume the proper role! Where would you think?"

"I want it to happen sooner. I want someone who's already inherited."

Lavinia threw up her hands. "Are you presuming that heirs grow on trees? If you refuse Romsey, are you imagining I can perform magic and conjure up another aristocrat for you?"

"I'm the prettiest girl in England," she boasted. "You know it, and I know it. Once we get to the city, and all the men see me, it will be easy to find the one I want. Besides, I'd hate to miss out on the fun of having them fight over me."

"What if Romsey turns out to be the best choice? If you snub him, he won't wait for you."

"He will wait. He's desperate; you said so yourself."

"Oh, to be sixteen again and so sure of everything."

"Better than being thirty-four and over-the-hill like you."

Lavinia considered slapping her, but instead, she stormed to the cupboard and poured herself a drink. She wouldn't brawl over the stupid issue. Penelope *had* to marry Jordan Prescott. There was no alternative.

The thick child didn't comprehend money, where it came from or how quickly it disappeared. Despite what Penelope believed, Lavinia wasn't about to pay for a London Season—not when Penelope had a perfectly good chance to wed immediately and save Lavinia a fortune.

She swilled her brandy, fuming over her plight. When she'd made her own debut years earlier, she'd been young and foolish like Penelope, and she'd coveted a titled husband, but her mother had convinced her to pick wealth over nobility.

She'd relented and rummaged to the bottom of the barrel by selecting Horatio Gray—a brewer! a tradesman!—and the fact still shamed her.

After he'd died, her initial act had been to sell the brewery and purchase the grandest mansion in the neighborhood, but how was she to know the upkeep would be so bloody expensive?

The bills piled up, the cash went out, until there was so little remaining.

Horatio had left several fat trust funds, but it was so difficult to manage such large amounts. She'd rapidly spent much more than she should have, and she'd become adept at shifting money and manipulating accounts, but she couldn't keep on forever. Something had to give—though she was positive no one would ever discover what she'd done. She'd been too proficient at hiding evidence of any fiscal ineptitude, and she'd never admit to malfeasance.

After all, desperate times called for desperate measures!

If she couldn't devise a solution, her sole option was to marry her neighbor and paramour, Robert Mason. He'd loved her so tediously, for so long, and he was constantly pestering her to proceed with the wedding, but—as she continually prayed for a reprieve—she used every machination to postpone the inevitable.

His standard of living was so meager, his assets so pathetic, that the very notion of stooping so low was too abhorrent to consider—unless, of course, she came to such a dismal fork in the road that she had no other choice. Then she'd latch onto him with nary a second's hesitation.

If only she hadn't frequently bragged about the size of Penelope's dowry! With the excessive sum having been publicly bandied, she had to be cautious. If she utilized the wrong penny at the wrong moment, she could attract dangerous scrutiny. The balance had to be given—intact—to Penelope's husband. There wasn't a single farthing available for an extravagant London excursion, which meant that Penelope had to wed Jordan Prescott.

When the dowry changed hands, Lavinia would be destitute, her house likely sold to satisfy creditors, and she'd be out on the streets. But the Prescott family couldn't let Lavinia, as Penelope's mother, wallow in squalor. She would ride Penelope's coattails to financial security.

As to Margaret, Lavinia wasn't concerned about her. They were on a sinking ship, and every woman had to save herself!

"Aren't you forgetting one thing?" Lavinia asked.

"What?"

She walked over behind Penelope as Penelope primped in the mirror. Lavinia enviously assessed Penelope's marvelous, youthful figure. Her waist was so tiny, her hips so curvaceous, her breasts so firm and pert, compared to Lavinia's, which were beginning to droop.

"I apprised you of what you'll have to do to keep your husband happy in the bedchamber."

"I never will!" Penelope insisted with the annoying certainty of a child.

"He'll stray if you don't. Could you bear to have him philandering with every hussy in town?"

"I'd kill him first."

"He'll touch you in despicable ways," Lavinia warned. "He'll take off your clothes, and he'll make you do things you detest. You'll have to agree. It's the price you pay for a good marriage."

"Are you trying to scare me? Or disgust me?"

"I'm merely telling you how it is. When picking a spouse, you have to factor in the physical traits of the man. When he's as handsome as Lord Romsey, the sex is easier to tolerate. But when you have to oblige an obese man, a bald man, or a cruel and revolting man—and you have to do it night after night—it becomes insufferable."

"I don't care what he looks like."

"You will," Lavinia asserted.

"I won't! There are too many other details that are more important to me."

"I'll decide what's best for you," Lavinia threatened.

"No, you won't. You don't know anything about me. I'm going to get everything *you* always wanted but never had, and you can't stand it."

She whirled away and strutted out, and Lavinia's anger surged. She'd informed Jordan that he could ruin Penelope whenever he was ready, and the prospect was increasingly satisfying to ponder. A bit of rape might be just the ticket to shove the arrogant girl off her pedestal.

Would Jordan dare? Could he be that ruthless? She'd heard so many terrible rumors about him. How badly did he desire Penelope's fortune?

Lavinia would have her way. Whether Penelope

consented or not, she would end up married to Jordan Prescott.

❧

R obert Mason was prepared to knock on the door to Lavinia's boudoir when it was flung open and Penelope sauntered out. He jumped to the side. He didn't like Penelope, had never trusted her, and often thought he might be downright afraid of her.

Lavinia claimed that she would wed him, but if it entailed playing father to Penelope, he was glad for the delay. He hoped Penelope would be wed herself before too long, so she wouldn't continue to be the wedge that had separated him from Lavinia.

"Hello, Robert." Penelope's voice was laced with sarcasm.

"Hello, Penelope. How are you?"

"I'm fine. What brings you upstairs?"

He patted his satchel. "I have some business to discuss with your mother."

"Business? Is that what they call it these days?"

She chuckled slyly, indicating that he had no secrets regarding his relationship with Lavinia, and she totted off. He observed her till she reached the stairs; then he entered Lavinia's room.

"Darling," Lavinia welcomed, "how sweet of you to visit. But it's really an awful time. I asked you not to stop by this week."

"Or next," he griped. "I know, but I missed you. Besides, you were adamant that we review your financial situation as soon as possible."

Recently, with her fiscal quandary at crisis levels,

she'd confided in him and pleaded for his advice. He was proud that she'd sought his assistance, but the papers she'd provided were extremely convoluted. Her income didn't match expenses, and he couldn't reconcile the two, so he couldn't make sense of her circumstances—other than to fear that she was facing bankruptcy.

"Have you studied my records?"

"Yes."

"Well?"

"There are many discrepancies with the numbers."

"I told you that I'm not a mathematician," she snapped.

"I realize you're not."

"That's why I need your help."

"It's a tad beyond my ability to decipher. Perhaps if we hired an accountant, he could—"

"No!" she declared much too vehemently. "I won't have strangers pawing through my private calamity."

She was seated at her dressing table, preening in the mirror, and he stood behind her, his palms on her shoulders. They were such a striking couple, her with her blond hair and blue eyes, him with his brown hair and brown eyes. His dark features were a startling contrast to her pale, iridescent splendor.

He'd loved her since he was ten years old, and she was eight, and he'd remained captivated through her horrid marriage to Horatio, as well as his own to a kindly woman whom he'd never appreciated. He wasn't able to sever his fascination to Lavinia, and he couldn't say why. He simply adored her in an insane, inexplicable fashion that never faded.

She could definitely be domineering and exasperating, but in spite of her flaws, he'd do anything for her. He'd proven over and over that he was willing to demean and debase and humiliate himself, but when the reward for his devotion was their eventual marriage, he couldn't desist. He'd been waiting his entire life to be her husband, and he was ecstatic to note that the outcome was closer than ever to becoming reality.

"You're very beautiful this afternoon," he advised. He was desperate to change the tenor of the conversation, to avoid the details of her doomed pecuniary plight.

"Do you think so?"

"Oh, yes."

"You're so good to me," she said as he bent down and nipped at her nape.

"I know what you want, Lavinia. I know what you need."

He slid down the straps of her negligee till he'd bared her breasts. She arched and stared at her reflection.

"Am I looking older?" she queried.

He was no fool. "Absolutely not. You get prettier every second."

She shifted around and grinned. "I do, don't I?"

"Yes, you do."

He was fibbing, not inclined to point out that her age was beginning to show. Her hair was sporting a few strands of silver, her waist was thicker, her breasts sagging, but he would never mention the differences. To his besotted eye, she was still as fetching as she'd been as a young girl.

He linked their fingers, determined to lead her over to the bed, but she pulled away, dashing his plan for a quick romp.

"Oh, Robert, not now. I couldn't possibly."

"Why not?" He was more surly than he'd intended to

be, but it had been weeks since she'd deigned to fornicate with him.

"I have the worst headache. I'm utterly sick about Penelope and Lord Romsey."

"Has he arrived?"

"Yes, but she claims she's going to London to make a better match."

"Better than a viscount? Why . . . that's ludicrous."

"That's exactly what I told her."

"We can't afford a trip to London."

"No, we can't," Lavinia agreed.

With marriage to Lavinia imminent, he considered any funds his own as much as hers, and he'd never permit Penelope to squander so much.

"You have to reason with her," he declared. "I'll help you."

"I knew I could count on you!"

She bounded to her feet and wrapped her arms around him. Her lush body was pressed to his, and his cock leapt to attention.

He drew her nearer, his hips grinding into hers, as he dipped down and sucked on her nipple. She let him briefly indulge, then she eased away, and he sighed with resignation. It was such a chore, luring her into the physical intimacy he enjoyed so much.

"Let's talk about my finances," she urged. "Have you any positive information to share?"

He hated to constantly be the bearer of bad news, but her circumstances were more grave than she fathomed. She had dug a terribly deep hole, and he could supply no shovel to rescue her.

"It's very dire, Lavinia. You'll probably lose the house."

"How soon?"

"Six months, maybe less."

"Gad! So fast!" She shoved him away and paced. "And the banker. Have you spoken with him?"

"Yes, but there's nothing he can do, Lavinia. You simply owe more than you can ever pay, and people are demanding their money. I warned you this would be the consequence of your borrowing so much."

"Don't nag!"

"I'm not."

When he was aware of how affluent she'd been after Horatio's death, it galled him to be silent. How could one single woman spend so much? It was a staggering amount, and she was mad to have frittered it away.

He hugged her. "Forget about your debts. Forget about this mansion and this beastly property. Marry me, and we'll be happy with what's left. All we really need is each other."

"Oh, Robert, I can't discuss this, not while Romsey is here, and Penelope's future is up in the air."

"You can't leave me hanging forever. I have to have some answers in my own life."

"Of course, you do."

"It's unfair of you to keep delaying. When you persist with your dithering, I wonder if you're serious in your affection."

"Don't be silly. We'll set the date. I promise!"

"Will we? Or should I move on? Your procrastination has me doubting your interest in a union."

While she strove to be tough and independent, the prospect of his abandoning her always garnered a reaction. Instantly, she took his hand and escorted him to the bedroom.

Hope sparked eternal!

"I've been so awful to you," she cooed. "Why do you put up with me?"

"Because I can't resist."

"No, you can't," she said. "All this talk of bankruptcy has me so tense. Would you rub my back?"

"Yes, darling. Lie down. I'll have you feeling better in no time."

As she shimmied out of her negligee and snuggled down on the bed, he tamped down a victorious grin. They would begin with a massage, but it would progress to other raucous and rough games. It would be a leisurely and satisfying afternoon—just as he'd intended.

❧

W hat the hell are you doing here?"
Charles Prescott, Earl of Kettering, sipped on a brandy and smiled at Jordan, pretending to be glad to see his son.

"Hello to you, too." He jiggled his drink, indicating the liquor. He hadn't been in Lavinia's residence fifteen minutes, and he'd already made himself at home. Before a full day had passed, the servants would think he owned the place. "The brandy is excellent. French, I'd guess. Would you like one?"

"I hadn't planned on it," Jordan snidely said, "but now that you've arrived, I'll have several."

He huffed to the sideboard, reached for a glass, then changed his mind and swigged straight from the decanter.

"Honestly, Jordan, you get more discourteous by the moment."

Jordan glared, his expression aggressive and hostile. "I repeat: What are you doing here?"

"Can't a father offer support when his son is about to tie the knot?"

"Since when are you concerned about my welfare?"

"I've always had your best interests at heart."

"We're all alone, Charles, so you can drop the paternal pretense."

Charles considered carrying on the charade, but it was such a waste of energy. He and Jordan knew each other well. They had few secrets.

He shrugged. "Light me a cigar, would you?"

"Light it yourself. Now tell me what you want."

"I was in the neighborhood."

"And . . . ?"

"I stopped by."

"And . . . ?"

"I wanted to see how you are."

"And could it also be—just perhaps—that you didn't have anywhere else to go? Admit it: You're here to sponge off Lavinia Gray for as long as she'll allow it."

Charles made a mock toast. "She's quite the hostess, and she adores having an earl as her guest. Why would I spurn her hospitality?"

"You're like a leech on a thigh. Why impose on the Grays? Why not simply travel to the family seat? There are plenty of caves in which to hide."

"My creditors are all searching there."

Charles sighed. It was a fine state of affairs when a peer of the realm, one of the premier citizens in the land, a man who regularly dined with kings, couldn't show his face on his own property.

The bill collectors were circling, eager to pounce

like wolves on carrion. His debt was so vast that not even his title could protect him. There were too many people, wanting too much that he didn't have. They were going for the throat!

"I imagine if you went home," Jordan taunted, "the crofters would turn you in for the reward. I hear it's grown extremely large."

"There's no such thing as loyalty anymore," Charles complained.

"Not for the likes of you," Jordan said, and abruptly switched subjects. "I'm not about to marry."

"Really?"

"Really."

Jordan was unflappable, not giving a hint of the truth, but Charles knew what it was: Jordan was contemplating marriage to a rich girl—the definitive word being *rich*—and Charles was intrigued by the news.

A bit of cash always made a female more attractive, and as soon as he'd learned what Jordan was about, he'd resolved that he should see the child for himself. Jordan might be broke, but that didn't mean that he should have first chance at an heiress.

Age before beauty, Charles had decided, and he'd headed for Sussex.

"Are you—or are you not—here to investigate a marriage to Miss Penelope Gray?"

Jordan cursed. "How did you find out?"

"I was gambling at White's and was informed over a roll of the dice."

"You were gambling? Who is still stupid enough to take your markers?"

"I'm an earl. They wouldn't dare refuse me."

"They're fools."

"Yes, they are, but they owe me for my patronage, and if I hadn't been wagering, I'd never have delved to the bottom of your intentions. I have to tell you, Jordan, it's a hell of a way for a father to keep track of his son and heir. I shouldn't have to have strangers apprising me of your business."

"You're claiming I should notify you? Why? So that you can poke your nose in and muck it up?"

"My arrival here is purely benevolent."

Jordan scoffed. "You haven't a generous bone in your body. You were born a mercenary, and you'll be one till the day you die."

"That's as may be," Charles concurred, not seeing any reason to contradict the obvious, "but I've been married five times and—"

"Six."

"What?"

"You've been married *six* times."

"Has it been that many?"

"Have the decency to honor your many children by remembering how many wives there were!"

Charles reflected for a moment, counting. "Yes, I suppose it has been six."

"And you drove each of them to an early grave."

"I can't help it if I choose women with weak constitutions."

"They're all hale and fit till they wed you. Then they drop like flies."

"As I was saying," Charles cut in, declining to quarrel, "I've had a good deal of experience with the marital condition, and I felt you could use my advice."

"Your . . . your advice?" Jordan appeared apoplectic.

"I can guide you, and hopefully, keep you from making some of the same mistakes I made."

"That is hilarious, Charles. Absolutely hilarious." He took another swig of brandy, then started out.

"Where are you going?"

"I'm off to warn the housekeeper to hide the silver."

Charles watched him depart, wondering why Jordan had to be so nasty. He and Jordan were always at odds, and he couldn't figure out where Jordan had obtained his moral leanings. Certainly not from Charles! It had to have come from his mother's side of the family.

He heard Jordan in the hall, talking with Charles's mistress, Anne, who was referred to as *Mrs. Smythe* but who had never been married.

"Are you positive I'm his son?" Jordan asked her. "Is there any possibility I might have been switched at birth?"

Anne laughed. "You look too much like him to be anybody else."

Jordan walked on, and Anne entered the parlor. On seeing her, Charles smiled. She'd been with him for nearly twenty years. At age forty, she was still slender and shapely, but her brown hair was streaked with gray, her astute brown eyes creased with lines. Yet he didn't care about the changes.

She was the only constant in his chaotic life, the last true-blue person in the entire country. She'd stayed with him through thick and thin, through marriage and heartbreak, through feast and famine, and for her loyalty he would always keep and protect her.

"Jordan is angry that I came," he pouted as she sat on the sofa with him.

"I told you he would be."

"He's an ingrate."

"He's a grown man. He doesn't want you here."

Charles huffed with indignation. "A son needs his father when there are vital decisions to be made."

"He doubts you'll be helpful."

"I shall prove him wrong."

"I'm sure you shall."

"A fellow has to be cautious when he weds—especially when the bride has so much money. All that cash can blind a man to what's important."

"Yes, it can."

"I must guarantee that he's considered all the angles before he proceeds." Charles nodded, having convinced himself he was doing the right thing. "He'll be thankful in the end."

Jordan would have benefit of Charles's shrewd counsel. And if—by chance—Penelope Gray determined that she didn't like Jordan, or if she should set her cap for someone else, someone who needed her fortune more than Jordan ever could, that was hardly Charles's fault.

Yes, everything would work out fine.

❦

Lavinia stared in the mirror, swabbing rouge across her cheek. As she rose to go down and have a brandy with Lord Kettering, she tamped down her excitement and avarice.

Kettering was handsome and virile, with Jordan's same blue eyes and dark hair, though Kettering's was peppered with silver. He had to be fabulously rich, too.

Though older than she would have preferred, he was incredibly attractive in every way, and she was enthralled.

Why should Penelope have all the luck? Why should Penelope be the one to marry into the aristocracy?

It had been Lavinia's dream, but Fate had tricked her. Now, with Kettering's arrival, Lavinia had an opportunity to rectify the past and secure the future.

After being married to Horatio for so long, after delaying Robert with various lies, she'd become an expert at coaxing and cajoling. Before the month was out, her own wedding plans would be progressing.

When she was through, Charles Prescott wouldn't know what had hit him.

She sauntered to the stairs and started down.

❧

P enelope dawdled on the verandah, peeking through the window into the parlor. She could see Lord Kettering on the sofa with Mrs. Smythe.

Penelope snickered. If Anne Smythe were a *Mrs.*, Penelope would eat her bonnet!

She didn't know Mrs. Smythe's true role, but she suspected her to be a fallen woman, parading around as a respectable lady; yet her position didn't matter. Mrs. Smythe was insignificant, and would have no part in how affairs played out.

Kettering was terribly old, but he was an earl! And he was a widower! He had to be fabulously rich, too. Not penniless like his son. Why should she settle for a mere viscount when the earl, himself, was present and available? With the title of countess as the ultimate prize, she would willingly pay any price to win it.

Surely, such an ancient, horrid man would be intrigued by the attentions of a fetching, young maiden. Surely, such a man could be flattered into doing all sorts of things he oughtn't.

The prospects for immediate gain were staggering. She smiled and strolled into the house.

CHAPTER FIVE

W hat are you doing in my room?"

"I missed you at supper."

Jordan sipped on a brandy and studied Margaret Gray. He'd suffered through an interminable meal with his father and the Gray family, though not Margaret, and her absence had eaten away at him. Obviously, she was avoiding him, and he'd wondered where she'd gone, but hadn't dared inquire as to her whereabouts.

With his father's appearance and subsequent charming of Lavinia and Penelope, Jordan was teeming with an ire and frustration that couldn't be squelched. He'd longed to spend some time with Margaret, so he'd wrongly barged into her bedchamber, once again, but after waiting for her for hours, he was incredibly angry.

She'd intrigued him against his will, and he blamed her for his enticement. He had a task to complete, one that didn't and couldn't include her, and he hated having her as a distraction. Yet, he couldn't stop thinking about her and the innocent kiss they'd shared in the woods.

Was she thinking of it, too? Had she wasted a single
second pondering him and the chemistry that drew them
together? Though it was absurd, he was dying to know
the answer.

She wasn't happy to see him—not that he cared—
and she scowled, trying to embarrass him into leaving,
but she didn't realize that he was beyond outrage or
shame. He'd stay till he was ready to go.

"My door was locked," she pointed out. "Any sane
person would have recognized that it indicates I don't
wish to be disturbed."

He held out the key so she could grasp how easily
he'd gained entrance. "Any *sane* person would, but as I
previously explained, no one has ever accused me of
being overly rational."

"How could anyone have a better opinion when you
constantly prove that you're deranged?"

He approached, liking how she stood her ground.
She was fearful, but curious, too, and captivated by the
sensations that flared whenever he was near.

"Where have you been?" he asked.

"If I thought it was any of your business—which I
don't—I'd tell you that I was at my school, preparing
lessons for tomorrow."

"I heard that you *work* for a living." He sounded snide
and snobbish, and she took the comment for the slur
it was.

"You're here to marry an heiress, yet you have the
audacity to condemn me for employment? What gall!
At least, I have the satisfaction of deserving what I
earn. When you're paying your bills with Penelope's
money, how will your pride stand it?"

She stomped to the wardrobe, stuffed her cloak and bonnet inside, and slammed the door. He walked over and trapped her in the circle of his arms.

"I'm sorry," he murmured. "I'm being an ass."

"Yes, you are."

"I didn't mean to insult you."

"Of course, you did."

She struggled, but when he wouldn't release her, she gave up the fight and slumped against him.

"You could get a job, yourself," she grumpily said. "It wouldn't kill you."

"A job!" He was aghast at the notion. "What would I do?"

"You seem like an educated fellow. You could be a clerk or a gentleman's secretary. Not everyone has to reside in a mansion with dozens of servants and fine wine at every meal. You could lower your standards."

He sighed. If he did as she'd suggested, what would become of his siblings?

His aggravation at Charles surged anew. He didn't want to be anybody's savior, and he detested being put in a position where so many others were relying on him. He recalled Johnny and Tim, Charles's ten-year-old twin sons, whom Jordan had met occasionally. He'd once visited the house where Charles had effectively abandoned them, only to discover that there was no food in the larder, no clothes that still fit them in the dresser drawers, and no tutors had been engaged in over a year.

"I have many brothers and sisters who need my assistance," he stated. "I'm afraid they'd starve on a clerk's salary."

"Why can't your parents look after them?"

"My mother passed away when I was a babe, and my father is . . . is . . ." He shrugged, unable to account for Charles. "He can't care for them."

"Well, re-enlist in the army. Isn't that what you're good at? It's rumored that you're some sort of . . . of . . . hero."

She muttered the word *hero* as if it were an epithet, and he chuckled miserably. By volunteering for every dangerous foray, he'd done his best to die in the army, but no matter how fervently he'd tried, he hadn't perished. He'd arrived home in London, hale and healthy and facing financial chaos, but he'd had his fill of death and destruction, and he wouldn't return to the war. Not that he'd reveal as much to Margaret Gray. Let her assume what she would.

"I was a lousy soldier," he lied.

"I'm sure that's not true. I'm sure you're proficient at whatever you attempt. You just require a shove in the right direction."

"And how about you?" He was eager to steer the conversation away from him and his problems. She was much more interesting. "I've been informed that you're an excellent teacher."

She was suspicious, as if she couldn't conceive of anyone saying something positive about her. "Who told you that?"

"Everyone to whom I've spoken."

"They're correct," she grudgingly admitted.

"Why do you do it?"

"Because I've been given so much, and it's only appropriate that I give something back. I feel it's my Christian duty, and I love children, but I'm continually chastised. I'm tired of all the nagging, so if you have negative opinions, I'd appreciate it if you'd keep them to yourself."

"I'm hardly nagging."

"You are."

"I'm actually amazed."

"By what?"

"By you."

She glanced up at him, and her verdant eyes were so wide and guileless that he had to bend down and kiss her. He seemed to have no other choice. For a brief instant, she allowed it; then she pulled away.

"What do you want from me?" she demanded.

"I don't know."

"You keep trifling with me—though I've practically begged you to stop. What am I to do?"

"Don't do anything. Just let it happen."

"But I don't want it to *happen*. I want you to leave me be."

"Do you really mean that?"

She frowned, considering. If she ordered him out, he wasn't certain he could oblige her.

His father's arrival at Gray's Manor had rattled loose his inhibitions. He felt as if he were perched on a cliff and about to jump over into open space. The slender threads of morality and sense that had tethered him to the civilized world had been severed.

In his wild condition, he would be a hazard to her, but he felt that they'd met for a reason, and he had to learn what it was.

"Well?" he pressed. "Should I go?"

"Yes," she said, crushing him; then she groaned. "No. Oh, I don't know what I want."

She pushed him away and went to the window to stare

out at the darkening sky. Dusk had fallen, and stars were beginning to twinkle. He came up behind her and rested his palms on her shoulders, and she elbowed him in the ribs.

"Don't stand here with me. Someone might see you."

"I don't care."

"Yes, you do. There'd be a big fuss, and you'd have to marry me." She peeked up at him. "Wouldn't that be your worst nightmare? Having to settle for a girl with nothing?"

"Have you paused to wonder why I was placed in the room adjoining yours?"

"The servants probably did it as a cruel jest."

"Perhaps it was Fate, taking a hand, giving us a chance to be together."

"Or perhaps," she countered, "it was merely the housekeeper's harmless error."

"Lavinia presumes that I'm in the bedchamber next to Penelope."

"Is that where you'd like to be?"

"No."

"The mistake will dawn on her eventually. She'll have you moved."

"What should we do in the interim?"

"There's a question for the ages: What should we do?" She gazed at the Evening Star out on the horizon. "Have you ever wished that you could simply close your eyes, say a few magic words, and become someone else?"

"I wish it all the time," he confessed.

"So do I, Lord Romsey. So do I."

"Call me Jordan."

"Will you leave, please? Will you make this easy on

me? I can't choose what I want. It's wrong for you to stay, but I haven't the fortitude to command that you go."

"It's not *wrong*. It's our destiny."

"What a romantic you are. I never would have guessed."

He wouldn't have, either. He knew better than to trust Fate, yet he couldn't deny the urge he felt to proceed.

"Come." He linked their fingers and tugged her toward the bed.

"Lord Romsey!"

She dug in her heels, desperate to halt his forward progress, and he sat on the edge of the mattress and peered up at her.

"I want this from you, Margaret."

"Lord Romsey . . . Jordan . . . I'm a spinster! I haven't the foggiest idea what it is you're asking of me."

"I'll just hold you for a bit."

It was a strange admission for him. He consorted with women for one purpose and one purpose only— that being sexual trysting—and he never sought more than physical alleviation. Female companionship was a corporeal necessity, usually a commercial transaction, too, with money paid for services rendered. He never dallied to be soothed or consoled, but suddenly, he couldn't wait to cuddle with Margaret Gray.

"Aren't you lonely, Margaret?" he inquired. "Wouldn't it be marvelous not to be so alone—just for a while?"

"Yes, it would be."

"Do you trust me?"

"Not for a second."

"Which is very wise," he replied, "but I won't hurt you."

"I can't imagine you'll do anything else."

"Lie down with me, Margaret. Don't be afraid."

He shifted onto the pillows, and when he tugged again, she came without further argument. She was draped across him, braced on her straightened arm, wary of him and what he was about.

"Relax," he coaxed. "It will be all right."

He pulled her down so that her chest connected with his, and the contact was electrifying.

"What are you going to do?" she queried.

"I plan to kiss you senseless."

"Will I like it?"

"Very much."

"Are you sure?"

"Very sure."

He rolled them so that she was on her back, and he was hovered over her. She looked so sweet, and it was horrid of him to coerce her into doing what she oughtn't. He was a worldly, sophisticated roué, who could effortlessly lure her to iniquity, but he couldn't desist. She was so wholesome and unsullied, while he felt soiled and contaminated. If he spent enough time with her, maybe some of her freshness and decency would rub off.

He brushed his lips to hers, and they both groaned with delight. The embrace was pure heaven, and he increased the pressure, his mouth seeking, playing. She joined in, reveling in the moment, in the novelty. His tongue flicked out, asking, asking again, and she opened and welcomed him inside.

Instantly, he was swept into the inferno. His hands were everywhere, caressing in slow circles as the anticipation spiraled. He nudged her legs apart, so that he was cradled between her thighs, and he flexed, her skirt a soft cushion that spurred him on. He dipped under her chin, to her bosom, and as he rooted at her cleavage, she writhed in agony.

"I feel terrible," she managed. "Are you positive you're doing this correctly?"

He chuckled. "I'm renowned as being extremely adept with women."

"I ache all over."

"If you're very nice to me, I'll make it go away."

"Then do so," she complained. "I can't bear this torture."

"The pain is part of the pleasure."

"I don't like it."

"You will."

He pinched her nipples, squeezing them through the fabric of her gown, and her hips started to meet his, thrust for thrust.

"Jordan!"

"This is what your body needs, Margaret. Don't fight it."

Her innocence thrilled him, but it unnerved him, too. What was he thinking? If they were discovered, there'd be the devil to pay. He could never marry her, as duty and honor would require.

Could he blithely wreck her life?

His lust was running at a fevered pitch, so he wasn't concerned about any consequences, but if he wasn't cautious, he'd behave in a dreadful, irrevocable manner.

"I want to show you something. It will feel wonderful."

"Get on with it!" she snapped. "If this . . . this . . . anguish will cease, I'll let you try anything."

It was the worst answer she could possibly give, for

in his stimulated state, he was desperate to interpret the comment as permission, when he knew it wasn't. He had to call a halt, but he couldn't. Not quite yet.

He unbuttoned her dress so that the bodice was loose, and he yanked at the front. In a thrice, a perfect breast popped into view. He clasped the tip, as she cried out and arched up, but he pushed her down.

"What a little hellcat you are," he murmured.

"Don't torment me."

"The *torment* has just begun."

He sucked the taut end into his mouth, continuing on till it was red and inflamed, and his agitation grew so intense that he was frightened. He was past the spot where he could prevent himself from doing permanent injury to her.

He drew away, stealing a final, brief kiss; then he rolled to the edge of the bed and sat up.

His breathing was labored, his pulse racing, his cock a wedge between his legs that throbbed and protested, demanding a satiation he daren't supply.

Tentatively, she reached out and stroked his arm.

"What is it?" she queried, confused. "Did I do something wrong?"

He smiled. "No. You were splendid."

"Then . . . what?"

"You simply arouse me beyond my limits."

"Is that a good thing?"

"Yes, my dear Margaret, that's a very, very good thing, but a man can get to a point where he can't stop."

"There's more to it?"

"Quite a bit more."

"What happens?"

"I'll show you someday."

"When?"

"I don't know."

With her sexual nature, she'd be game to try whatever he suggested, which was precisely the reason they had to slow down. If neither of them could temper the pace, they were on a fast road to perdition.

"Why not keep on?" she inquired.

"I need to reflect on this. It was awful of me to come in here and pressure you."

"Oh, now you say so! After you've ravaged me to Hades and back again!"

"I enjoyed it very much, though." He grinned. "That's why I must reflect."

"I'm an adult, Jordan. If I decide to gad about like a common trollop, it's my own affair."

"There's nothing *common* about you. That's the problem. You're very fine."

Too fine for the likes of me! he almost said, but didn't.

She sat up, too, her dress clutched to her bosom. Her hair had fallen; her lips were moist and swollen, her cheeks flushed with desire. She looked rumpled and adorable, and he was flabbergasted at how eager he was to begin again. When his room and hers were in such proximity, how would he stay away?

He wasn't a saint, and he didn't pretend to be. He was a mortal man, with human drives and passions, and he wanted her so badly that it scared him.

"What now?" She appeared young and lost.

"I think I'd better conclude my dealings at Gray's Manor and be on my way as swiftly as I'm able."

She studied him, her face blank and unreadable. "It's probably for the best."

"It probably is," he agreed.

"Will I . . . I . . ."

"What?"

She waved away the comment. "Don't mind me. I was merely about to ask if we could be together again before you go, but it would be madness."

"Yes, it would be."

"I have to remember that I don't like you. It will help me to . . . well . . ."

He leaned in and kissed her.

"I wish I were a different man. I wish I were the man you need."

"Believe me, so do I."

He stood and walked away, while she remained on the bed. A thousand remarks hovered in the air, but he couldn't speak any of them aloud, and he wasn't surprised. What could possibly be appropriate?

"Perhaps after I'm married," he finally said, "I can assist you in some fashion. I can provide funds so you could move away or you could—"

She shook her head, her sad, wise expression silencing him. "Don't make promises that you could never keep. It's cruel."

"I'm sorry."

"I survived long before you arrived, and I will endure long after you're gone. You needn't worry about me."

"I won't, then."

But he would. He'd always wonder about her and be troubled.

"Go," she urged, gesturing for him to leave.

He dawdled, wanting to say something pithy and defining, but what?

Without another word, he spun away, and went to his

room, and he shut and locked the door, but the walls soon closed in on him. He couldn't abide that she was so near but so hopelessly far away.

He rushed to the hall and down the stairs, out into the cool night, racing away as if the Hounds of Hell were on his heels.

CHAPTER SIX

Lavinia peeked out her door, and when she finally espied Lord Kettering strolling down the hall, she breathed a sigh of relief. She'd been huddled in the shadows for two hours, watching for the moment he exited his room and headed down to breakfast.

She was wearing a sheer negligee, the neckline cut very low to reveal her splendid bosom, so he would get an eyeful of what he could have with scarcely any effort.

For days, she'd been sending him signals, but she hadn't been able to entice him. Either he was entirely disinterested—which she would never believe—or he was being absurdly coy. When she was so obviously ready for a greater intimacy, what was to be gained by delay?

He neared, and she pulled open her door, pretending that she thought he was the maid.

"Abigail, you've come! I need you to—" She cut off and fiddled with the bodice of her negligee, acting as if she were embarrassed by her state of dishabille, but drawing his attention to it, too. "Oh, Lord Kettering! I didn't know it was you. Pardon me."

"Good morning, Mrs. Gray."

"I've told you over and over: You must call me Lavinia."

"Certainly, so long as you will call me Charles."

"I will; I will."

She dropped her hand, and his expression brightened at the sight of her breasts. For once, her hint registered. He chuckled and glanced down the corridor to ensure they were alone.

"You're a very beautiful woman, Lavinia."

"Do you think so?"

"I've wanted to tell you, but I hated to seem too forward."

"I don't find you forward, at all. In fact, you've been a total gentleman."

"Have I?"

"Yes."

"I can be naughty, though."

"Can you?"

"Would you like me to show you what I mean?"

"Oh, yes."

As she stepped back to allow him entrance, she tamped down a triumphant grin. There wasn't a man alive who could resist her, and Charles Prescott was no exception. He'd just needed a little prodding.

After a few tumbles in her bed, wedding bells would chime. She could practically hear herself being addressed as Countess of Kettering, and at the notion she was quivering with glee.

"Would you like a brandy?" she asked.

"No, thank you. I'll be too busy."

"I was hoping you'd say that."

"Why fool around? When I see something I want, I like to seize it immediately."

"So do I."

He reached out and caressed her breast, and her nipples leapt to attention, which surprised her. Usually, she loathed carnal contact and couldn't warm to male advances. Maybe with Charles, she would ascertain what had so many women tittering behind their fans. She still didn't know. As far as she was concerned, sex was a lot of sweating and grinding that held no appeal whatsoever.

Would Charles Prescott ignite the spark that had been missing?

She led him into her bedchamber, then turned to face him, and she preened, not doubting for a second that she looked fabulous.

He smiled. "Very nice, Lavinia. Very nice, indeed."

"For you, Charles. All for you."

"I just love a generous woman."

He tugged at the straps of her negligee, yanking them down so that the bodice drooped to expose her bosom. He inspected her, his gaze keen and enthused, then he snuggled her to him, and he dipped down to suck on her nipple. The move excited her in a way she'd never been before, and she cradled him closer, urging him to feast.

He taunted and played until her knees were weak, so she eased onto the bed, and drew him down with her. They tumbled together in a swirl of arms and legs, and he paused to trace his thumb across her lips.

"You have the most fascinating mouth."

"Yes, I do," she agreed.

"I wonder if you have any good uses for it."

"Oh, yes, darling. I know a very interesting one that I'm positive you'll enjoy."

She smirked. Horatio had been a rutting bull, who'd forced her to learn many disgusting deeds, which was now a benefit as she seduced various lovers to her schemes. She could do any ghastly thing without revealing her level of revulsion. When she performed fellatio, men were putty in her hands—poor, malleable Robert being the prime example.

Charles assessed her in a curious manner, waiting for her to proceed. He reclined on the pillow, and for a moment, he appeared bored and cynical, as if her low behavior was what he'd been expecting all along.

Which couldn't be right, and she frowned. Apparently, he wasn't sufficiently titillated, and she had to try harder.

She scooted down his body until she was directly over his crotch, and she unbuttoned his trousers, baring him and pumping him with her fist. His cock was firm and rigid, ready to be pleasured, and giving no hint of his advanced age.

With great determination, she licked him from base to tip, over and over, the suspense building, until finally, she glided over the crown. He sighed with contentment, which spurred her on, and quickly, he was at the edge. He clutched at her neck, and he let go, his hot seed spewing into her throat, and she swallowed it down.

Feeling smug and satisfied, she nibbled up his torso. She was prepared for praise and gratitude, but to her horror, he was evaluating her blandly, and she was rattled by his lack of appreciation.

She scowled. "What is it?"

"I take it that your dear, departed husband didn't request such base conduct from you."

"Why . . . what do you mean?"

"I *mean* that I apologize."

"For what?"

"You seem like such a worldly creature that I assumed your husband must have taught you to . . . well . . ." He was struggling to be kind. "I shouldn't have pushed you to do something for which you're so thoroughly untrained and unqualified."

"You . . . you . . . didn't like it?"

"It was fine," he claimed, but his aversion was so evident that she was mortified.

"You didn't like it!" she repeated, growing angry. "Just say so. I'm not a child. I can bear the truth."

He shifted away and stood, stuffing his privates into his pants and arranging his clothes. "I'm a man. Of course, I *liked* it."

"Then what are you implying?"

"I merely think you need a bit of practice. That's all." As if she were a pet dog, he patted her on the head. "Perhaps while I'm here, we can work on your skill. I'm always happy to help others improve themselves."

He turned and left, and she flopped onto her back and glared up at the ceiling. She felt as if she'd auditioned to be his countess but had blown her chance. How could she persuade him to let her have another?

She had a vision, of thousands of England's most gorgeous women, lined up to kneel before him, to suck him dry, and she was certain they all knew how to do it better than she ever could.

It was clear that Horatio had failed to impart some facet of instruction that was desperately necessary, and her confidence was shattered. When she recalled how often Horatio had made her please him with her mouth, when she thought of the early years, as she'd hid from him, as she'd begged for a respite, and all that time, she'd been doing it wrong!

She'd never been more humiliated, and she couldn't imagine how she'd show her face around the house while Kettering remained in it.

Silence descended, and with his exit, the sensual ambiance vanished. She couldn't abide the smell or taste of him. Suddenly nauseous, she leapt off the mattress, grabbed for the chamber pot, and vomited for all she was worth.

※

Penelope peeked out her window to the verandah below, watching for the instant Lord Kettering stepped outside to eat breakfast on the terrace. When he did, the intrepid Mrs. Smythe was absent, so he was alone and fair game.

She sneaked down the rear stairs and into the garden, skirting the verandah, but aware that he could see her from his perch at the table. She ignored him and continued down the path toward the gazebo by the lake.

From the day he'd arrived, she'd sensed his heightened regard. He constantly and furtively observed her, but they hadn't been able to chat privately.

If she couldn't get him off by himself, how was she to permit the elderly oaf to seduce her?

She'd reached the trees, and she paused, glancing over at him with a look that couldn't be misconstrued; then she went on. Men had never been a mystery to her, and Kettering definitely wasn't. He'd appear shortly. She walked to the lake's edge and picked a flower, sniffing it while listening for footsteps. Very soon, she heard him approaching.

She whirled around, feigning surprise at seeing him, but to her amazement, he didn't join in the charade. He marched over to her, not pretending that they were doing anything but engaging in an illicit tryst.

"So, Penelope, you've managed to lure me away. It took you long enough."

His audacious beginning caught her off guard. She'd been positive that she'd be in charge of the encounter, and she hadn't planned on his seizing control. She'd assumed him a thick, slow buffoon who would be easy to coerce and finagle.

"I . . . I . . . haven't been trying to get you anywhere. How dare you follow me out here! My mother would have a fit if she knew."

"Yes, I'm sure she would. Shall we go speak to her together? We can tell her what a little trollop you are."

"Why . . . you despicable . . . insulting . . ."

She couldn't guess at the words refined people flung at each other when they were quarreling. Instead, she huffed away, but he gripped her arm and pulled her to a halt.

"Let's not play games," he said. "I detest them."

"I don't know what you mean."

"I can read it in your eyes. You're thinking, 'Why settle for the son when I could have the father?' "

She yanked away. "You are so full of yourself."

"Am I?" His gaze blatantly wandered to her bosom. "You're so hungry to be my countess. Are you presuming you're the only female who's ever contemplated such a conclusion?"

"As if I'd crave your stuffy old title! If I accepted it, I'd have to accept you, too!"

"Yes, you would." He assessed her, then gave a mocking bow. "My mistake, Miss Gray. I misinterpreted your interest. I hope you're very happy in your life with *Viscount* Romsey."

He started away, and she panicked, stunned that he hadn't fallen for her sly advance. How would she ever orchestrate another secret appointment with him?

Like an idiot, she called, "Wait!"

He glared at her, then strolled back. "I don't have the patience for your nonsense. What do you really want?"

"I . . . I . . . wouldn't be adverse to our being better acquainted."

He snorted. "You make it sound as if we're about to have tea." He leaned in, his body connecting with hers, his chest pressed to her breasts, his manly parts wedged to her thigh. "If you're serious, you'll have to entice me with something that's a tad more exciting."

She knew to what he referred, and she gulped with trepidation. "I understand."

"Do you?"

"Yes, my mother explained everything."

"How terribly modern of her."

"I'm not afraid to try it," she boldly claimed, but the tremor in her voice belied her words.

"Aren't you? I've been a widower for years, so I have girls proposition me all the time."

How humiliating! Her world was so small, her opportunities so limited, that she'd imagined she was the only one to have thought of it!

"You're lying," she accused.

"I'm not. They all wish I'd pick them, but I never would. Aren't you curious as to why?"

"Yes."

"Because they're silly children, who don't appreciate a man's needs."

"I could give you whatever you require."

"Could you?"

He cupped her breast, cradling it and clasping the nipple. Lavinia had often taunted her with horror stories of how she'd eventually be touched like this, so Penelope was aware of what could transpire, but she hadn't anticipated it from *him*. Not when she scarcely knew him. Not when they'd just sneaked off for their first rendezvous.

It was evident that he was much too mature and sophisticated for her, but she wasn't certain how to extricate herself from the degrading encounter without seeming even more of a juvenile.

"Bare your breasts to me, Penelope."

She blushed bright red. "What?"

"You heard me. Do it."

"I don't want to."

"But you can't suppose I'd consider you as a bridal candidate without knowing what I'm getting. I'm a lusty fellow, and I can't abide squeamish females. I have to learn if what's hidden beneath the gown is worth having." He gestured to her chest. "Let me see."

Pondering, delaying, she gnawed on her lip, not sure if this was the best course. She was desperate to scurry off to her room like the ninny he envisioned her to be, and she was disgusted with herself for being such a coward. She'd always viewed herself as so very brave.

An important aristocrat like Kettering would expect her to behave like an adult, and if she planned to captivate him, she had to give him something to want. He'd asked to see her breasts. Where was the harm?

"Well, Penelope," he chided, "what's it to be?"

She pulled on the front of her dress, exposing herself, her nipples tingling as the breeze brushed across her skin.

He stared and stared, then finally stated, "I like big teats. Yours are very small."

Her pert bosom was her most appealing feature—or so she'd believed—so she hadn't realized her figure was lacking. Why hadn't Lavinia told her? It wasn't like her mother to ignore such a hideous flaw.

She'd never been so mortified, and she mumbled, "I'm sorry."

"I'll get over it. I can get over almost anything if there's enough cash involved."

He bent down and put his mouth on her nipple. He sucked very hard, biting with his teeth as she struggled to escape.

"Stop it!" she commanded. "You're hurting me!"

"Am I?"

"Yes."

He halted and straightened. "Do you think I care?"

Tears flooded her eyes, her shame escalating. "I can see that you don't."

"You're so foolish."

"I'm not! I wanted to please you."

"You're too immature to *please* me. Can't you grasp that fact?"

"Give me another chance!"

"Another chance! You'll be lucky if I don't take a switch to you. Don't you know anything about men? I could rape you without consequence. Maybe I *should* talk with your mother."

"But you asked me to . . . to . . ."

"Why would I have you as my bride? You'll have to provide me with a reason why I should bother."

"I'm rich."

"And whores are cheap. I pay them when I'm finished, and I don't have to fuss with them again. If I married you, I'd have to chat with you over the breakfast table every morning for the rest of my life. At the moment, it doesn't seem like much of a bargain."

"I'd do whatever you demanded," she boasted. "I'd never complain."

"Wouldn't you? In light of what I've already observed, I'm convinced you'd be a constant pain in my ass."

"I could satisfy you better than any harlot."

"Now that I doubt." He clutched her nipple, squeezing till she winced. "I'm sick of you. Cover yourself, then go to the house before someone sees us."

"Perhaps I want someone to see us."

"I'd rather throw myself off a cliff than be caught with you."

She glared, wishing she'd had the foresight to bring a pistol with her. If she had, she'd have shot him right through the middle of his black heart.

"I hate you!" she seethed.

"No, you don't. You yearn to be a countess too badly. You're like a dog at a bone. Next time I'm alone, you'll show up to pester me."

"I won't. I'm quite certain of it. I never intend to speak to you again."

"Fine by me."

She stormed away, having been positive that he'd arrived at Gray's Manor because he was sniffing after her fortune. Every man in the world loved her because of her money, yet he acted as if her wealth had no meaning, as if it conferred no special status.

She reached the rear door and rushed to her room. Then she paced for hours, as she plotted and stewed. She would get even. She couldn't predict how or when, but she would, and when she did, he'd never be the same.

❧

Anne Smythe sat at the table on the verandah, munching a scone, but her appetite had fled.

From a parlor window, she'd spied as Penelope Gray had flitted into the woods, as Charles had sauntered after her. The horrid girl had just stomped back, and Anne could only imagine what Charles had done to her. He hadn't reappeared yet, but he would, and Anne pushed her plate away and went inside as Jordan was coming out.

"Anne"—he halted and scrutinized her—"are you all right?"

She shook her head. She was such a fool! Such a stupid, stupid fool! She'd persuaded herself that this occasion would be different, that Charles had been telling her the truth and they would finally marry.

"He's here because of Penelope Gray's dowry," she admitted. "He's going to try to ruin her and force a marriage."

"Of course, he is," Jordan agreed, though gently. "How could you have presumed he planned to do otherwise?"

"I'm so sorry."

"Why should you be sorry? You're not his mother."

"But I let him travel to Gray's Manor. I could have

dissuaded him, or convinced him to visit elsewhere, but he said that . . . well . . . oh, it doesn't matter now."

"Why stay with him, Anne? Leave him. Stop tormenting yourself."

"And where would I go? I've been with him for two decades. This life is all I have, all I know."

"When I'm wed and settled," Jordan proposed, "you'd be welcome to come live with me."

He'd offered before, and she was ashamed to be forty years old and to recognize that it was her only option. "I'm sure your new bride will be happy to have Kettering's mistress as a permanent guest."

"Perhaps not, but we'll figure something out. I appreciate your loyalty to him. I'll always help you."

"I know." Out in the trees, she saw Charles strolling toward them, a confident grin on his face, and her rage surged. "You can't let him get away with this—for Miss Gray's sake as much as your own."

"I won't."

"How will you prevent it?"

"I'll talk to her mother. Don't worry."

"You should probably chat with her at once."

"I'll make it a point."

She continued on into the mansion, momentarily disoriented as she left the bright sunshine and entered the dim corridor. She dawdled, waiting for her vision to adjust, her temper to calm.

She'd been twenty years old and much too vulnerable when she'd cast her lot with Charles. Her fiancé had been killed in an accident, and her parents had both died within months of each other. She'd been on her own and frightened about the future.

In those days, Charles had been so much like Jordan,

handsome and virile and so very masculine. He'd always possessed the heart of a charlatan, but in the beginning, she hadn't understood what he was like. She'd been bowled over, seduced by his promises, and she'd willingly allied herself with him. There'd been no coercion.

Because she'd loved him, she'd remained with him at twenty-five, at thirty. She'd been with him through several marriages, the *other* woman who hoped to eventually take center stage, but what was her excuse now when it was so obvious that her dreams would never come true?

As he chased after Penelope Gray, and prepared to humiliate Anne, once again, after swearing he wouldn't, why did she stay? What was the reason?

She had no idea.

Her world was collapsing, falling away brick by brick, and the notion made her feel wild and reckless.

She started down the hall, when she literally bumped into a man who'd been approaching from the other direction.

"Pardon me," he murmured as he steadied her.

He was a striking fellow, tall and dark, with brown hair and eyes. He was her own age, or a few years younger, and he was well built, his sturdy frame exhibiting a robust physique.

"The fault is mine," Anne insisted. "I apologize."

"Not necessary." He smiled. "I'm Robert Mason, Mrs. Gray's neighbor."

"Oh, hello, Mr. Mason."

"You must be Mrs. Smythe."

"Yes."

"I've heard a great deal about you."

"How terrifying!"

"All of it good," he quickly added, which she knew was a lie.

It was scandalous in the extreme for Anne to have barged in at Gray's Manor, but it was a mark of Charles's notoriety that he'd been allowed to bring Anne into a gentlewoman's home and pass her off as a *friend* of the family.

Mr. Mason hadn't released her arm, and normally, she'd have been upset that he hadn't. With her being Charles's mistress, she was regularly the target of unsolicited attention, but in her current mood, she didn't mind.

It had been an eternity since a handsome man had noticed her, and if he wanted to tarry for the next hour—for the next day!—she was eager to oblige. In fact, in light of her restless emotional condition, she might agree to do anything he requested.

He frowned, studying her. "Have we met previously?"

"I'm sure we haven't."

"You're so familiar."

"I was thinking the very same."

She didn't know if he was speaking the truth, but on her end, the comment was false. There was nothing about him that she recognized, but she was content to linger and gaze into his exquisite brown eyes.

He noted that he was holding her arm, and he dropped it and moved away.

"It was very nice to *bump* into you," he said, amused.

"And you, as well."

She gave him a hot look that was impossible to misinterpret, and she was stunned by her audacity. She never behaved wantonly, never cheated on Charles or even flirted. Not once in all the time they'd been together. Yet suddenly, she'd practically propositioned a stranger.

Whatever the message she'd been sending, he received it with no difficulty. He rippled with surprise as he calculated her intent.

"I hope to see you again very soon," she boldly declared.

"I hope so, too."

"Are you ever about after supper?"

"I'll make it a point to be."

"Marvelous."

He nodded, confused but intrigued, and he walked on.

She left, too, heading for the stairs and away from Charles and the confines of her life that were slowly choking her to death.

CHAPTER SEVEN

"D ammit!"

At Jordan's curse, muttered in the adjacent chamber, Margaret jumped. A crash followed as, in a fit of temper, he smashed something against the wall.

She was amazed to hear him storming about. He always seemed so calm and collected, so in control of every word and action. What could have happened to put him in such a dither?

Tiptoeing to the door, she pressed her ear to the wood, listening as he let fly with a string of epithets. When he smashed another object, she couldn't resist spinning the knob and peeking in. Unfortunately, she hadn't paused to remember that he was in the dressing room, complete with hip bath, soaps, and towels. To her dismay—she refused to call it *delight*—she had stumbled upon him in the same state of undress in which he'd initially found her.

He was attired in a pair of tan breeches that fell to just below the knee. His shirt was missing, as were his shoes and stockings, and she couldn't help but gape.

His back was to her, and as she studied his wide shoulders, his thin waist and hard thighs, he whipped around and barked, "What the hell are you doing home at this hour of the day?"

"The children are busy with summer chores, so there are no classes for a few weeks."

Apparently, she'd interrupted his washing. His hair was damp and swept off his forehead, his skin moist and smooth, and the sight of his naked chest did something funny to her insides. It was broad and manly, covered with a matting of dark hair that was thick on the top, but it tapered to a line in the center, and descended into his pants to destinations she couldn't begin to fathom.

The buttons on his breeches were undone, and she couldn't keep her brazen eyes from drifting down. With ease, she was metamorphosing into a shameless hussy!

Since the occasion when he'd kissed her senseless, she'd been in a fine fettle. Her body was alert and alive, aching in spots she'd never previously noted, and her pleasant demeanor had vanished. She was surly, out-of-sorts, her patience exhausted.

She was desperate to be with him again, and she'd been in a veritable frenzy of anticipation, night after night, expecting that he'd relent and join her, but he hadn't, and his disinterest was driving her crazy.

"What do you want?" he snarled.

"With all the noise in here, I was merely checking to see if you're all right."

"I'm so bloody dandy, I could strangle somebody!"

"Well . . . good. I'll just be going."

He resembled a wild animal that was ready to attack, so she retreated, eager to escape before he pounced.

She took a step, then another, and she'd made it through the door when he lunged after her, approaching until they were toe-to-toe. He towered over her, trying to intimidate her with his size, with his temper, but she wasn't frightened.

His anger was blatant and exciting, and she reveled in it. She was thrilled to have him so near, to have all his concentration focused on her, and it occurred to her that she might do anything to keep it.

"Why are you poking your nose into my affairs?" he demanded.

"I told you: I was checking on you."

"I don't need you hovering."

"So, go away. Did I ask you to follow me in here?"

He gripped her waist. "Don't you know how dangerous it is to taunt me when I'm in such a foul mood?"

"Me? Taunt you? I was minding my own business, in my own bedchamber, till you started rampaging like a monster."

"A monster? Yes, that's exactly how I feel."

He picked her up and twirled them so that they fell onto her bed. They bounced on the mattress; then he rolled and pinned her down.

Having no notion of what to do next, he stared at her, and his expression was filled with such longing and confusion that it was almost comical. He was on edge and keen to lash out, but he wouldn't be violent. His energy had to be channeled in another direction, into conduct she couldn't describe but relished.

She reached out and placed her hands on his chest. His skin was warm and soft, and at feeling her he was pushed off the cliff where he'd been perched.

He initiated a searing kiss, his tongue in her mouth,

his fingers in her hair. He seemed to be searching for something, or pleading for something, though she wasn't sure what it was. She felt as if she were on a ship at sea, that she was being tossed in turbulent waves and about to sink to the bottom. She had to hold on and hope that he would guide her safely to the shore when the tempest had passed.

"Touch me all over," he ordered. "Don't stop for a single second."

"I won't."

At his command she realized that she'd been lying like a statue, and she leapt into the foray, stroking his shoulders, his back, even daring once to dip down and massage his buttocks.

Her caress was like lightening, electrifying him, and his passion grew more intense, his need more powerful. Her own body was in an awful state, her pulse pounding, her nipples throbbing.

He settled himself between her legs, his torso fitting there as if it had been specially created to welcome him. His privates were wedged to hers in a way that she recognized and craved, and as he clutched her to him and began to thrust, her hips met his with an equal vigor.

"What are you doing to me?" she managed on a gasp.

"I've explained this before: I'm making love to you. Pay attention."

"But you keep flexing into me. Why?"

"It's how a man makes love to a woman, how a husband makes love to his wife."

"I don't understand."

"Does it feel good?"

"Yes."

"Then you don't need to *understand*. Just do it for me."

"Beast!" she chided.

"Yes, I am. I'm a beast, and you're crazy to be with me like this."

"I'm not afraid of you."

"You should be."

"I'm not."

He was fumbling with her gown, struggling with the buttons, but in his frustrated condition, he couldn't free them.

"Bloody dress! Next time I come in here"—her heart soared at the prospect of there being a *next* time—"have your clothes off prior to my arrival. I want you naked and waiting for me. Save me all this trouble!"

He was jerking at the fabric and about to rip the garment in half. She had such limited apparel and couldn't have him destroying any of it.

"Stop!" she scolded. "If you need me to remove my dress, we can discuss it like civilized people. I won't permit you to tear it to shreds as if you were some sort of barbarian."

"I want it off now!"

He gave a ferocious tug as material split and buttons flew. With a smirk of satisfaction, he rolled them again so that he was on the bottom and she was draped across him, her breasts spilling into his hands. He squeezed the two mounds, pinching the nipples, and she hissed with pleasure.

"This is how I desire you," he said. "This is all I contemplate, all I ponder. My dreams of having you like this—they consume me!"

"That can't be true."

"Have you any idea how I've longed for you?"

"No."

"Can you imagine how difficult it's been to be right next door, to yearn for you so badly but not be able to have you?"

"I *can* imagine." She'd been dying to be with him, too, but she couldn't bear to suppose that he'd felt the same.

He rooted to her breast and took the tip into his mouth, nursing as a babe would its mother, though with none of the tenderness. He was rough and insistent, and he seemed to know what she needed when she wasn't aware herself. She didn't want gentle treatment or placid interaction. She wanted fire and heat, and he gave all she required and so much more.

He kept on and on, until she was writhing in misery, in ecstasy. He shifted from one nipple to the other, going back and forth, back and forth, and she worried that she might explode.

"Desist!" she eventually implored, and she tried to squirm away, but he wouldn't release her.

"You can't quit until I decide you're finished."

"But you're killing me! I can't stand much more."

He was inching her skirt up her leg, pulling it higher and higher, until he was at the juncture of her thighs. He pressed down with the heel of his hand, providing a modicum of relief, but it wasn't nearly enough.

"Jordan, please . . ."

She didn't know for what she was beseeching. She wanted the agony to cease, but she wanted it to go on forever.

"Yes, say my name," he murmured. "Say my name as you beg me."

"Jordan! Oh!"

He slithered into her drawers and through her womanly hair, when suddenly, he slid a finger inside her. A second joined the first, and he stroked them in a rhythm that made her body tense and ripple.

"Has any man ever touched you like this before?"

"Are you mad? Who would have?"

"So I'm the only one?"

"Of course, you are! Do you think me a trollop?"

He grinned. "Let me show you something."

"What?"

"You'll see."

He sucked on her nipple as his thumb flicked at a spot she'd never noted prior. He jabbed once, again, again, and she shattered into a thousand pieces. She was blinded by rapture and careening across the universe. A harsh noise rang out, and she thought it might be herself, wailing with bliss, which couldn't be possible. She was much too restrained for such a shocking exhibition.

Finally, she reached a peak and floated down, landing safely in his arms, and he looked very smug.

"My goodness," she breathed.

He chuckled. "You are so easy."

"What was that?"

"It was a very stunning example of sexual pleasure. It's called an orgasm or a climax."

"Can it occur more than once?"

"Yes, it can occur over and over."

She gazed at the ceiling, disconcerted and wondering if a person could become addicted. Was it like a dangerous drug? Would she be chasing after him, cornering him in dark alcoves and demanding he do it again?

"Did I . . . did I . . . cry out?"

"Very loudly."

"Aah! Do you suppose anyone heard me?"

"Let's hope not."

He adjusted her dress, covering her; then he snuggled her onto her side and spooned himself to her. They cuddled in the quiet, and it was the most precious, most splendid moment of her life. She shut her eyes, absorbing every smell, every sound when, in a slow, deliberate motion, he flexed against her bottom.

"I'm so hard for you," he muttered, and he quivered, seeming distraught.

The comment puzzled her, and she tried to rise up and turn around, but he wouldn't let her.

"What do you mean—you're *hard*?"

"Lie still." He pushed her down.

"Jordan!"

"I told you to lie still!"

"Why should I?"

"Because I want you—in such a thoroughly masculine fashion—that if you wiggle your ass at me one more time, I can't say what I might do."

"I don't understand you, at all."

"I wouldn't expect you to."

"Quit talking in riddles. I detest it."

He took another leisurely flex, and he moaned.

"Are you in pain?"

"Yes."

"Can I help you?"

"No."

She elbowed him in the ribs. "Don't be such a grump."

"When I'm this miserable, I can't act any other way."

She froze. Was he claiming he hadn't enjoyed what

they'd done? Was he hinting that he'd found her lacking in her amorous abilities? For pity's sake, she was a spinster! How could she know any different?

She struggled around enough so that she could frown at him.

"Why would you be *miserable*? As I am the one who's been ravaged, you'd better say something nice. And be quick about it!"

"Stop looking at me like that."

"Like what?"

"You have the most seductive eyes."

"I do?"

"You make me want to take you and damn the consequences."

"*Take me* how?"

He sighed with exasperation. "I've never been in bed with a virgin before, so I didn't realize it could be so tedious."

"What a horrid thing to tell me."

She scrambled away to storm out in a huff, but he clutched her even tighter and nestled her down again.

"There's more to it," he whispered.

"Then explain it to me."

"I can experience the same ecstasy as you."

"But you didn't?"

"No, and it makes me grouchy. I'm so aroused that even my teeth are aching. I can barely keep from proceeding."

"So go ahead. What's preventing you?"

"There are other . . . uh . . . aspects to it."

"And I want to do them!"

"You just think you do," he declared.

"No, I'm pretty sure I mean it."

"It involves my ruining you, my taking your virginity."

"How does that transpire? I've always wondered."

"It's for your husband to demonstrate."

She scoffed. "As if some *man* would marry me. Especially after this!"

"It requires something totally magnificent, but totally reckless, and if we carried on and you later wished you hadn't, you couldn't ever fix what we'd done."

"You're speaking in riddles again."

"Just believe that I like you too much to hurt you that way."

At his admission, she smiled. "You do?"

"Yes. You provoke me beyond my limits. I don't know what to do with you."

She gazed at the far wall, the marvelous words sinking in. In the past, she'd never thought much about marriage, but now that she'd met him, it dawned on her that there was an entire side to it that she'd never considered. What would it be like to have a man like Jordan for her own? The prospect had her seriously reflecting on what she'd missed by remaining a spinster, and suddenly, it seemed like so very much.

She yawned, and he laughed.

"I'm tired."

"I bet you are. Sex can be rather draining."

"Will you show me what to do someday? Will you teach me how to please you?"

After a lengthy hesitation, he murmured, "I will."

He grabbed for a blanket and covered them with it, sealing them in a snug cocoon. She reached over her shoulder to caress his cheek, and he kissed her hand.

"Why were you angry?" she inquired.

"When?"

"When I first heard you in the dressing room, you were very upset."

"My father is here."

"I know. I was introduced to him."

"He can be difficult."

"Really? He seemed very charming to me."

He snorted. "Charming, yes. He's definitely charming, but you should be wary of him."

"Wary? Of your father? Would he harm me?"

"Well, you don't have any money, so he probably won't notice you, but he's capable of any treachery."

"Your father?" she queried again, not quite able to accept it.

"Yes. Hush now. Rest for a bit."

He pulled her closer, and shortly, her eyelids drifted shut. She dozed, content in the circle of his arms, but when she awoke, he was gone, the bedchamber next door eerily silent, and there was no sign that he'd ever been there with her, at all.

CHAPTER EIGHT

I t's not fair that such a horrid child should have so
   much money."

"No, it's not." Anne toasted Charles with her glass
of brandy.

"Why would Fate waste a bloody fortune on someone so unworthy?"

"I believe that's why it's called *Fate*," Anne said.
"There's no rational explanation."

She'd had too much to drink, which was dangerous.
In light of her ill humor, she might say anything, even
things she didn't mean, even things she couldn't retract
later on.

She didn't usually overindulge, but her reckless mood
was growing stronger by the second, and she was desperate to tamp it down.

Would Charles steal Jordan's fiancée? Would he marry
again after swearing to Anne that he wouldn't? Could he
really behave that badly to the last two people on earth
who still tolerated him?

If he made a play for Penelope Gray, then Anne would

have to make a play of her own. She couldn't stay with him, and she yearned to ask him outright, to demand a straight answer, but she was too much of a coward.

If he admitted that he was about to seduce Miss Gray, Anne would finally be pushed into a decision. But where would she go? What would she do?

By hooking up with Charles as she had, she'd lost contact with friends or relatives who might have assisted her in a crisis. She was on her own, with Jordan as her sole ally, but his financial situation was even more precarious than hers, and she wouldn't add herself to his burden of responsibilities.

She'd have to depart with only a satchel of clothes and not a penny in her pocket. The notion was terrifying and had kindled the strange temper that she couldn't shake.

Charles was preening in the mirror, dressed for bed, and planning that she join him for their regular nocturnal romp.

"What do you think?" He glanced over at her. "Am I a handsome dog or what?"

"Very handsome, Charles."

"The ladies still titter over me."

"Yes, they do."

"I'd love to have all Miss Gray's money in my bank account. It would certainly solve many of our troubles."

"It certainly would."

At a prior period in her life, when she'd been younger and more naïve, she might not have grasped the subtle message he was sending, might not have guessed how his mind was leaping forward to justify the conduct that he would perpetrate shortly. But she was no longer a girl, and he was no longer a mystery.

She stared him down, refusing—for once—to pretend she didn't understand the ramifications of his scheme.

"You're old enough to be her grandfather," she said very quietly.

For a brief moment, he let her see the resolve behind the façade; then he masked it and chuckled as if his remark had been a joke.

"Of course, I am. She'd never notice an elderly fellow such as myself. Not when there's a dashing buck like Jordan sniffing about."

"Don't do it, Charles," she warned. "I'm begging you not to—for both Jordan's sake and my own."

"Anne!" He scoffed as if she were mad. "Are you presuming I'm interested in Miss Gray? You and I will marry—as soon as I hear from my attorneys about that last lien that was filed. We can't wed till I have a home to take you to. It wouldn't be fair."

"Swear it!" she tersely urged. "Swear to me that you mean it!"

"How could you doubt me?"

His expression was so sincere. If he hadn't been born an aristocrat, he could have had a brilliant career on the stage. He was so credible, and he was absolutely lying.

She swigged her brandy and walked to the door.

He scowled. "Where are you going?"

"I'm tired this evening."

"But you know I wish to fornicate."

"I have a headache."

It was a blatant fib, one he couldn't help but decipher. Yet he shrugged off the snub as if he couldn't care less, which was a further indicator of how set he was on Miss Gray. When he was prepared to copulate, he never let Anne decline, and she never did. If he allowed her to leave, he was already so immersed in his plot to ensnare Penelope that there could be no other outcome.

"Good night," she murmured.

She hurried out and shut the door with a determined click.

❧

H ello, Mr. Mason."
      "Hello, Mrs. Smythe."
      Robert pulled to a halt, stunned to have stumbled on her in a downstairs parlor at such a late hour.

He'd been huddled in Lavinia's library, poring over her financial records, still trying to make sense of them but having no luck. He couldn't figure out the numbers, and in light of her inheritance from Horatio, she seemed to have had too much income at her disposal over the years, which increased his confusion over her predicament and how best to rectify it.

His head was throbbing with questions, and he definitely welcomed the diversion Mrs. Smythe presented. She was over in the shadows by the window and sipping on a brandy. The house was silent, and he'd thought everyone was sleeping, so he couldn't imagine why she was roaming the halls. Perhaps she was an insomniac as he was himself.

She was clad in her nightclothes, her magnificent brown hair brushed out and flowing down her back, and she was wearing a very sheer negligee and robe, evidence that she'd tried to slumber but couldn't. To his amazement, on seeing him she wasn't embarrassed over her dishabille, and she did nothing to conceal her shapely form or hide what he shouldn't be permitted to view.

His manly instincts were stirred. He hadn't forgotten the hot look she'd flashed the first time they'd met, and he'd been dying to learn what she'd implied by it. Maybe he was about to find out!

She approached, a saucy smile on her ruby lips, the indomitable glide of her curvaceous hips bringing her so close that her fabulous breasts were nearly touching his shirt.

"We're all alone," she stated.

"Yes, we are."

"Did you know I'm not really *Mrs.* Smythe?"

"No, I didn't."

"I've never been married." Her speech was slurred, a sign that she was intoxicated. "I just say that I was. For Charles's sake. Actually, I'm his . . . mistress."

She uttered the word *mistress* as if she was eager to astound and offend, and he frowned, anxious as to where the encounter was leading. It seemed as if she was about to proposition him, which was such an outrageous prospect that he couldn't credit it.

If he had any kind of manners, he'd escort her to the stairs, point her toward her bedchamber, then depart, but apparently, his chivalrous tendencies had fled.

"Are you married, Mr. Mason?"

"I'm a widower. I have two sons."

"I don't have any children. Charles insisted I not."

"I'm sorry for you," he replied, meaning it.

"Don't be. I could have chosen another path."

"Could you have?"

"Oh, yes, but I assumed that Charles was the man for me."

"But he wasn't?"

She stepped in, her body pressed to his, her breasts,

stomach, and mound of Venus setting off wildfires of sensation in various charged spots.

"You're very handsome, Robert."

He gulped. "Am I?"

"I realize that you're just a country gentleman, but have you ever fantasized over what it would be like to fuck a genuine London harlot?"

The crude remark was beyond him, and he couldn't respond as she reached out and traced a finger across the bulge in his trousers. With the gesture, there was no mistaking her intent. She wanted him.

Why would she? Did it matter why?

"Mrs. Smythe—" He couldn't finish the sentence. He was a moral fellow, but she was throwing herself at him. Was it wrong to catch her?

"Since I'm about to screw you blind," she boldly pronounced, "you should probably call me Anne."

"Anne, I think you've had a little too much to drink."

"You're right, I have, and it's given me the most keen insight."

"In what way?"

"I'm curious as to what it would be like to have sex with you."

"That's the alcohol talking."

"Perhaps."

"You'll regret it in the morning."

"No, I won't. I'm positive I'll be delighted."

She gripped the waistband of his pants and started to open them. Like a frozen ninny, he watched her. The interlude had an unreal quality to it, as if he were in the middle of an erotic dream. At any second, he was certain he'd awaken, but he didn't.

The buttons on the placard were easily freed, and she slithered her naughty hand inside to circle his enthused cock. The pleasure was so severe that he was in danger of swooning like a girl.

She cupped him, gauging weight and girth. "You're very fine, Robert. Very fine."

At the compliment, his balls swelled, and his phallus extended even farther—if that was possible. He was close to pushing her onto the sofa and having at it, and he felt as if he were back in his dormitory at school, listening as the older boys regaled each other with their preposterous, virginal stories. They'd all pretended that the indecent, anonymous trysts had truly occurred, but Robert had always secretly regarded them to be boasting.

Now, he wasn't so sure. This sort of raucous incident might be extremely common. How could he be thirty-six and not have known?

He was dawdling like a statue, was stammering and gaping, but if she was bent on seduction, he was eager to have it happen.

"Get down on your knees," he commanded to see if she would obey. "Take me in your mouth."

Without hesitation or complaint, she dropped down, and he almost fell over in shock. Did women really act this way? She'd mentioned she was from London. If this conduct was typical, he might have to relocate to the city!

She drew his rod from his trousers, and she licked the crown, lapping at it until he was oozing with sexual juice, and he was quickly spurred to the point where he was about to embarrass himself. It was the most unbelievable, carnal episode of his life. How could he be expected to muster any restraint?

He wound his fingers into her hair, noticing how soft it was, how beautiful she looked, and he began to thrust, but he'd been goaded to insanity, and he jerked away before he spilled himself like a callow boy.

"What do you want from me?" he demanded.

She gazed up at him, her brown eyes poignant and weary. "Is it that difficult to understand?"

"Yes."

"If you're confused, I'm happy to explain it."

"You're naught but a whore."

He had no idea why he'd said such a terrible thing to her, but she shrugged off the uncouth taunt.

"Yes, I am, though it's recently dawned on me that—over the years—I haven't been paid nearly enough."

She rose slowly, gracefully, and she glared at him; then she wrapped her arms around him and kissed him. He wasn't immune to the embrace, and he clutched at her with an equal fervor.

There was a sofa behind her, and he shoved her down and knelt on the rug. With no finesse, he tugged at the hem of her negligee, yanked at her thighs, and impaled himself between them.

He flexed once, twice, and he came in a hot rush, crushing himself to her, shooting his seed deeper and deeper. The moment was so decadent, his deplorable betrayal of Lavinia so satisfying, that he was more aroused than he'd ever been. The climax went on and on, and he reveled in it, barely able to keep from braying like the beast he was.

Finally, it ebbed, and he ground to a halt. He scowled

at her, conjecturing as to what she thought. Not that he cared. She was a trollop who, for reasons he couldn't fathom, had let him take her on the couch in the front parlor. Yet, a man had his pride.

He knew how to make love to a woman, but her salacious advance had caught him off guard, so he hadn't done it very well. Rattled by his actions—and hers—he eased away, not sure of what to say.

She straightened her nightgown and smirked. "I guess I didn't have to explain it, after all. You figured it out on your own."

Without another word being exchanged, she stood and left. He hovered in the quiet, his cock hanging out, sweat cooling on his brow, as he pondered what he'd just set in motion.

He had to fornicate with her again. There was no other choice.

※

P ull."

"I'm pulling! I'm pulling!"

"Well, pull harder!"

Penelope gave a particularly vicious wrench on the corset laces, and Lavinia let out a whoosh of air. She was determined to have her waist cinched to the size of a twig.

"How's that?" Penelope asked.

"It will have to do."

Lavinia assessed her profile in the mirror, wondering if she shouldn't ring for a maid's assistance, but she was in a hurry to finish dressing and get downstairs.

There were entirely too many females in the house, and Lavinia was resolved to be the only one who held Charles's attention.

After what she privately thought of as the fellatio disaster, he hadn't deigned to dally with her again. She was still humiliated and so desperate to rectify the situation that she'd considered practicing on Robert, seeking his advice as to what he liked and didn't, but she wouldn't grovel to learn what she needed to know.

If it killed her, she would tempt Charles back to her boudoir.

She selected her most stylish gown from the wardrobe, and she had Penelope help her put it on.

"Honestly, Lavinia," Penelope chided, "what's the occasion?"

"I'm hosting an earl. Can't I look the part?"

"It won't do you any good."

"What do you mean?"

"You're obviously hoping to entice him, but it won't work."

"Why shouldn't I try for him? He's a rich, charming aristocrat. And he's a widower. I was married to an aged man once, so I know what it takes to keep them happy."

Penelope snorted. "Are you claiming that Father was . . . was . . . *happy* with you? My Lord, but that's hilarious."

"Horatio was very, very happy with me. I was his whole life!"

"Right!"

Lavinia seized Penelope's wrist and pinched with sufficient force to make her wince.

"Shut your rude mouth before I shut it for you."

They glared, eye-to-eye and toe-to-toe, and Lavinia insisted, "Lord Kettering could do much worse than me."

"You're so old, Mother. You can't seriously assume that he finds you attractive."

"I'm not *old*. I'm only thirty-four."

"You're positively ancient. If he wanted an elderly—"

"Elderly! How dare you!"

"As I was saying, if he wanted an *elderly* wife, he'd have settled on Mrs. Smythe years ago." She primped her perfect blond curls, adoring her reflection in the mirror. "When he weds, he always picks a debutante."

"Where did you hear such an idiotic rumor?"

"The housekeeper was telling one of the maids. I guess he's been married several times, and the brides get younger with every wedding."

Penelope had a sly grin on her face, and Lavinia froze.

The treacherous, duplicitous monster! She thought to make a play for Charles herself!

Lavinia clasped Penelope's arm and whirled her around.

"You will marry Lord Romsey as I've arranged."

"Maybe. Maybe not."

"I brought him here specifically for you. You will do as you're told."

"And what if I don't? What if I'd rather have the Earl? Why should you get him? If you think Romsey is so grand, you can keep him for yourself."

"You spoiled child! I've done everything for you. Everything! Yet you would repay me with perfidy?"

"Why would it be perfidy? I say—when there's a title to be had—it's every woman for herself."

"You . . . you . . ."

Lavinia slapped Penelope as hard as she could. Penelope shrieked, and in an instant, they were wrestling on the floor in an all-out brawl.

"I'll murder you before I let you have him," Lavinia threatened.

"Well, it won't be up to you, will it? The choice will be Charles's to make. We'll see which of us he likes best."

Lavinia howled with rage, and she bucked and rolled till she was on top and pinning Penelope down. Her fingernails were bared like a cat's claws, ready to scratch Penelope's eyes out when, without warning, a pair of male hands grabbed her and yanked her to her feet.

She whipped around, about to lash out at the interloper, but when she found herself confronting Robert, she blanched.

She couldn't have him discover the reason for the fight! Robert was convinced she was about to marry him. And she might have—if Charles Kettering hadn't ridden up the drive and presented such a marvelous opportunity.

Hastily, she smoothed her features, patted at her hair, and tugged at her twisted corset.

"Lavinia! Penelope!" he scolded. "What's come over the two of you? They could probably hear your caterwauling all the way in the village. You have guests!"

He helped Penelope rise, and as she stood, she flashed Lavinia a look of seething hatred; then she turned to Robert, all innocent smiles and cordiality.

"Mother and I were just having a small disagreement."

"About what?"

"Ask Lavinia. She'll tell you all about it." She snickered and strutted out, stopping at the last second. "Robert, are you still planning to marry Lavinia?"

"You know I am."

"What fabulous news! I'm certain she can't wait."

She laughed and waltzed out, leaving Lavinia to explain the cryptic comment, and Lavinia decided she understood why some animals ate their young.

CHAPTER NINE

Margaret heard a floorboard creak, and she spun around, stunned to note that Jordan had followed her to her dilapidated schoolroom.

Despite Lavinia's protests, Margaret had used an abandoned crofter's hut at the edge of the property. The children who came for lessons, as well as their parents, were accustomed to the squalor, but Jordan Prescott was a different kettle of fish altogether. If he teased or berated her, she'd be very hurt.

Though it was foolish, she wanted his approval and esteem. The dislike she'd harbored for him had vanished, and it was gradually being replaced by emotions that were much more complicated. She was fascinated by him—both as a person and as a man—and her budding intrigue was dangerous.

After their previous tryst in her bedchamber, she hadn't seen him again. He'd been markedly absent, seeming to know when she'd take supper, or arrive for afternoon tea, and he was never present.

At night, she huddled in misery, wishing he'd relent and visit her, but ultimately being glad when he didn't.

He was trying to behave, which was for the best, but still, she couldn't comprehend how he ignored the passion that sizzled between them. Even now, with him loitering over in the doorway, she could feel the energy sparking, her body humming with the delight she experienced whenever he was near.

"Hello, Lord Romsey."

"Call me Jordan, or call me nothing." He pushed away from his perch in the threshold and came toward her. "I thought your students were busy with summer chores. What are you doing here?"

He approached, skirting the worn slab of wood that passed for her desk, until he was directly in front of her.

"Why must I explain myself to you? I wouldn't think my whereabouts, or how I spend my time, to be any of your affair."

"Can't a man be curious?"

"Why are you following me?" she countered.

"I saw you walking, and I was dying to know where you were headed."

"So you deemed it appropriate to spy?"

"Yes," he said without a hint of remorse.

She braced, certain he would touch her, but he didn't. He kept his hands pinned behind his back, and she was so disappointed. She gestured around the dark, dank space. "Are you content with what you've discovered?"

He whipped away, as if he didn't like being so close to her. He fussed with one of the children's slates, thumbed through a ragged storybook.

His censure clear, he frowned. "Why do you do this?"

"Do what?"

"Teach the neighborhood urchins."

"Why shouldn't I?"

"You're a gently bred female. It isn't seemly for you to be working."

"I don't consider it to be work."

"What do you *consider* it to be?"

"I'm merely being helpful to those in need."

"You get paid! It's just not right."

He uttered the comment as if she were prostituting herself, and she wanted to shake him. Who was he to chastise and condemn?

He was in Sussex to marry Penelope for her money. At least Margaret had the satisfaction of laboring for the few pennies she was given. How would he describe what he was prepared to do? How could he live with himself?

"Would it be better if I did it for free?"

"It would be better if you didn't do it, at all."

"I'll keep that in mind." She picked up her bonnet and tied the bow; then she started out. "Good-bye, Lord Romsey."

"Where are you off to now?" he had the audacity to inquire.

"I'm sick of your boorish attitudes and your stuffy opinions, and I have no desire to linger while you spew more of them. I'm returning to the house, where I promise to be idle for the rest of the day. Will that make you happy?"

She tried to stomp past him, but he blocked her exit.

"Move!" she demanded.

"No."

"I won't stay here with you. Not when you're being so critical." She was so proud of how much she'd built, with what little she'd had, and she hated his scorn.

"What is the real reason?"

"The *real* reason for what?"

His scathing regard swept the decrepit area. "You can't convince me that you enjoy this."

"Actually, I do, and you're an incredible snob."

"Me?"

"Yes, you. I've been given so much. Why is it so difficult for you to accept that I'd like to give something back?"

"You assume you've been given much?" He studied her tattered cloak, her frayed bonnet, and his disdain was cruel. "Pray tell, what—precisely—have you received?"

"My uncle, Horatio, took me in when I was a girl. He offered me a home, clothes to wear, food to eat."

"As any guardian should."

"He provided for me, when he could have declined. And I love children. I won't ever have any of my own, so—"

"Why would you say that?"

"Not everyone is born rich—as you well know. I can't snap my fingers and produce a dowry."

"Maybe someone will marry you anyway. Maybe some lucky fellow will decide he likes you no matter what, and money—or the lack of it—won't be an issue."

"And maybe pigs will sprout wings and fly."

"Maybe."

He stepped in, the tips of his boots slipping under the hem of her skirt, and he rested a hand on her waist. He looked angry and exasperated with her, and she couldn't imagine why he would be. Why would he care what she did?

"Stop carping at me," she murmured.

"I'm not."

"I'm doing something worthwhile."

"I understand that."

"No, you don't." She glanced away, amazed when she added, "I can't bear my life. I have to occupy my time, or I'll go mad."

There was a long, charged interval, where he assessed her in a thrilling fashion, then he muttered, "I want to kiss you again."

Her heart pounded. "You do not."

"Don't tell me what I want or don't."

"You never even think about me."

"Now that, my darling Margaret, is where you're wrong."

He dipped under her bonnet, the rim in his way, and, growling in frustration, he tugged it off, and threw it on the floor. His mouth connected with hers, sweetly, tenderly. He held her as if she was precious and cherished, and the silence settled around them, so that there was just him, and her, and the quiet summer afternoon in the woods.

He pulled away, and it dawned on her that she could never have enough of him, not if he stayed a hundred years, and the realization made her terribly sad.

Deep in thought, he traced a thumb across her lip and asked, "Would you be my mistress?"

Had she heard him correctly? "What?"

"You know what I said. I won't embarrass the both of us by repeating it."

She gaped at him, stunned and impossibly hurt.

"When would this occur? Would it be before or after you have my cousin's fortune in your bank account?"

It was his turn to glance away. "Well . . . after."

"So you'd marry her, then your first act would be to set me up as your paramour. Would I have a fine house in town?"

"If that's what you wanted."

"And a beautiful wardrobe?"

"That goes without saying."

"My own carriage, and a box at the theater?"

"Of course."

"As you crept between my bed and Penelope's, we'd have to devise a schedule so she didn't suspect where you were on the evenings you were away. Don't you find the notion a tad disconcerting?"

"Margaret . . ."

"Obviously, she'd have your children. Your *legitimate* children. Would I have some, too? Would I be graced with a gaggle of little Prescott bastards?"

A muscle ticked in his cheek. "You make it sound so tawdry."

"That's because it would be." She scooped up her hat and pushed by him. "Don't raise the subject again. It insults me when you do."

She walked into the bright sunshine, and she blinked against the glare. To her surprise, there were tears in her eyes, but she'd die before she'd let him see them. She started toward the manor, her heart heavy, her musings morose.

Was this all there was for her? A brief fling with a handsome man whom she didn't even particularly like? Would there never be more?

He was advancing on her from behind, and she

increased her pace, but he easily caught her. He slipped his arm into hers so that it appeared as if they were taking a stroll.

He shrugged. "I'm sorry. I had to learn your response."

"I can't believe your gall."

"Why shouldn't I have suggested it? Such an arrangement is common, and we'd both benefit."

"I'm not positive how females behave in the city, but I'm not some London doxy. I'm just a very private gentlewoman, from a small, rural estate, who's getting by as best she can. I have no idea why your roving eye has fallen on me, and I take no pleasure in our acquaintance."

"Don't you?"

At his pointing out the carnal implication of her statement she blushed. "You know very well what I'm saying."

"Yes, I do." He sighed as if he had the weight of the world on his shoulders. "Would you at least agree to be my lover while I'm here?"

She chuckled. "You grow more outrageous by the second."

"Does that mean your answer is *no*?"

"My answer is *no*." She was very firm, but as she peeked up into his magnetic blue eyes, her resolve wavered.

She'd never meet another like him, and her life was all drudgery and monotony. What if she dared to reach out and grab for some excitement? What if she dared to take what she wanted? Had she the courage?

"It would be so wrong," she insisted.

"Probably, but let's do it anyway."

"You're a man, so I suppose it's only natural you'd think that way."

"At night, when you're all alone, don't you ever wish I'd join you?"

"I admit it: I do, but that's in the night, in the dark. When I awake to the full light of day, I'm glad you stayed away."

Looking young and hesitant, he stared down the path and kicked at a rock. "It's hard not to come to you. I contemplate it all the time. After the other morning, when we—"

She placed her fingers on his lips, stopping whatever he might have confessed. She was thrilled by the news that he was pining for her, but she'd already discovered that, where he was concerned, she had no self-control.

If he declared a heightened affection, she'd never be able to maintain her moral stance. She'd leap to iniquity, and when he wed and left her, where would she be?

"We're adults, Lord Romsey. We might have sinful impulses, but we don't have to act on them."

"When you're in the throes of passion, you call me Jordan."

"And you are a beast to remind me of it."

"If I sneak in some evening, will you send me away?"

"Yes, I will."

It was a bald-faced lie, but she hoped he didn't recognize it as one. When she was so desperate to be with him, the prospect of her exercising any willpower and fending him off was laughable. If he was determined to enter, she'd be happy to let him.

Oh, she was so weak! So lacking in principle! She'd always pictured herself as a strong woman, a decent woman, but a few stolen kisses had altered her completely.

"How is Penelope?" she inquired. She was anxious to switch the topic and interject some sanity so he remembered why he was at Gray's Manor. "Any progress on the marital front?"

"I'm fairly sure that she hates me"—he grinned—"but I'm wearing her down."

Margaret chuckled and they walked on, ambling arm-and-arm, as if they were close friends. She allowed him to escort her all the way to the house and in the rear door, and she reveled in his elegant manners and gallant charm. When they parted, she was proud of how well she managed to hide her sorrow that he could never be anything more to her than he was at that very moment.

❦

L avinia gazed out the window, watching as Margaret and Lord Romsey promenaded through the garden. They were a handsome couple, and it was enjoyable to observe them as they passed under her perch, unaware of her elevated scrutiny.

They were entirely too cordial, as if they knew each other well, as if they'd established a relationship of which Lavinia was totally ignorant.

When would Margaret have had the chance to become so familiar with him? And she was extremely *familiar.* Lavinia had no doubt. She studied how Margaret leaned toward him, how she smiled whenever he spoke, and Lavinia rippled with unease.

What was Margaret's game? Was she making a play for Romsey? Was she planning to snatch him right from under Penelope's nose?

The little tart! If that was her ploy, Lavinia would kill her.

She went to the mirror and dabbed powder on the scratches Penelope had inflicted during their physical altercation. When she witnessed them, her rage bubbled up, but she refused to be distracted.

She and Margaret had to have a chat, and she proceeded to the other wing of the mansion, to Margaret's bedchamber, certain that was where Margaret was headed. She was climbing the stairs as she heard Margaret and Romsey approaching from the other direction.

She halted and peeked around the corner, blatantly spying, listening to them joke and carry on like bosom companions. Romsey deposited Margaret at her door, then continued on to the adjacent room as if it was his own.

Lavinia scowled, waiting. Shortly, Romsey exited, having changed his coat, and he left the way he'd come.

As his strides faded, she stomped over and peered inside, and she was stunned to see his clothes. He . . . he . . . was in the room next to Margaret's!

Lavinia quivered with fury. When she'd told the housekeeper to lodge him by Miss Gray, she shouldn't have had to specify to which *Miss Gray* she was referring. How could the competent servant have made such a ghastly error?

She marched to Margaret's door, knocked once, then entered without being invited. Margaret was seated at a small writing desk by the window.

"Hello, Lavinia," she welcomed, but she couldn't conceal her annoyance at Lavinia's unannounced appearance.

Lavinia scanned the space, searching for anything out of the ordinary, for any sign of trouble, but everything seemed satisfactory. "How long has Lord Romsey been in the bedchamber next to yours?"

"Since the day he arrived."

"Why didn't you tell me?"

Margaret's expression was all innocence. "I thought you meant to put him there. Why would I comment?"

Lavinia went into the dressing room that was conveniently and dangerously situated between the two bedchambers, but it revealed no mischief, either.

When she stormed back, Margaret had risen from her chair and was assessing Lavinia as if she'd gone mad.

"I saw the two of you sauntering in the yard," Lavinia accused.

"Yes, we were."

"Why were you together?"

"I'd visited my school, and I ran into him in the woods as I was returning. He escorted me home."

"That's all?"

"Yes, that's all." Margaret frowned. "Honestly, Lavinia, what's come over you?"

Lavinia advanced on her, and though she wasn't much bigger than Margaret, her wrath made her seem much larger. Margaret had always been too confident, too sure of herself. She paraded around like a bloody queen, acting as if *she* were lady of the manor, instead of a penniless orphan who was tolerated because of Lavinia's benevolence.

"Swear to me that there's nothing between you."

"Between whom?"

"Don't play dumb with me, Margaret. It doesn't become you."

"Between me and Lord Romsey?" She was aghast at the suggestion.

"Yes."

"I swear."

"He's going to marry Penelope."

"I know that. Everybody knows it."

"No matter what you hope, no matter how hard you pray, he'll never pick you. If you assume so, you're a fool."

"I can't imagine why you're saying these things to me. You're speaking as if I . . . I . . . have designs on him."

"Let me be very clear: His debts are so vast, his responsibilities so enormous. He has to choose Penelope—or another girl just like her."

"I realize that."

Lavinia scrutinized her, then nodded. "Good. Don't forget it, for if you betray me, if you try to snag him for your own, I'll kill you. Do we understand one another?"

"Kill me! You're being entirely too melodramatic, and I have no idea why you're behaving this way. I don't even like him. Penelope can have him—with my blessing."

"He needs to spend more time with her, so that he can get to know her better. I don't want to see you with him again."

"You won't."

"I'm sending the maids to move his belongings over to the other part of the house, so he can be nearer to his intended."

"Fine."

"Fine."

Lavinia stepped into the hall, her mind racing, her misgivings not assuaged.

Margaret hadn't seemed distressed by the news that Jordan would be relocated, but still, one could never be too careful, so she would have to watch Margaret like a hawk. There were too many plans in the works, too many irons in the fire, and Margaret could not be allowed to interfere with any of them.

CHAPTER TEN

Jordan heard the door open, and he jerked awake and peered through the dark. Someone was sneaking in, but who? And why?

He prayed it wasn't Charles in need of assistance, Penelope hoping to be ruined, or Lavinia wanting to tryst, but he couldn't imagine who else would dare. Not any of the housemaids, certainly. He had no desire to become involved with Lavinia's servants, so he'd maintained a polite distance.

Through hooded lids, he focused in, concluding the intruder was female, and as she neared, he braced. She reached out to touch him, and before she could, he clasped her wrist and pulled her onto the mattress, rolling them so he had her pinned down.

She gasped, and he froze.

"Margaret?"

Terrified and mute, her heart pounding, she gazed at him, her eyes glimmering in the pale moonlight. He pictured her creeping through the deserted halls, destined for his room and determined not to be discovered.

What had happened that she would have risked so much?

Surely, she knew what sort of response her conduct would garner from him. He wasn't a saint, so if she was willing to crawl into his bed, he was willing to let her, but where would that leave them?

His goal of wedding an heiress was his paramount consideration. Margaret could be compromised beyond redemption, with the whole household looking on, could wind up pregnant and abandoned, but Jordan could not behave honorably and marry her.

He was about to enter a bog, where a wrong step would suck him to the bottom. The only logical course was to refuse what she was offering, but his cock was full and heavy between his legs, and his entire being— down to the smallest vein and pore—was ecstatic over her appearance.

"Margaret," he said again, "what are you doing here? What are you thinking?"

"You know what I'm thinking."

"But . . . but . . . why?"

"After Lavinia had your belongings moved, it was so quiet without you, and I couldn't bear it."

She stunned him by initiating a torrid kiss. He perceived passion and lust, but desperation and despair, too, and her level of anguish gave him pause.

Should he do this? Could he do this?

He broke off and drew away, and she took his hand and laid it on her breast, the erect nipple branding him with the shock of the erotic moment.

"What is it you want from me?" he inquired.

"You once asked me if I was ever lonely, and I am—most of the time. I want to stay with you. I want you to fill a few of my hours, so that I'm not quite so alone."

He eased away from her, glad he'd had the foresight to don a pair of drawers before he'd slipped under the blankets. Usually, he slept in the nude, and if he'd been naked, there was no telling what he might have done to her.

He fussed with lighting a candle, using the chore as an excuse to delay. As the flame sputtered and grew, he'd assumed it would provide increased illumination—of both his room and the best path to take—but only the bed was clearer.

As to his choices, and what they should be, he hadn't a clue.

"If I agree to this," he ultimately said, "I won't let you leave. It's all or nothing with me. In a few minutes, if you change your mind and wish you hadn't come, I won't permit you to skitter out like a frightened rabbit."

"I won't want you to stop." She looked as bleak as he felt.

"I'll insist on having you more than once. I'll insist on being with you every night—for as long as I remain at Gray's Manor."

"I understand."

"You couldn't possibly."

"I ask one thing in return."

"What is that?"

"You must try not to hurt me."

Rankled, he frowned. "Despite what you may have heard, I'm not the type to brutalize a woman."

"I don't mean physically. You have to swear that you won't break my heart when you go." As if it was already aching, she rubbed the center of her chest.

This would be her first sexual relationship, and he the first man who'd ever showered her with any genuine attention. As a virgin and spinster, she couldn't be aware of how a carnal association might seem like something else, something more. She would become fond of him, might even love him when they were through, but her feelings would have no bearing on what he elected to do with Penelope.

"I can't make you any promises," he warned.

"I know. You've been very blunt—from the beginning."

"If Lavinia strolled in this very second and caught us, it wouldn't matter to me. Your reputation would be destroyed, and she could shout and demand reparation, but I couldn't marry you—my responsibilities lie elsewhere."

"I realize that. I'm not seeking anything from you. I don't *want* anything from you. Just let me have tonight. Please. Don't send me away. I can't go."

She was content to give all, with no guarantees, and the notion bothered him enormously.

He wanted her to care! He wanted her to at least pretend—here at the outset—that he was important to her. She had him feeling as if he were merely a tool, an empty vessel she would use to assuage her loneliness, and stupidly, he yearned to be so much more.

Her poise and resignation had him angry, both at her and at himself. But how could he decline to seize what he so urgently craved?

He tugged off her robe, then undid the tiny buttons at the front of her nightgown. The bodice flopped loose, supplying him with a hint of the paradise hidden beneath.

"Take it off," he ordered.

"All the way?"

"Yes."

He wanted her to comprehend that this was her choice and her doing—rather than his own. It was a pathetic attempt to mollify his nagging conscience, but he wouldn't be deterred, nor would he lament.

She didn't hesitate. Bravely, she faced him, and as she grabbed the neckline and jerked it to her waist, only the slight blush on her cheeks betrayed any discomfort.

"No regrets, Margaret."

"No, none, at all."

He captured her mouth in a hot and hungry kiss. She joined in, having abandoned all restraint. She was eager to participate, and he planned to take full advantage.

He dipped to her breasts, and he suckled and played, nursing at one, then the other as he yanked her nightgown down and off and pitched it on the floor. She was naked, her glorious body splayed beneath him. He settled himself between her thighs, his naughty fingers slithering down to cup her, then slide inside. She was so tight, so wet, and he eased her open, exploring, stretching her for what was to come.

"I want to show you something," he murmured.

"What?"

"It may seem strange at first, but let me do it."

"You may try whatever you wish," she assented. "I'm happy to allow it."

"It will feel very, very good."

"I'm sure it will."

He nibbled down her stomach, and she writhed and giggled as he tormented and teased. She didn't recognize his destination until he arrived at her womanly hair, and as he spread her nether lips, she tensed, but didn't resist.

He licked her with his tongue, and she arched up and tried to squirm away, but he wouldn't release her.

"What are you doing?" she gasped.

"I'm making love to you—but differently from before."

"You said I'd like it."

"You will."

"I don't."

He chuckled. "Relax, Margaret. Let me pleasure you."

"It doesn't feel *pleasurable*."

"It will. I promise."

He reached for her breasts, pinching the nipples, as he continued his work down below. The contact was electrifying, and she arched up again, struggling to buck him off.

"Oh, do stop, Jordan! I'm begging you!"

"Just another minute."

"I can't stand it."

"Almost there."

She was at the edge, and he jabbed once, twice, and she came in a rush. Sensation swept her away as she soared to the heavens, then down, and as she quieted, he was meandering up her torso.

He'd never had a paramour who was so easy to arouse, and he was enchanted. His only regret was that he wouldn't have more time to teach her, to enjoy her.

He initiated another stormy kiss, and as she tasted the tang of her sex on his lips, she groaned with delight.

"I can't believe I let you do that to me."

"I'm a shameless rogue. I admit it, but you're not exactly a timid virgin." He smiled at her, thinking he'd never witnessed a more lovely sight. "You know, most men agree that it's exceedingly difficult to bring a female to orgasm."

"They do?"

"But not you."

"What are you implying?"

He leaned in and whispered, "You may be a gentlewoman, but you possess the soul of a harlot."

She swatted at him with the pillow, but he laughed and tugged it away. Their gazes locked, the interlude growing even more intimate.

"I want to see you naked," she said. "I'm curious."

"Oh, Margaret . . ."

"You've seen me and touched me."

"I'm afraid to let you."

"Afraid? You?"

"If I remove my drawers, I'm scared about what might happen."

"Have I asked you to restrain yourself?"

"No, and therein lies the problem. One of us needs to keep a level head."

"Why?"

Why indeed? "Because passion can spiral out of control, and once the genie's out of the bottle, we can't shove him back in."

"Please, Jordan. I want it."

"Sweet Jesu!" he muttered. "Those eyes! When you look at me like that, I can't refuse you."

Without warning, she squeezed his nipple, much as he did to hers, and he flinched.

She yanked away. "Have I hurt you?"

"No, it feels splendid."

"Really?"

"Yes."

"May I do it again?"

"Of course. When we're here like this, anything is allowed."

Tentative, then more bold, she took both of his nipples and twirled them, the motion excruciating but superb.

"Would you like it if I sucked on them, too?"

"Oh, yes."

She riffled through his chest hair and latched onto his breast. As she teased with teeth and tongue, his air rushed out in a whoosh.

He shifted and stretched out, then guided her hand into his drawers.

Her expression was filled with surprise and a great deal of interest. "What is this? What is it called?"

"It has many names: a phallus, a cock."

She was stroking him, judging weight and girth, and he moaned in anguish.

"For what is it used?"

"For mating—and for pleasure."

She scowled. "I don't understand."

He reached down and probed her sheath. "I would push it inside you—"

"Inside?"

"Yes, as I've been doing with my fingers. It feels very good."

She flopped onto her back. "Show me what you mean."

"No."

"Why?"

So many whys! "Because there is a thin piece of skin here, and if I entered you, I would tear it."

"So?"

"It can't be repaired, so later on, if you decided to

wed, your husband would know that you'd lain with another."

She scoffed. "We've discussed this before: I'll never marry."

"You can't predict what the future might hold." Oddly, he was unnerved to talk about her marital prospects. He didn't like picturing her with another man, didn't like the idea of another man enjoying what Jordan was quickly coming to consider his own.

"Trust me: I shall never wed. So show me!"

"I could make you pregnant."

"How?"

"After I penetrated you, I would flex and flex, and it creates a friction that is very stimulating. It causes a white cream to erupt from the end. The cream contains my seed, and it can plant a babe."

"You're joking."

"No."

She was still stroking him in a seductive rhythm, so conversation was becoming more and more difficult. He couldn't concentrate on her words. There was only her hand and its incessant tempo.

"I want to see it," she insisted.

"No."

"I'm not listening to you anymore."

She growled with exasperation, and before he could stop her, she'd bared him for her inspection.

"Oh my," she breathed, glancing down. "Would you look at that? It's so big."

"It can be."

"I'm confused about how it fits into me."

"I'll demonstrate someday—but not today."

He was in agony, a driving need sweeping over him

like no other he'd ever experienced. He yearned to throw her down, to take her and be done with it, but he wasn't ready to steal her chastity, and she definitely wasn't ready to surrender it.

She scooted down to have a better view, to ogle and fondle, and the sight of her—perched at his crotch, her ruby lips inches away—was his ultimate undoing.

He dragged her up the bed, and she frowned as if he'd gone mad, when in a way he had. He was mad with lust.

"What is it?"

"I have to come," he ground out.

"What should I do?"

"Hold me tight."

"Like this?"

"Yes, just like that."

He pulled her close, his cock pressed to the soft skin of her belly. Then he thrust again and again, and he let go, flying high, thinking the sensation might never end. Finally, he arrived at the peak and floated down. His body relaxing, his mind reeling, he shuddered to a halt.

He was quiet, wondering what to say. It was her initial encounter with male desire, yet he'd behaved like an unschooled ass, and he hated that he might have to explain or defend.

He simply wanted her to leave so that he could regroup and figure out how they should carry on.

But no, he mused, scowling. He didn't want her to leave. He wanted her to stay; he wanted her to stay forever.

He rippled with dread. What was happening to him? He was as flustered as a lad after his first orgasm. Why did she have such a disturbing effect?

At recognizing his frantic mood he chuckled and

forced himself to calm. Yes, he'd been extra titillated but only because he'd recently suffered a dearth of feminine companionship. He'd been loaded like a gun, prepared to fire, so it had been easy for her to prime the pump. It didn't mean anything more than that.

He smiled at her, relieved when she smiled in return.

"Are you all right?" he asked. "I didn't hurt you, did I?"

"Why would you have? I'm not made of glass."

"No, you're not."

"I'm still a virgin, aren't I?"

"Yes."

"How frustrating you are!"

She sighed and clasped his phallus again, and even though he'd just come as if there were no tomorrow, his unruly rod leapt to life.

He slapped away her questing fingers, unable to believe he could respond so soon and so vehemently.

"Good Lord, but you're insatiable. Let me catch my breath, would you?"

She grinned, as he rose and proceeded to the dressing room to fetch a washing cloth.

"Where are you going?"

"I thought I should clean us up."

"Well, hurry back," she commanded. "I'm tired of waiting for you to get on with it."

He shook his head, curious as to what he'd set in motion. How fast and how furiously would it spin out of control? Where would they all be at the conclusion?

He couldn't bear to imagine.

CHAPTER ELEVEN

I believe I'll call it a night."

Anne faked a yawn and stood, desperate to escape the parlor and the small group that was engaged in after-supper conversation. There was such an unpleasant undercurrent of intrigue and scheming that if she didn't flee—immediately—she just might start screaming and never stop.

Mrs. Gray and her daughter were hissing like a pair of venomous snakes, while Jordan and Charles were trading barbs, not able to conceal their hostility. Charles was stirring the pot by flirting with both women, which outraged everyone for differing reasons. Jordan was disgusted by it, Mrs. Gray was jealous, and as for Penelope, she acted as if whatever attention Charles paid her, it wasn't as much as she deserved.

Mr. Mason was off in the corner, observing all and wondering about the festering animosities.

It was the first time Anne had seen him since her embarrassing, drunken advance, and though she'd tried to ignore him, she couldn't help how her gaze kept stealing in his direction.

She couldn't imagine how low his opinion must be. She persuaded herself that it was all Charles's fault, that his obnoxious philandering had driven her to the very dark, very handsome Mr. Mason, but she wasn't a trollop, and she had no idea what had spurred her to such indecent conduct.

Until she'd knelt in front of Mason and unbuttoned his trousers, Charles had been her only lover. She'd been a virgin when she'd initially succumbed, and in all the years after, she'd never so much as glanced at another man. Her reckless mood hadn't abated, though, and she didn't like it that Mason was so close by and such an easy target at which to steer her misbehavior. With the slightest provocation, she would seduce him again, and the discovery was extremely unnerving.

She couldn't remain in his company, and she peered around the room, but no one had heard her declaration that she was off to bed. With so many plots hatching, she was invisible, which was fine by her. They could taunt and conspire all night, but she didn't have to watch.

She moved toward the door, pausing next to where Charles was seated on the sofa, and she whispered, "Will you be needing me later?"

Though he strove to mask it, he peeked at Mrs. Gray. "No, I'm quite tired myself. I'll see you in the morning."

She departed, refusing to be upset or shocked. If he wanted to consort with Mrs. Gray, if he could make a play for the daughter while he was fucking the mother, what was it to Anne?

Still, it galled to be faced with such hard evidence of

his infidelity. Had he ever cared about her? Had he ever cared about anyone but himself?

She didn't have to answer the question. She was fully aware of how much she'd given, how much he'd taken, and how little she had left.

She walked down the hall and out onto the verandah. It was beginning to rain and sprinkles dotted her hair and dress. She tarried, calming herself, enjoying the respite; then she wandered into the garden and down the winding path. For a thrilling moment, she pondered whether she should keep on walking and never come back.

How long would it take for Charles to realize she was missing?

At the edge of the trees, she halted and turned to scrutinize the mansion. To her amazement, Mr. Mason stepped out the rear door. Clearly following her, he studied the grounds, trying to see where she'd gone, and he espied her lurking in the shadows.

Behind her, the gazebo beckoned, the lights from the house reflecting off the lake. With a nod to him, she went to it and waited on the stairs as he slowly and deliberately marched toward her. As he neared, she panicked and rushed into the decorative building.

What was she doing? Was she planning to tryst again? Was this really what she wanted? She didn't think so, so what was the matter with her? Why couldn't she get her roiling emotions under control?

He arrived, and they stared and stared. Arms braced at his sides, he inspected her from head to toe.

"Why?" he ultimately asked.

"Why what?"

"Why did you have sex with me the other evening?"

"Why not?" she blithely responded, as if she frequently trifled with strange men.

He narrowed his focus, assessing, contemplating. "You're not a whore."

"I am," she insisted.

"No, you're not, so I can't figure you out."

"What's to *figure?* I wanted to. I'm not some timid country Miss. I'm an adult woman, and I can do as I please."

He reached out and caressed her breast, and she let him. She didn't pull away, didn't clout at his hand, or huff with indignation. Her nipple leapt to attention.

"You like having sex, don't you?"

"Yes," she baldly admitted.

Anymore, she wasn't too keen on having Charles as her partner, but the act itself was always agreeable, and she wouldn't deny her base disposition. If Mr. Mason didn't like it, he could jump off a cliff.

"Are you truly Lord Kettering's mistress?"

"Of course, I am. Why would you suppose I travel with him?"

"What would he say if he learned what you'd done with me?"

"I suspect he'd beat me, then toss me out without a penny."

"Then why did you proceed? Why risk so much?"

"I don't know."

"I want to do it again."

"So do I."

She couldn't believe the words had slipped from her mouth. Was she mad? She'd heard that women occasionally lost their mental faculties as they aged, so perhaps her advanced years were causing her to become deranged.

"I like it rough and hard," he stated. "I don't want to hold back."

"You can do it however you wish. I don't mind."

She felt wild, as if she were about to be hurled into an abyss. She grabbed for the waistband of his trousers, and she drew him to her, delighted by his erection.

"Are you and Mrs. Gray lovers?" she queried.

"Yes."

"For how long now?"

"We commenced shortly after her husband passed away—although I've been fond of her since we were children."

"You never dared to commit adultery?"

"No, never."

"How noble of you."

"Isn't it though?" Oddly, he added, "We're to be married soon."

"Really?"

"Yes."

Mrs. Gray was so conniving and vicious, while he was straightforward and open. They were a peculiar match. "Do you imagine she'll make you happy?"

"Very."

"Are you sure?"

"Yes." He didn't appear too certain.

"Why are you telling me about her?"

"I'd presumed myself an honorable man, but I am betrothed to her, yet ready to fornicate with you, which means that my integrity is more questionable than I'd fathomed. I can make you no promises, so you shouldn't

have any misconceptions about the sort of man I am."
His smile was grim. "As I shall have none about the sort
of woman *you* are."

"What would Mrs. Gray do if she found out about us?"

"She'd pitch a screaming fit."

"She's smitten by Lord Kettering."

"Yes, she is."

Anne could see the tension in his shoulders, the
clenching of his jaw. "And how would you react if she
slept with him?"

"I wouldn't tolerate the news very well."

"Is that why you're out here with me? Are you eager
to betray her, hoping to make her jealous?"

"I don't understand why I followed you. When you
left, it just seemed as if I should come after you. I
couldn't stop myself."

He wouldn't confess the truth, but she knew what it
was: He was a man, so he thought with his cock. He'd
chased after her because he was anxious for them to
have another bout of raucous sex, and he was correct in
assuming they would philander.

For some reason, she was desperately attracted to
him. It was an insane need that had been growing since
they'd first met. He lusted after her, too, and while his
motives might be purely physical, it was so bloody refreshing to have somebody want her for something.

She flicked at the top button on his trousers, then at
the next, and the next. The placard was loose, and she
reached in and took him in hand, expertly sliding her
thumb across the sensitive crown. Without being asked,
she knelt down, pushed the fabric aside, and sucked
him into her mouth.

She had no pride, no shame. Charles had taught her well, and if she was going to cheat, she would do it in grand style.

She cupped his balls, but to her surprise, he jerked away and yanked her to her feet.

"What's the matter?" she inquired.

"Not like that," he said. "Not yet."

"Then what do you want?"

"I'll show you."

He led her to the cushioned bench, and he eased her down and came over her. He was a big man, and she enjoyed feeling his weight on her.

He evaluated her curiously, and she was humored by his expression. He was clearly confused—by her lack of inhibition, by her enthusiasm to do whatever he demanded—and her zeal had him flummoxed.

"What is it?" she finally said.

"I want to fuck you lying down together like this," he explained, "and I want you to watch me the whole time."

"Fine."

"I want you to be glad that it's me, and if you can't be genuinely glad, then I want you to pretend that you are."

"I don't have to pretend. I *am* glad it's you."

Her comment had a palliative effect. He fussed with her skirt and settled himself between her thighs; then he took his cock and guided it to her center, forcing it in without hesitation or preparation.

She winced, but raised no complaint. She was used to brutal handling, and had endured much of it when Charles was being a beast.

Mason was immobile, apparently waiting for the protest he expected, and when none occurred, he started to flex. He was braced on his palms, and he held himself over her, not changing the tempo, not doing anything to arouse her, not speaking or touching her except where their bodies were joined.

He kept on for an eternity, and gradually, the experience metamorphosed into something besides an awkward and illicit tryst. His motions gentled, the regard in his eyes warmed.

"You're so beautiful," he murmured.

The tender remark made it seem as if she were young and pretty again, and she kissed him with a frantic passion. Isolation and despair were suddenly crushing her, and she felt more alone than she'd ever been, as if they were the last two people on earth, as if—should she let go of him—she'd float away.

He was a tether to the world she had relinquished eons ago, the one where she'd been a normal woman with ordinary hopes and dreams, before she'd abandoned them for Charles Prescott.

The power of his thrusts increased, the culmination approaching, and she didn't want him to finish. Once he spilled himself, he'd leave, then she'd have to proceed to her room, and the notion of being by herself, of ruminating in the dark, was the most depressing thing she could imagine.

With a low growl of satisfaction, he stiffened and came, his cock buried deep; then he exhaled a heavy breath and drew away.

As if they were strangers—which they were—he sat up and straightened his clothes, so she sat up and straightened hers, too. They peered off across the yard, not looking at each other, and she knew she should say something, but what?

Eventually, he shifted toward her.

"You seem very sad," he said.

"Not sad. Just quiet."

"I didn't do that very well."

"Didn't do what?"

"I didn't make love to you."

"I didn't expect you to."

"Do you always demand so little for yourself?"

She shrugged. "This isn't a Grand Passion, Mr. Mason. It's merely a hasty tumble in the gazebo. In a situation such as ours, I don't anticipate much."

He snorted, then inquired, "Will Lord Kettering seduce Lavinia?"

"He might, but he'll marry Penelope."

"I thought she was destined for Lord Romsey."

"She is."

"Would Kettering cuckold his own son?"

"We'll see."

She wasn't about to discuss the two Prescott men, or the fiscal crises driving them. Both Mrs. Gray and Miss Gray were aware of Jordan's money troubles, but Anne was certain neither of them understood Charles's urgent condition. They were probably both salivating at the prospect of wedding a wealthy aristocrat, but whichever one wound up with him, she would be in for a huge surprise.

"How long will you and Kettering stay at Gray's Manor?"

"Until he's ready to go."

"Then what?"

"I haven't the foggiest."

He stared at the house, then at her. "I want to do this with you in my bed sometime."

"I'm sure it would be divine."

"If I asked you to stop by my residence, would you? My boys are visiting their grandparents for the summer. It would be quite discreet."

"I believe I would, yes."

"And would you arrive early and spend the entire day?"

"I would."

Was she really contemplating such an outrage? Could she carry through? To what end?

"Why have you invited me, Mr. Mason?"

"I don't know."

"You must have some idea."

"I just want it," he said, unable to expound.

She nodded. She felt much the same. By being with him, she was filling an empty spot that had grown so vast it constantly echoed with the reminders of all that was missing. No home. No family. No friends.

Just Charles Prescott, and the ashes of what remained of their relationship. Would she ride it to its tortured conclusion? Or would she have the courage to flee before he tossed her over yet again?

"I'll come as soon as I can."

"I live just through the woods. It's a quick walk."

"Which will make it easy to slip away."

"Yes." He reached for her, dragging her across him so that she was over his lap and on her knees.

She scowled, questioning, and he muttered, "I must have you again before I go."

"All right."

"I want to do it over and over. May I?"

"You don't have to be so bloody polite. Just take me. Take me however you'd like. I'm happy to oblige."

He loosed her dress and tugged it down so that her

breasts swung free. At seeing them, he rippled with delight and cupped them, thumbing the nipples. Then, he pulled her closer and as he suckled, she let out an odd sound, a sob of pleasure, or perhaps relief. It had been so long since she'd been touched with awe or affection.

His hips rose, and his phallus found its target all on its own. He began his slow, methodical thrusting, and she gazed out at the water on the lake, wondering who she'd become, for she hadn't a clue, and she was terrified over what would happen next.

CHAPTER TWELVE

Charles puffed on a cheroot and studied the dark, cloudy sky. As he'd huddled in the shadows, he'd seen Anne walking back from the lake, but he didn't waste any energy wondering why she was out there by herself. He was too busy with more pressing concerns.

A door furtively opened, and he glanced over, smirking as Penelope sneaked out onto the verandah. The foolish child! He'd known she'd follow him and had specifically gone for a smoke so that she would have an excuse.

She threw herself in his path at every opportunity, as did Lavinia, and he relished how both women fawned over him. In the end, though, there could only be one choice—that being Penelope and her fortune—but he liked having them on the hook, and the sexual possibilities were intriguing.

He'd participated in many instances of *ménage à trois* and was pondering whether he shouldn't instigate a few trysts with Penelope and Lavinia in his bed together.

He'd never had a mother and daughter duo, and the incestuous prospects were almost too thrilling to contemplate.

Penelope had espied him, but he ignored her and strolled farther down the path, certain she would keep coming. She was like a fish on a hook. All he had to do was reel her in.

Shortly, he was waiting on a garden bench, and as she stomped up, he pretended to be surprised by her appearance.

"What are you doing here?" he asked.

"What did you want?" she snapped in reply.

"Me? Nothing."

"You did, too. You wanted something. You intentionally lured me out."

"You are so full of yourself. I merely sought some peace and quiet. I get tired after so much socializing."

He finished his cigar, tossed it onto the grass, and snuffed it out with his heel.

"You've hardly spoken to me since that day at the gazebo. Why not?"

"I don't like you, and I never fraternize with adolescent girls. I find them boring in the extreme."

"I suppose you like my mother better."

He was amused by her jealousy. "Yes, I like your mother very much. She's very charming, very feminine."

"But she's so old!"

"To a man of my years, she doesn't seem so."

"I don't believe this!"

She paced, and he relaxed, watching her strut and fret.

Suddenly, she whirled to face him. "Take a good look at me, you disgusting roué! I'm the prettiest girl in a hundred miles."

"Yes, but you have the personality of a shrew, and I like my women to be sweet and biddable."

"Like my mother?"

"She understands how the game is played. She knows how to curb her sharp tongue and make me happy."

"*I* could make you happier."

"Could you?"

His question hung in the air. She was an innocent, but she wasn't stupid. She recognized the sexual innuendo, and she evaluated him, sifting through her responses as she calculated which behaviors would bring her the fastest success.

"Let me prove it to you," she begged.

"How?"

"My mother has been exceedingly explicit in describing what's required. Tell me what to do, and I'll do it without complaint."

His nose wrinkled with distaste. He hated the entire notion of maternal guidance. If a child knew what was to occur in the bedchamber, it took much of the excitement out of the encounter. He liked to be the one to teach them, to browbeat them as they grew anxious.

Where was the fun in fucking a virgin if you couldn't scare her just a bit?

"I may be inexperienced," Penelope boasted, "but I'm not timid. I'm eager to oblige you."

"Let's see."

"Let's see *what?*"

He held out his hand. "Come here."

Her bravado faded. "Why?"

"I want to look at your teats again."

"You already saw them once."

He scoffed. "You are such an impertinent tease. Go away and leave me be."

She was conflicted—yearning to storm off, yearning to stay—and he grabbed her wrist and tugged her onto his lap. She struggled, but only for a second as she remembered that she'd vowed to do whatever he demanded.

He smirked again. It was like taking candy from a baby.

"If you hope to entice me to matrimony, you'll have to exhibit a tad more interest in carnal affairs."

"I'm interested! I am!"

He eased her back so she was draped across his arm, and he slipped his fingers into her dress, pushing the fabric away from her breasts. He gazed at her tiny nipples, then bent down and sucked on one of them till it was raw and inflamed; then he pulled away.

"This is the sort of pursuit I enjoy."

"I know. I let you do it, didn't I?"

"I realize that you're hot to wed an earl, but I warn you: I will do the same—and much worse—every morning, noon, and night. I won't permit you to refuse me."

"I wouldn't dream of it."

"Lift your skirt."

"What?"

"You heard me. Raise the hem to your waist."

She hesitated, then reached down and did as he'd commanded. She had on drawers, and he undid the string and jerked them down so that her privates were exposed.

She groaned with embarrassment, but he ignored her. *She* was the one seeking an alliance, and if he agreed, she would gain many boons through their association, so she had to pay the price.

"A lovely puss," he murmured. "Is it virginal?"

"Yes."

"You're sure?"

"Of course, I'm sure. If some buffoon had stuck his rod up there, don't you think I'd recollect?"

"Has any man touched you here before? Not your father? Not a kindly neighbor? Not a friendly uncle?"

"No."

"Has any man so much as peeked at it?"

"No," she said again.

He slid a finger inside, relishing how tight she was, how he could make her gasp and squirm. He probed much longer than he should have; then he stopped and shoved her to her feet. He stood next to her, watching as she straightened herself.

"Why are you treating me like this?" she challenged. "I don't have to put up with it."

"No, you don't."

"If you don't quit being such a bully, I'll tell my mother."

"Be my guest. She'll be delighted to learn what a little harlot you are."

She lashed out to slap him, and he snatched her wrist and gripped it so firmly that she winced in pain.

"If you ever hit me," he threatened, "I'll hit you back."

"You're a swine!" she seethed.

"I definitely can be, but you've been very clear that you'd like a match with me anyway."

"Maybe I've changed my mind."

"Have you? If so, speak up. I'm happy to let my son have you—although you should know that I plan to live for many decades, so you may never hear the word *countess* attached to your name."

"I hate you."

"Which I deem a rather poor remark from a female who claims she'd like to be my bride."

They were silent, with her glaring, while he smiled and acted as if he hadn't a care in the world. And he didn't really. She could marry him or not, and if she declined, he'd find another stupid, rich debutante to ruin.

"I don't wish to wed Lord Romsey," she eventually grumbled. "How could I convince you to have me instead?"

He nearly shook a triumphant fist in the air. "You need do nothing. I'll handle the details."

"How can I know you're sincere?"

"You'll have to trust me."

He probably should have proceeded, then and there, by forcing her down on the bench and raping her, but he had to orchestrate the conclusion so that the appropriate people saw what he'd done.

He imagined that it would take a crowbar to pry Penelope's dowry away from Lavinia, so he had to devise the perfect place and time for her downfall to occur.

"Will you propose," Penelope nagged, "or talk to Lavinia, or what?"

"Your mother is set on your marrying Jordan."

"I won't do it—no matter what she says."

"Are you certain?"

"Positive."

"Good. We'll arrange events so that Jordan won't ever want you."

"What will I have to do?"

"If your mother has informed you, I shouldn't have to explain it."

"We'll have marital relations?"

"Yes. What did you suppose?"

"When?"

"Whenever you decide you're ready. Just sneak to my room. Any night is fine by me. You'll stay till morning, and the maids will stumble on you. It will all be accomplished quite easily."

"I can't come to your room!"

"Then you'll never have me as a husband, will you?"

He had no intention of going to her. *She* would have to take the steps for it to transpire, so that there was never any doubt as to who had instigated the dirty business. In the future, if she was miserable, she'd never be able to throw the scandal in his face. It would be her doing and none of his own.

Finally, she spun and stormed off. He chuckled, satisfied with his scheme; then he strolled inside, wondering which woman or women would join him before the evening was through.

❧

Lavinia tiptoed into Charles's bedchamber. A candle was burning, and he was awake and propped against the pillows, so obviously, he'd been waiting for her, and she could barely keep from preening.

On several occasions, she'd stopped by, accepting his not-so-subtle hints that she'd be welcome. Where was his fancy London mistress now, hmm?

Mrs. Smythe was in her own bed, that's where! Lavinia was the woman he wanted!

She was thrilled with the progress of her seduction and felt that, very soon, he'd realize he couldn't live without her. Perhaps there would be a double wedding. Penelope could marry Jordan, and Lavinia could marry Charles.

"I didn't think you'd ever arrive," Charles complained. "I was about to call it a night."

She walked over, shrugging out of her robe so that she was clad only in a sheer negligee. "I can't come until everyone is asleep. You know that."

"Your standards are so provincial."

"Would you rather have your son and my daughter gaping at me as I saunter down the hall?"

"Who cares about them? Their opinions are irrelevant."

Lavinia wasn't concerned about them, either, and she couldn't figure out why she was being so cautious. What was it to her if others learned that she and Charles were carrying on?

"I'm sorry I was late, darling." She loathed apologizing, but he expected that she would. "Let me make it up to you."

"Please do."

He never demanded she perform fellatio, but from the first, she'd begun in this fashion, and it had become a routine she couldn't break.

Just once, she wished something else might happen, that *he* might arouse her, that *he* might show some awareness of her sexually, but he never did, which was extremely aggravating.

She pasted on a smile and snuggled next to him. He didn't like a lot of nonsense, no kissing or cuddling or even much caressing. He liked her to get down to business, so she took him in hand and pumped him into a fine erection; then she nibbled down to his phallus. Within seconds, she had him in her mouth, and he was thrusting with the bored control at which he excelled.

He was well-endowed, could flex for an eternity, and unfortunately, once he deigned to let loose, her jaw would be sore, her neck aching from the strain, but she wasn't about to protest.

If she didn't suck him off, she was sure Mrs. Smythe would, and before the week was out, Lavinia was determined to have Smythe sent away. Lavinia was the only woman Charles needed, and she was certain she could convince him that it was time for Smythe to go.

She was tired of waiting for him to finish, so she stroked his balls and fingered his anus, and his seed shot down her throat. Like a seasoned courtesan, she swallowed it down, and after the final drop was spent, she pulled away and wedged herself into his arms.

"You're improving," he admitted, and she tamped down a smirk.

"It must be all the fabulous practice I've been getting."

"It must be," he agreed.

They both laughed, and she licked her lips, pretending she enjoyed the abominable taste, the disgusting smell.

"You're a marvelous lover, Charles," she lied, buttering him up.

"Aren't I, though?"

"I just love making you happy. I do make you happy, don't I?"

"Who wouldn't be content after a good blow job?"

"But I do it because I adore you."

"Do you?"

"Yes. I'd do anything for you."

"Would you really?"

She gazed up at him, her blue eyes open wide and promising any number of decadent acts if he would only give her some hint of a returned affection.

"Tell me one of your fantasies," she urged. "Select a deed no woman's ever previously done for you." He hesitated, so she pressed, "There must be a way I could show you how much you mean to me."

"Actually, there is something that's always titillated me. It's very . . . well . . ." He waved away the idea. "Never mind. It's too awful to mention."

"Tell me! It can't be that naughty. And even if it is, so what? We're adults; we can do whatever we like. It's no one's affair but our own."

"I'm embarrassed to say it aloud."

"Oh pish-posh! Go on! Go on!"

He was quiet forever; then he murmured, "Is Penelope a virgin?"

It was the last question she'd anticipated, and she was careful not to reveal her shock. "Well . . . yes."

"You're positive?"

"Yes."

He nodded. "I enjoy a *ménage à trois* as much as the next man, but I've never tried it with a mother and daughter."

"A . . . a . . . mother and daughter."

"It would be incredibly invigorating."

"The . . . two of us?"

"Yes."

She was stunned, and she struggled for calm. She'd never considered that he might wish for something so impossible. While she didn't have any qualms about letting him fuck Penelope if that's what it would take to keep him, she recoiled at the notion of his seeing the two of them naked and together.

For a woman of thirty-four, Lavinia looked fantastic, but her body couldn't compare to Penelope's youthful torso. Gad! She had to dissuade him!

"Since Penelope's a virgin," he was saying, "we could initiate her into intercourse as a team."

"A team?"

"It would be so stimulating to have you kissing her, or perhaps sucking on her nipples or licking her pussy. You could arouse her; then I would relieve her of her chastity."

"You'd like me to put my mouth on her?"

"Yes, but if you're not comfortable with that scenario, you could simply hold her down while I raped her."

"I don't think she'd be willing."

"Of course she wouldn't be. She'd fight like the dickens, but it doesn't seem as if the two of you get on all that well. Wouldn't it be amusing for you to help me force her?"

There was some satisfaction to be gleaned from restraining Penelope while she screamed and begged for mercy, but still, Lavinia was aghast. The last thing she would ever do was bring Penelope to Charles's bed, for she was terrified that she would never be able to pry the child out of it.

Once Penelope was there, Lavinia would be but a distant memory.

Then again, if Charles ruined Penelope, no man would have her—not Jordan, not anyone—so there would be no need to dangle her fortune in front of suitors. The money would be useless as bait, so Lavinia could keep it and spend it on herself. She wouldn't have to have Robert pawing through her records, searching for financial escape routes.

Oh, what was best?

She needed to stall, needed an opportunity to plot and prepare. She couldn't upset Charles by refusing his request outright, so she had to lie and placate him while she calculated the odds.

Now that she recognized Penelope to be her biggest and only rival, she had to get rid of the annoying girl, so that she had Charles all to herself. With so much at stake, Penelope couldn't remain at Gray's Manor. Lavinia had to take immediate steps to guarantee a speedy departure.

She chuckled, feigning interest in his scheme. "It's humorous to picture, isn't it?"

"Very."

"Penelope would pitch a fit."

"I'm sure she would, but she'd learn a valuable lesson, too."

"That being?"

"She's quite out of control. We could teach her who's in charge."

"Yes, darling," she cooed, "let's do it. When would you like to proceed?"

"How about Saturday night?"

Saturday! Three nights away! She had to take action—and fast!

Could she have Jordan married to Penelope in three days? She didn't know, but if there was any way in hell it could be accomplished that quickly, she was the person who could organize it.

"Saturday should work," she coolly replied.

"I'll want to start early and go at it till dawn."

"What fun it will be."

"Thank you, my dearest Lavinia."

As he used an endearment for the first time, as he kissed her tenderly, passionately, Lavinia soared with elation.

"You're welcome, Charles."

"You're the woman for me."

"I am, Charles. I am."

"You know just what I want. You know just how to please me. I'm very grateful."

"I'm ecstatic to hear it." Lavinia swelled with pride. Finally—finally!—she was making progress.

"I'm so excited by our plan," he said, "that I can't wait. I have to have you again."

Before she could revel in her triumph, or steer the discussion to their pending union, he was rolling her onto her stomach.

"I'm going to sodomize you," he explained, his finger already in her ass, the tip of his cock not far behind. "I need a really tight hole, so I can shut my eyes and pretend it's Penelope's virginal puss."

He entered her, giving her an inch, then another, and she buried her face in the pillow to hide her agony. She'd never previously allowed such a hideous thing to be done to her, though Horatio had occasionally tried and been soundly rebuffed, so she hadn't understood how much it would hurt.

After he was fully impaled, he gripped her hips and thrust—slowly but deeply—and she prayed that he would end more swiftly than he did when he was fucking her in the mouth.

Penelope would pay for this! She would pay for every bloody humiliation, and if it took the rest of Lavinia's life, she would extract a suitable compensation.

CHAPTER THIRTEEN

I just received a letter from your housekeeper in Chelsea," Jordan announced.

"Why would she write to you?" Charles inquired.

"She thought I could apprise her of your whereabouts."

"Why would she be looking for me?"

Jordan glared at his father. "The liquidation of the property is finished. The house is sold, and the new owner is coming next week. The staff is packing to leave. She's asking what to do with the boys."

"What boys?"

"Your ten-year-old sons, Johnny and Tim! You recall Johnny and Tim, don't you?"

"Well, of course I do. Don't be smart."

"What should I tell her?"

Charles walked to the sideboard and poured himself a brandy, which he made a great show of drinking. "Tell her whatever you'd like."

"Shall I have her send them here?"

"For God's sake, no!"

"What should I say, then?"

"You're an expert at handling delicate situations. You figure it out, then let me know the details."

Lavinia chose that moment to saunter in, and she proceeded directly to Charles and snuggled herself into his arms—unconcerned that Jordan was observing. They cooed like a pair of lovebirds, and Jordan wanted to gag.

He wouldn't discuss the fiasco in front of Lavinia, so he stormed out and raced to his room, where he tarried, steadying his breathing and trying to concentrate. His fury was so potent that he could taste it. He was desperate to be left alone, and he detested being burdened with Charles's problems.

Johnny and Tim didn't deserve the adversity that had landed on them simply because they were Charles's sons. They needed attention and security and a safe haven where they could laugh and play.

Why did he have to be the one to give it to them?

He yearned to lash out at somebody, but who? The person to blame was Charles, but as Jordan had learned after many years of trying, it was impossible to make his father feel guilty about anything.

He went to the window and gazed out at the night sky, contemplating the hoard of Charles's forgotten and discarded children. Jordan scarcely knew Johnny and Tim, but he sagged under the weight of his anxiety for their future. He wondered if they were afraid, if they were hungry or being mistreated.

Were they hoping Charles was worried about them? Were they staring down the lane at each passing horseback rider and carriage, expecting a message to arrive, that Charles had finally made arrangements, that he'd remembered they needed him?

He could see stars, and he shut his eyes and uttered a

foolish wish—for happiness. That's all he'd ever really wanted, but it had always been so bloody difficult to attain. With his plans to marry Penelope, he had to face the fact that not only would he never be happy; he'd never even achieve the smallest amount of contentment.

From now on, there would only be duty and responsibility and a good deal of misery besides.

Charles was about to make a move for Penelope, so Jordan had to forge ahead and propose. He couldn't continue to dawdle, putting off a decision, as he flirted with Margaret Gray. No matter how he might pine for a different ending, he couldn't marry her.

Disaster loomed, and he had to inform Lavinia that he was ready; then he had to wed Penelope as fast as he could. Yet instead, he was fumbling around like a blind man and praying for a miracle.

He whirled away from the window, poured himself a brandy, and gulped it down. He poured another and gulped that, too. The quiet closed in on him, till he felt as if he were the last man on earth and about to fall off the edge. He couldn't bear it, so he tiptoed to the hall and sneaked out, his feet carrying him in the precise direction he shouldn't go.

A wild, reckless energy was gushing through him, one that was so powerful and so pervasive that it scared him. With how crazed he was, he might do anything, without regret or limit, and for once, he didn't care.

He approached Margaret's door and entered without knocking. It was nearing midnight, but she wasn't in her bed, and he frowned until he heard her in the adjacent chamber, in what had been their shared dressing room. He could smell warm water and realized that she was washing, perhaps even taking a bath, and at the notion that he might have stumbled on her all naked and slippery, his cock stirred.

He walked over, and as he appeared in the threshold, she was lounging in the hip bath and sipping on a glass of wine. She cast him a glance that was shrewd and wise, and he was swamped by the uncanny perception that she'd known he was coming—when he hadn't known himself.

"Hello, Jordan."

"Hello."

"I didn't think you'd ever arrive."

"I wasn't going to."

"What made you change your mind?"

He shrugged. He wasn't about to confide how wretched he was, or that he intended to reach out and grab for what he craved, before circumstances guaranteed that he never could again.

"I want to have you," he said, "in a sexual way. As a man does with his wife."

"Are you positive?"

"Yes."

"You constantly say that, but you never mean it."

"This time, I do."

"Really?"

"Yes."

"What about Penelope?"

"What about her?" he crudely shot back.

"Will you marry her when we're through?"

"Yes, Margaret. There can't be any other ending."

She nodded. "I just need to be sure we're both very clear."

"I have been from the start."

"Yes, you have." She assessed him as if she could see

inside to the tempest that raged. "You're upset. What happened?"

"Nothing happened," he claimed. "I'm simply tired of never getting what I want."

"And you want me?"

"For now. For tonight."

"Then I am yours. For now. For tonight. I make no promises for the morrow."

"Neither do I."

She stood, unashamed of her nudity, the water sluicing down her torso as she stepped out of the tub and onto the floor. His torrid gaze wandered down, taking in her perfect breasts, the tuck of her waist, the curve of her hips, and he suffered such a wave of desire that his knees nearly buckled.

He strode to her and swept her into his arms, her damp body pressed to his all the way down.

"Have you any idea," he told her, "how badly I want you, how badly I've always wanted you?"

"Tell me," she replied, her mouth finding his for a sizzling kiss. "Tell me how much."

Her hands were on his trousers, fussing with the buttons, and within seconds, her fist was wrapped around his cock. As she stroked him, he hissed with a frustration created by weeks of restraint.

Gripping her thighs, he lifted her, forcing her back to the wall, her legs circling his waist. His phallus throbbed with need, his discipline shattered. Being much too rough, he dipped down and bit her nipple, not caring if he hurt her, or if she was afraid. He was beyond the point where he could trifle and tease.

"I'm going to fuck you," he coarsely said. "I'm going to fuck you so hard."

"What does that mean? That word? I don't know what it means."

"Yes, you do. You know!"

He slipped his fingers between their bodies, and he pushed them into her. She squirmed and strove to escape the brutal treatment, but he wasn't about to release her. Not until he'd sated the rampaging beast that was demanding to be let loose.

Still holding her, he spun away from the wall, and he took her to her bedchamber, to her bed, and he laid her down, then came down on top of her. He stretched out, crushing her with his weight, and he started in on her breasts again, sucking and playing, until her hips began to thrust in a rhythm with his own.

He blazed a trail down her stomach, to her center, and he pried her thighs apart and delved inside. The tang of her sex was an aphrodisiac that lured him to his doom. He had to be naked, had to have his bare skin gliding across hers, and he rose up on his knees and yanked at his shirt, desperate to tug it off, but lust had him so disordered that he couldn't remove it.

She rose, too, and she struggled with the buttons, but she was even more impatient than he, and when she couldn't free them fast enough, she seized the fabric and ripped the garment in half.

She jerked at his pants, his shoes and stockings, both of them fighting to have them off as swiftly as possible. Finally, she drew him down to her, sparks cracking as flesh connected with flesh.

"If you stop now," she warned, "I'll have to kill you."

"I won't stop. Not even if you beg."

"Don't toy with me, Jordan."

"I'm not."

"If you don't follow through to the end, you're a dead man."

From her virulent expression, he was fairly certain she wasn't joking. They'd reached this spot, or one very close to it, several times, but he'd refused to proceed. An odd chivalry kept making him cautious, but he was worn down by his vacillation. He couldn't bear to harm her, yet he could no longer delay or demur. He could only carry on.

The passion had continued to simmer and was easily heated to a full boil. He plundered her mouth, as he caressed her everywhere. She was moaning, writhing in agony, and as his fingers slithered down, as he slid them into her, she came in an instant.

She arched up and cried out, and he kissed her again, swallowing the sound of her joy. As it concluded, he was over her, his phallus positioned exactly where it needed to be.

"Finish it, Jordan," she demanded.

"I intend to."

"Don't leave me like this."

"I won't." He smiled, his heart swelling with indescribable emotion. "I'm so glad I'm to be your first."

"Yes . . . yes . . . now get on with it!"

"I want you to always remember that it was me."

"I will."

"Swear it! Swear to me that you'll never forget."

"I never could."

He had a vision of another man making love to her someday in the future. He would be the man she needed, the man who could love her, and Jordan shoved away the disturbing image.

"No regrets," he murmured.

"None."

"I couldn't stand it if you were sorry after we're through."

"I won't be."

He pulled her thighs even wider; then he took his cock and inserted the blunt crown.

"You're so tight," he muttered through clenched teeth.

"This doesn't feel right."

"It will."

He pressed forward, easing in, and she wriggled with the initial stirrings of virginal alarm.

"You're too big," she insisted. "You'll never fit."

He'd planned to go slow, to prepare her for the awkwardness of joining, but an animalistic urge was sweeping him away, and he couldn't desist. Quaking with restraint, he clutched her flanks and forged on, coming up against her maidenhead, her female anatomy blocking his way.

She struggled in earnest. "Jordan, wait!"

"No."

"You're scaring me."

"Relax."

"I can't!"

"It will be over soon."

"Jordan!" she pleaded, but he couldn't listen.

At that moment, he was all male, all beastly sexual drive, and he flexed once, again, again, and though she fought and implored, he couldn't heed her. He kept on and on, and suddenly, he burst through and was buried to the hilt.

She groaned in anguish. "It hurts."

"I know"—he held himself motionless as he kissed

her nose, her cheek—"but it will pass. Take a deep
breath. Let it out."

He dawdled as long as he could, but he was in a
frantic state. He began with deliberate penetrations,
but rapidly, he increased the pace until he was rutting
into her like a madman. With no consideration for
her untried condition, he simply took and took some
more, and much before he was ready, a huge orgasm
commenced.

He spilled himself in her womb, his seed spewing
precisely where he'd had no intention of it going. He'd
meant to retreat, to do the appropriate and sane thing,
but the brute within had guided his actions.

Was he deranged? Was he eager to leave her pregnant? What if he had? What if she was?

He pushed away the troubling rumination, focusing
on the joyous interlude and naught else. In the morning,
he'd be sorry. But not now. Not when he was still trembling with ecstasy.

His erection waned, and he pulled out and slid to
the side, snuggling himself to her as she studied him
curiously.

"Are you all right?" he eventually asked.

"You can't tell me I'm still a virgin."

He chuckled. "No, you're not."

She reflected, then nodded. "I'm glad it was you."

"So am I." He rubbed her stomach. "You'll be sore
for a day or two, but it will fade."

"I'm fine now." She stretched and smiled. "Can we
do it again?"

"Again?"

"Can't you . . . ah . . ."

"I can do it again," he hastily declared, "but you should rest."

"I'm not tired."

"Minx." He wrapped his arms around her and hugged her close. "Give me a minute."

She cuddled with him, her soft hands stroking and soothing.

"Am I pregnant?" she inquired.

Obviously, a woman could become pregnant from her first sexual encounter, but he wasn't about to frighten her by admitting it. The prospect would cause needless worry and would most likely turn out to be nothing.

"No, you're not."

"How can you be certain?"

"You're just not."

She didn't believe him, but she didn't argue, and he was relieved. If she'd questioned him as to why he'd risked so much, he couldn't have explained in a thousand years.

He pictured her belly swollen with his child, her skin healthy, her eyes aglow with pending motherhood. The sweet image rattled him, and he yearned and regretted as he'd sworn he wouldn't.

"I wish things were different for me," he said. "I wish I could make a different choice."

"Hush!" she scolded. "Don't say that to me. Not when we're here like this."

"Why not? It's true."

"But you have me hoping we could change the ending, when we both know it's not possible."

"If I . . . if I could have altered my path, would you have had me? If I could have married you rather than—"

She pressed a finger to his lips, cutting him off. "Don't ask me."

"But I need to hear your answer."

She glanced away, staring at a spot over his shoulder. "No, I would never have married you. We wouldn't have suited."

For a long while, they were frozen, as he pondered whether she was sincere, thinking that she couldn't have been, but he was surprised by how the rebuff wounded.

He mumbled, "I'm sure you're correct."

"Of course, I am." A strained quiet ensued; then she added, "Don't be sad, Jordan."

"I'm not."

"Let's be happy for what *is*, for this precious period that we've managed to steal for ourselves."

He hated that she could be so blasé, that she could exhibit such aplomb, but if she could act nonchalant, he could, too.

"I want you again," he told her, and he flexed against her leg, letting her feel the sudden state of his arousal, and she laughed.

"I guess you can do it again."

"I can *do it* all night if you can keep up with me."

"Oh, I can, my dear Jordan. I definitely can."

He rolled her onto her back and started in again. Dawn would bring plenty of opportunity for lamentation, but for now, there was only delight to be had, and he would take all she could give—and more than that. Much more than that.

CHAPTER FOURTEEN

Margaret huddled in the window seat of her room, her robe cinched tightly, a knitted throw draped across her shoulders to ward off the chill. She gazed at Jordan as he slept in her bed. He was exhausted from their night of passion, resting on his stomach, the covers pushed down to his bare bottom.

Before meeting him, she hadn't known that a man's body was so beautiful, hadn't realized that the sight of him, nude and reposed, could be so thrilling. Oh, how she wished she could keep him there forever. How she wished the glorious interlude would never end.

Outside, dawn was breaking, the morning commencing much too quickly. He'd have to leave soon, and should have left long ago, but she hadn't had the fortitude to insist. With each passing minute, they were courting disaster, but she didn't care.

She could be branded a harlot, assaulted by Lavinia, kicked out onto the road, tarred and feathered in the village square, and it would all have been worth every joyous second.

She hadn't understood how it could be between a man and a woman, hadn't grasped how effortlessly a woman could plunge to the spot where she'd tumbled. Her heart ached with the knowledge of how much he meant to her. How would she let him go? How could she watch in misery as he married Penelope?

He kept saying he had to have an heiress, but what if he chose another path? What if he wed for happiness?

They were smart people; they could figure out how to be together. She just knew they could!

Over on the bed, his eyes fluttered open. He held out his hand, and she walked over and took it, easing a hip onto the mattress.

"What time is it?" he asked.

"Very late. After five already. The sun's nearly up."

He yawned. "I should be going."

"Yes, you should," she agreed, but she was relieved when he didn't move.

"Are you all right?" he inquired.

"Just sad," she replied.

"Sad? Why?"

She wouldn't feign indifference. Finally, she'd found something that mattered, something she wanted more than anything. If she didn't make an attempt to keep him, she'd always regret her silence. He might refuse her, but at least she'd learn where she stood, and she wouldn't be left wondering.

"I fibbed to you last night," she said.

"About what?"

"I told you that we wouldn't suit, but I was lying. We'd get on fine."

"Yes, we would."

At the small concession, her pulse raced. "I don't want you to marry Penelope."

"I don't want to, either."

"Marry me instead."

There! She'd blurted it out! Yet to her dismay, he didn't seize on the opening she'd supplied.

He didn't smile; he didn't speak. He merely stared, appearing dumbfounded.

"Oh, Margaret . . ." he breathed.

"We could be so happy!"

"Perhaps," he equivocated.

"We're friends, and you seem to have a genuine fondness for me. We could build on that."

"But you don't have a dowry," he gently reminded her.

"To hell with a dowry!" she blithely declared. "Don't you crave more for yourself than the . . . the . . . chattels a pile of cash can purchase?"

"You know that I don't seek it for myself. There are so many people counting on me. They should be able to count on my father, but you've met him. His life is in shambles, and he's not concerned about how it's affected anyone but himself."

"So you have to save everybody for him?" Though she didn't mean to be curt, she'd hurled it as an accusation.

"Yes. It's his tenants and employees who've worked for our family for generations."

"I don't care about any of them!" she selfishly claimed.

"It's my siblings, too. There are no funds to buy them clothes, or feed them, or send them to school. Someone has to help them, and it won't be the Earl of Kettering."

"So? What is it to me?"

"The other day, I received a letter from two of his young sons. They're about to be tossed out of their home, and they have nowhere to go. Should I shrug my shoulders and permit it to occur? Should I ignore their plight?"

Growing desperate, she shamed herself by confessing, "I love you."

"You don't."

"I do."

"Margaret, sex is an extremely emotional experience, and afterward, some women become overwrought. It happens frequently."

"Are you saying I'm suffering from some sort of carnal hysteria?"

"Well . . . yes."

"My feelings have naught to do with the sex we had!"

"They do, too!" he insisted. "It can't be anything else. I won't let it be anything else."

"Are you afraid to hear that I love you?"

"No, but what good does it do?"

"I want you to know how important you are to me."

She felt as if she was begging for crumbs of his affection, and she braced, waiting for a reply that would indicate a similar sentiment. To her undying mortification, he was stonily silent, assessing her as if she'd gone mad.

"Have you any feelings for me in return?" she pressed.

"Yes."

"Then, please apprise me of your opinion, because it's suddenly dawned on me that I haven't a clue as to what it might be."

He was quiet, weighing his responses, but why would he need to? She'd been very candid. Why couldn't he be the same? Why was it so hard to tell the truth—unless there was nothing to tell?

"Don't do this, Margaret," he ultimately pleaded.

"Don't do what?"

"This entire evening was so grand, and we'll never have another like it. Don't ruin the moment by demanding more than I can give you."

"You could find a way to be with me—if you really wanted me."

"Spoken like a true romantic, but it won't pay the bills. And I have so many."

Slumping with defeat, she eased away from him. She considered stomping off, but she couldn't make herself go. She doubted they would be able to sneak away for another rendezvous, and during these last, painful minutes, she couldn't bear to be separate.

She stared out at the brightening sky and had never felt so alone, had never been so lonely.

"What if I'm pregnant?"

"You're not."

"What if you're wrong? What if I am?"

"I don't know."

She supposed it was as much of an answer as he could convey, and the fact that it was so disappointing and so unsatisfactory only underscored how foolish she'd been to assume she could sway him or alter his course.

He stroked her back, and she let him, needing his warmth, his touch.

"Why don't you go?" she suggested.

"I can't—not when you're so angry."

"I'm not angry."

"I can't change who I am."

"I understand."

"If there was any other way . . ."

She leapt at his words, pitifully brimming with anticipation over what he'd implied. "Now that I've humiliated myself, can you at least throw me a bone? Humor me and confess that you'd have had me if circumstances had been different."

"You know I would have."

"I don't know that, at all."

He drew her into his arms, and she didn't put up a fight. There was such an air of finality that she could almost taste it. Time was growing short, his window of opportunity closing. He had to reach a decision about Penelope, had to marry her or depart. He couldn't continue to linger, day after day, with no proposal tendered and no wedding planned.

"Let me ponder this," he mused.

"All right."

"There has to be a viable solution for us. Maybe I can think of something."

"Maybe."

She shut her eyes and offered up a prayer, not asking for much but a small miracle.

The cock crowed out by the barn, heralding the morn, and he pulled her onto the bed and rolled them, so that she was beneath him.

"I want to have you again before I go," he said.

"I'd like that."

She'd hoped that he'd dawdle and seduce, but it was

so late, and she could sense his urgency, though he did his best to hide it. With no wooing or preparation, he slipped off her robe and entered her, and she couldn't keep from wincing. Several hours earlier, she'd been a virgin, so she was sore and raw.

"I'm sorry," he murmured.

"Don't be."

He smiled, though it was tremulous and strained. "I can't ever get enough of you."

"I'm glad."

Very rapidly, it was over. A few thrusts, a few kisses, and he was finished.

The cock crowed again, and he peered outside, gauging the increasing light. Mentally, he'd already left her, his thoughts a thousand miles away.

"I have to go."

"And be quick about it." She hugged him tight and whispered, "I love you."

She'd been certain that, here at the end, he'd echo the sentiment. But he didn't. He frowned and moved away. Hurriedly, he tugged on his trousers, and she lay in the awful quiet, observing him.

Soon, he was dressed. He bent down for a parting kiss; then just as he stood, the door burst open. The interruption was so unexpected that all Margaret could do was blink and blink, her mind struggling to grasp what her eyes could plainly see.

Lavinia loomed in the threshold, an irate, hulking menace that was no apparition. She was absorbing every detail of the sordid tableau, with Margaret and Jordan frozen like a scene in a scandalous painting. Margaret broke the moment as she grabbed for the quilt and covered herself.

Lavinia smirked, her furious gaze locking with Jordan's.

"I've been waiting in your room for an eternity," she explained, "so we could discuss Penelope. When you didn't return, I did some investigating. It didn't take me long to figure out where you were."

"If you believe my whereabouts are any of your business," he insolently remarked, "you're absolutely deranged."

"Margaret is my niece, and you are a guest in my home. If those two facts don't make it my *business*, I don't know what does." She pointed toward the hall. "Get out of here! At once!"

Jordan's cheeks reddened, but like a chastened child, he slinked out without argument or backward glance. Margaret was abandoned to face the consequences on her own, yet she couldn't blame him. She only wished that she could have scurried away, too.

They listened to his strides fading, and as the silence descended, she wondered if she'd ever see him again.

Lavinia hissed, "I will speak with you in the library in one hour. I suggest you have your bags packed."

She spun and marched out, and Margaret fell onto the pillows, exhaling a heavy breath.

What would happen now? She wouldn't hazard a guess. It seemed her worst fear had been realized, and she was about to be tossed out. Would Lavinia follow through with her threat? Did Margaret have any right to refuse to go? Who might help her?

Depressingly, she couldn't conjure the name of a single person.

Ready for any catastrophe, she climbed out of bed and began to dress.

R obert sprawled in his chair, cursing his offer to aid Lavinia in unraveling her convoluted finances. Try as he might, he simply couldn't get the numbers to match up.

Grumbling about ungrateful females—and idiotic, long-suffering males—he recommenced adding the lengthy rows of sums. He checked the totals, then checked them again, and again, but no matter how many times he tabulated, they made no sense.

Her enormous expenditures were easy to calculate, but it appeared as if she'd had an income that was triple any amount she should have had. Yet there was no indication as to where the extra cash had originated.

So . . . either she had a secret and vast stash of money she'd never mentioned, or he should have paid closer attention to his mathematical instructors when he was in school.

He'd had the best education England could provide, so he didn't think his problem was the result of poor teaching by his professors. Though it irked him to admit it, Lavinia was probably involved in some scheme that would land him—as her future husband—in an impossible jam.

Why, oh why, had he agreed to assist her?

Though he loved her desperately and beyond reason, he couldn't deny how devious and cunning she could be. On occasion, she exhibited a vicious nature, one that she hid well and was rarely displayed, but he'd known her since he was a boy, and she couldn't fool him. She likely had a nefarious plan in the works, and he'd thrust himself directly in the middle of it.

They'd both need rescuing.

He'd have to pester her for details, would have to sit her down and press until she spilled all, but the notion of confronting her, of bickering and nagging till she confessed her mischief, was so distasteful that he couldn't bear to consider it.

He wanted to marry her and live happily ever after—as he'd always dreamed. What he didn't want was to learn that she'd done something horrid, and he refused to dig for evidence of fiscal misconduct.

He had to be wrong. There was no other option.

With a groan of annoyance, he dipped his quill in the jar of ink and began adding yet again.

※

As Jordan entered his room, Lavinia had arrived before him and was lounged in a chair, watching the minutes tick by on the clock. He peeked over; it was after six.

"How dare you do this to me!" she growled as she rose to her feet.

"To you? When I started my affair with her, *you* never crossed my mind."

The flip statement enraged her further—as did his condition. He was a mess, his clothes askew, his shirt torn by Margaret during their frantic coupling. He hadn't bothered to put on his shoes, and they dangled from his fingertips.

He deposited them in the armoire, then proceeded to the cupboard and poured himself a stiff whiskey. He leaned against the wall, sipping it as if he hadn't a care in the world, but on the inside, he was livid.

What should he say? What should he do? How could he defend the indefensible?

"I demand an answer from you," she badgered. "Where would you come by the temerity to seduce her?"

"What are you? My mother?"

"Shut your rude mouth."

Keen to quarrel, she stomped over till they were toe-to-toe, but he was too rattled to reason clearly, and too confused to make sound decisions.

"So I've been off fucking," he crudely admitted. "I still don't understand why you'd have the gall to comment."

"You've dallied with me on exactly one occasion, and you've hardly looked at Penelope—even though I specifically gave you permission to ravage her. It's enough to have me suspect that you prefer boys. But lo and behold! It's not boys you favor. It's my mousy, indigent little niece."

"Think what you will." He shrugged, declining to talk about Margaret or his unrelenting desire for her. "Now if you'll excuse me, I've been *up* all night, and I intend to take a nap."

He tried to walk away, but she clutched his arm and yanked him to a halt.

"You're through trifling with Margaret. Do you hear me?"

"Don't order me about."

"You forget that *I* am the trustee of Penelope's fortune. *I* shall decide upon whom it is bestowed. How badly do you want it?"

He shook her away. "Not as badly as you seem to suppose."

"Fine, then. Leave my house. This instant!"

He felt like a rabbit snared in a trap. As Lavinia was aware, when he had such a contemptible history, it was impossible to find an heiress. There were so few rich girls, and typically, they quailed at the sight of him. While he didn't expect much in a spouse, he would not have one who wept with terror when he was near.

"What do you want, Lavinia?"

He'd capitulated—they both recognized it—and she preened, knowing she'd won. He would never see Margaret again, would never have the chance to apologize or say farewell, and at the notion he was so bereft that he could barely keep from falling to the floor and blubbering like a babe.

"Your father is scheming to wed Penelope!"

"Of course, he is. It's been his ploy all along."

"Aren't you going to fight for her?"

"*Fight* for her? Good God, Lavinia, why would I? It's just about money."

"A lot of money!"

"Yes, a lot of money."

"But you can't let him have her!"

Jordan scowled. She was so upset, when he couldn't imagine why. Perhaps she wanted Charles for herself. Poor woman! He thought to warn her, but didn't.

She'd be perfect for Charles. She'd make him miserable each and every day for the rest of his life. If Jordan was lucky, she'd drive him to an early grave.

"You're her mother," he calmly rationalized. "You want her to marry *me*. If he asks for her hand, say *no*."

She scoffed. "I doubt he'll inquire politely. In fact, I believe he plans to ruin her and force a union."

He could only nod. "I'm certain you're correct. He's not known for his scruples."

"You have to stop him."

"What can I do?" He'd never been successful at thwarting Charles. If he was, he wouldn't be in the predicament where he currently found himself. "If you're begging me to speak with him, it would be a waste of breath. He'll act however he pleases and damn the consequences."

"He can't have her!" she vehemently insisted.

"So kick him out of your home. Send him away. You're very clever. Make up some pretext to get rid of him. Tell him . . . tell him . . . you have other guests coming and not enough space to accommodate everybody."

"But I don't want him to leave," she muttered.

She blushed, ashamed at having divulged a weakness, and he rolled his eyes. How could she fancy Charles? How could she fail to see the snake slithering under the smooth exterior?

"So it's like that, is it?"

"Yes, it's just like that. I want him to stay and Penelope to go." She poured her own drink and gulped it down. "I'm tired of your petty delays. You traveled to Gray's Manor—at my invitation—to pursue a match with my daughter, but you've been so busy fucking my niece that you've scarcely noticed her."

"That's because Penelope has made her feelings very plain. She thinks I'm old and boring and that I have a violent past. She loathes me."

"Her opinion is irrelevant. She'll do as I command. So what's it to be: Will you have Penelope or won't you?"

Her question sucked all the air out of the sky. The earth seemed to stop spinning. His heart ceased to beat. He couldn't give her an answer! Not now! Not yet!

She tarried, waiting, waiting, and when he didn't respond, she continued.

"This is a one time offer. You have the next sixty seconds to snatch her up, and I'll dispatch a messenger to London to retrieve a Special License. We can have the entire affair finished by tomorrow afternoon. If not by tomorrow, then by Saturday for sure."

His knees were shaky, his tongue tied. What was best?

He had to have that money! He had to have it! Yet, an affirmative reply would kill Margaret. She'd never forgive him. He'd never forgive himself. Not after the night he'd spent with her. Not after his tepid vow that he'd devise a way for them to be together.

He couldn't behave so callously toward her. He couldn't! But what alternative did he have?

"You're in a blasted hurry all of a sudden."

"Yes, I am. I admit it. If you agree to have her, I'll sign a letter that immediately places half the dowry in your bank account. The other half will be transferred after the ceremony."

He could practically smell those piles and piles of pound notes. "That's fast."

"All I ask in return is that you take her away as soon as the last *I do* is uttered. You'll get in a carriage with her and go—and you won't ever bring her back."

"Your motherly affection leaves much to be desired."

"I don't care how you view my relationship with my daughter. I merely seek to have her married and out of my hair as rapidly as the deed can be accomplished. Are you the man to handle it for me or aren't you?"

"And if I refuse?"

"I'll put her in a carriage myself—today—and escort

her to London, where I'll find someone else who's smart enough to grab her fortune." She glanced over at the clock. "Your sixty seconds start now."

He studied her, the clock, her again. The ticking was inordinately loud as he tried to work out a solution. He could have Penelope, or he could have Margaret. He could have the money and Penelope, or he could have Margaret and nothing.

Did he really want Margaret? If he chose a path of poverty with her, over the enormous obligation he owed to so many, how could he ever convince himself that it was the proper conclusion? If he took the cash, he could rectify so many ills. If he declined it, he could do nothing at all for anyone.

Could he selfishly pick Margaret?

He was a man of the world and had no illusions. At present, he lusted after her, yet his infatuation wouldn't persist. He knew how swiftly passion could burn, how promptly it could fizzle out. His carnal peccadilloes were always fleeting, and though he'd liked Margaret more than most females, his interest in her would wane. Then where would he be?

He would be poor and unable to discharge any of his responsibilities. He'd hate her for luring him away from his duty, and he'd hate himself for having let her.

"Your minute is up," Lavinia snapped. "What's it to be? Will you marry Penelope or won't you?"

Steadying himself, he filled his glass and swigged the contents.

"Yes, I'll marry her."

"A wise decision."

"Yes, it is," he concurred without a hint of mockery or regret.

"I'll have a footman depart for London at once. I'll notify you the moment he arrives with the license. Maybe we could still hold the ceremony later tonight. You could consummate and ride off with her in the morning."

"Whatever you wish is fine with me. Keep me posted."

"I will."

Smiling in triumph, she sauntered out, and he went to the window and gazed outside. The sun hadn't peeked over the horizon, but he felt as if he'd lived a lifetime since he'd awakened in Margaret's bed.

When she learned what he'd done, how would she react?

"I'm sorry, Margaret," he murmured, "I'm so sorry."

He sank into a chair and blindly stared at the wall.

CHAPTER FIFTEEN

"I won't do it."

"You will."

"I won't. You can't make me."

Lavinia glared at her lazy, recalcitrant daughter, who was still abed and too indolent to rise and show her mother any deference. If Penelope persisted with her rebelliousness, Lavinia's rage was so intense that she couldn't predict what she might do.

"I don't know where you acquired the notion that you can defy me, but I suggest you tamp it down."

"I'm not afraid of you," Penelope claimed.

"Aren't you?"

"No. You're jealous because Lord Kettering likes me best, so you're forcing me to marry Lord Romsey to get me out of the way."

"Let me be very clear: You will wed Romsey—or your precious fortune will vanish. You'll no longer be a snooty heiress. You'll be poor like everybody else. You'll be nothing, at all."

"That money is mine!"

"No, it isn't. It's held in trust, and I am the trustee, with full rights to disburse of it in any fashion I choose. So far, I've *chosen* to utilize it as your dowry, but if you continue with your insolence, I'll change my mind."

"You have to use it for my benefit!"

"Who's to say I haven't? I can fill my files with hundreds of false invoices, proving that I've spent every penny seeing to your welfare and that it's all gone. Robert will lie for me and swear the expenditures are genuine."

"No one will believe you!" Penelope insisted, though not as vehemently. The first inklings of alarm were sinking in.

"Why wouldn't they? It will be your word against ours. Who will people find more credible? A respectable widow and her reputable companion? Or an impudent, hysterical child?"

"If you don't allow me to have my dowry, I'll never forgive you!"

"Are you supposing I care?" Lavinia chuckled. "Actually, I'd be perfectly happy to keep it for myself, and I don't know why I didn't consider it before. Perhaps *I* shall become the heiress in the family."

"You wouldn't dare," Penelope seethed.

"Wouldn't I? Gad, but you're so naïve."

Lavinia had no doubt she would win the argument. Penelope's entire life revolved around the fact that she was affluent. Her wealth defined her, gave her substance, and if it was suddenly snatched away, she'd be all but invisible.

Ultimately, she would yield, for she had no other

option. She would marry Jordan, he would take her away, and Lavinia would be free to pursue Charles without interference.

Penelope's temper got the better of her. She leapt off the bed to attack, but Lavinia was ready for her, a leather belt hidden in the fold of her skirt. As Penelope stormed over, Lavinia lashed out, smacking Penelope across the face. The blow stunned her, and she lurched away and fell to her knees, clutching her cheek.

"You hit me! You hit me!" she wailed over and over.

"Yes, I did, and if you sass me a second time, I'll strike you again, and I'll keep on striking you until I've beaten some sense into you."

"I hate Lord Romsey!"

"So what? No woman has ever been permitted to marry for love. Why should you be any different?"

Lavinia leaned down and gripped Penelope by the back of the neck, her nails digging in, so that Penelope cried out and squirmed in agony, and Lavinia reveled in the petty torment. She'd been too lenient, so Penelope had never learned how little her own wants or needs mattered when compared to Lavinia's.

"What is it to be?" Lavinia demanded. "Will you have Romsey? Will you seize the chance to instantly be a viscountess and subsequently a countess? Or will you refuse and be an impoverished nobody?"

"Let go!"

"Not until I hear your answer."

Lavinia squeezed, deeply enough to draw blood, and Penelope collapsed onto the rug, a quivering, complaining ball of fury, but her ire was no match for Lavinia's. With Charles as the prize, Lavinia felt insane, so desper-

ate to win him that she could murder Penelope without
a twinge of conscience.

"Well?" she hissed. "I'm waiting!"

"Yes, yes, I'll marry him."

Grinning with triumph and malice, Lavinia shoved
her away. "I'll send your maid to help you dress for the
ceremony. We will proceed the moment my footman returns from London with the Special License."

"You can't expect me to go through with it today!"

"I can, and you will." Lavinia bent down again, which
caused Penelope to recoil in terror, and Lavinia relished
the girl's fear. "I can see how your mind is working.
You're plotting to foil me, but you won't be able to."

"I will! I'll get out of this horrid betrothal if it's the
last thing I do."

Penelope glared, her loathing unveiled, and a frisson
of apprehension slithered down Lavinia's spine, but she
shook it away. Penelope was a child, Lavinia her lawful
and sole parent, and she would behave as Lavinia commanded.

She strutted to the door, stopping for a final glance,
thrilled by the sight of Penelope on the floor, disheveled and beaten down.

"By the way," she taunted, "you won't be going anywhere."

"What do you mean?"

"I'm locking you in. You'll stay here in your room
until the vicar arrives; then I'll escort you down to the
ceremony."

"Bitch!" Penelope hurled.

"Aren't I though?"

Lavinia stepped into the hall, spun the key, and sauntered off.

I've been thinking."

"About what, darling?"

Charles smiled at Lavinia. She really was a gorgeous woman, but she was too old for him to take seriously, and she was broke. She concealed it, but he could sniff out penury like a dog tracking a wounded fox.

She was in dire straits, and he had no idea why she was giving away Penelope's dowry. If the girl had been *his* daughter, he'd have kept the funds for himself.

"We'd talked about my ravaging Penelope," he said.

"Yes, we did."

"I've been on pins and needles ever since we discussed it."

"Have you?"

He pulled her to him, his regard washing over her, and it wasn't feigned. He truly did find her attractive, and he was always partial to a female who performed fellatio without his having to request it. "I'm so hard—just from pondering it—that I can barely stand up straight."

She chuckled and rubbed herself against his erection. "I can tell."

"Can you?"

"Oh, yes."

"Why wait till Saturday?" he urged. "We should do it tonight. Wouldn't that be fun?"

"It would be"—she frowned and sighed—"but a slight problem has surfaced."

"What is it?"

"Jordan finally spoke to me, and he's settled on Penelope, after all. I was sure he wasn't interested, but he claims he's smitten. I couldn't refuse him."

At the news, Charles panicked, but he hid it well.

"Of course, he wants her! He needs her money. But why would his decision alter our plans?"

"I can't provide him with a bride who's not a virgin. He'd cry foul. Why . . . he might sue me for damages! Our family would be a laughingstock. Penelope would never be able to show her face in public again." She pouted. "Neither would I."

"But I'm so eager to dally with the two of you."

"It's just not meant to be. I'm so sorry."

She patted the front of his trousers, then walked on, and he went to the sideboard and poured himself a drink. He sipped it as he contemplated his next move. He'd read Penelope's signals correctly. She wanted *him*. Not Jordan. So what had happened in the past few hours?

Perhaps Jordan had bribed Lavinia. Or perhaps he was blackmailing her. Whatever the basis, Charles had to halt any wedding. Victory was so close that he could nearly taste Penelope's fortune, and he wouldn't let it slide through his grasp.

Penelope abhorred the notion of marrying Jordan, and Charles was happy to do his part to guarantee that Penelope got exactly what she wanted.

❧

I s it true what I heard?"

"About what?"

Robert watched Lavinia as she sat at her dressing table and primped in the mirror. "Has Romsey asked for Penelope's hand?"

"Yes, isn't it grand? We'll be shed of her in no time— by tomorrow at the latest."

"Will he stay on at Gray's Manor?"

"No. He's leaving immediately, and he's taking her with him."

Robert rested his palms on her shoulders. "So . . . all of our dreams have come to fruition."

"Yes, they have."

His fingers glided down, hesitating at her bosom, but when no complaint was raised, he covered her fabulous breasts. He caressed the soft mounds, as she moaned and arched, but he couldn't shake the impression that her response was faked.

On several occasions, he'd copulated with Anne Smythe, and she was always so excited to be with him, so keen to try whatever he suggested. He'd been sneaking around with Lavinia for so long that he'd forgotten how wonderful it was to have a partner who enjoyed the sexual act.

"With Penelope gone," he pointed out, "we can be wed right away."

"Yes, we can."

"Let's set the date."

"The date! Oh . . ."

"Yes, the date, Lavinia. What reason is there to put it off yet again?"

She eased away and peered up at him, her grin flirtatious and sly. "I have a thousand tasks to complete before I send her on her way. It isn't every day that a mother sees her only daughter married!"

Where Penelope was concerned, Lavinia didn't have a maternal bone in her body, so he understood her comment for the delaying tactic it was, and he tamped down his frustration.

"What about the Earl?" he queried.

"What about him?"

"Will he remain after the wedding?"

"I don't know why he would."

Her smile was steady, her eyes guileless and open wide, and she looked so innocent, but Robert didn't believe her. Then again, he was so jealous of Kettering that it was difficult to think clearly about the man.

Robert had invested so many years in pining for Lavinia, had embarrassed and disgraced and demeaned himself in his quest to wed her. She'd insisted they'd be together in the end, that the instant Penelope's future was secured, she would be ready to tie the knot.

If she'd changed her mind, what should he do? How much longer would he wait? *Why* would he wait?

"You know, Lavinia, if I were to find out that you're stalling, that you've no intention of following through—as you've repeatedly promised you would—I can't predict how I might react."

"Why . . . whatever do you mean?"

"I've been poring over the ledgers you gave me."

"So?"

"You have too much money. From where did it come?"

"Too much?" She laughed, but nervously. "Are you mad? If I'm so accursedly well-off, why am I so broke?"

"Don't lie to me. I've calculated the numbers. They don't add up, and I'm extremely curious as to why not. I demand you explain yourself—or else!"

"Or else *what*?" She studied him, then jumped to her feet, her gaze growing hard. "Are you threatening me, Robert?"

"No, I'm just stating the facts. You've made me privy to some of your secrets, but I shan't protect you unless you can convince me as to why I should."

"Obviously, I made a mistake in assuming I could trust you."

"If you supposed that I'd cover for you, or that I'd hide immoral conduct, then yes, you have."

"Return my records! At once! I'll solve my own problems without any of your halfhearted assistance." She rippled with indignation. "I can't imagine what possessed me to presume you'd help."

She spat the word *help* as if it were an epithet, and it was all he could do to keep from throttling her. He'd do anything for her—anything!—as he'd pathetically proven time and again.

"Where did you get the extra money?" he hissed. "Tell me!"

"There is no . . . no . . . extra."

"If you aren't candid with me, you'll leave me no choice. I'll have to take steps. . ."

"To what? What are you implying? Are you insinuating what you seem to be?"

He paused, trying to decide his purpose, but quickly, he backed down. He didn't believe for a second that she was a thief, but if she was, he'd rather die than reveal her duplicity. What if it amounted to felonious behavior? He could never be responsible for instigating legal proceedings against her. She could wind up in prison!

Still, it was clear that she was up to no good, and he was angry at his foolishness.

When would he ever be strong enough to separate

himself from her? He was like a fly, trapped in her spider's web and about to be eaten alive.

"I'm not accusing you of anything," he declared. "I merely want to marry you."

The dangerous moment passed, and her attitude warmed. "I realize how much you do, and it will happen very, very soon. I swear." In an apparent truce, she snuggled herself into his arms and confessed, "I shifted a bit of cash from Penelope's dowry. Just to tide me over. Is that so terrible?"

If that was indeed what she'd done, it was much more than *a bit.* It was a bloody fortune, but he hated to quarrel, and he was so desperate for the discrepancy to be an innocent error.

"I guess not."

"Can you forgive me?"

"Yes, but you'll have to put it back," he warned, "before the balance is transferred to Lord Romsey."

"I was planning on it." She smiled a sultry, inviting smile. "I can see how tense you are. Let me relax you."

She always recognized when she'd pushed him too far, and it was her habit to smooth over any discord with a bout of sex. She was so fussy at doling it out that when she offered, he agreed as if he were a dog in need of petting.

For once, though, the prospect of crawling into her bed, of flexing away as he stared into her bored face, held no appeal whatsoever.

He thought of Anne Smythe, of how raucous she could be, of how there was no pretense with her. She told you what she liked, and she told you what she didn't, too. There was no mystery to it.

"I don't think so," he said, refusing her for the first time ever.

She grasped that she'd been rebuffed. "Why . . . what is the matter with you?"

"I'm busy." He set her away, unable to abide her cloying touch. "By the way . . ."

"What?"

"You were correct in deciding you shouldn't have shared your files with me. I'll return them in the morning."

He left her with her jaw dropping in shock. The firm rein with which she'd controlled him had begun to slacken, and he was thrilled to have rattled her. The ungrateful shrew could fix her own damned problems.

In a reckless mood, he marched down the hall, and as he would have proceeded toward the stairs, he continued on to Mrs. Smythe's room. He halted, glanced both ways, and, seeing no one, he slipped inside without knocking.

She was at a writing desk by the window, occupied with correspondence, and when she looked up, there was a flicker in her eye that he assumed was surprise, but which might also have been a smidgen of delight.

She didn't ask what was wrong or why he'd come, didn't order him out or do anything but murmur, "Lock the door."

He complied, then walked over to her, and he took her hand and led her to the bed. He urged her down so that she was reclined on the mattress, her knees bent, her calves dangling over the edge. He lifted her skirt and wedged himself between her thighs, tickled to note that she wasn't wearing any drawers.

Without discussion or wooing, he leaned in and licked

his tongue across her, and the taste of her spurred him to decadence. There was something about her that drew him in, that drove him on, and though he didn't understand it, he wasn't about to deny its potent force.

He delved and explored, but in a smattering of minutes, he was too aroused to resist. He tore at the buttons on his pants, loosed his straining cock, and shoved it into her. In a mere five thrusts, he came and came and came. She wrapped her legs around his waist and held him tight until it ended.

On the few occasions they'd philandered, they'd scarcely spoken a dozen words, yet he felt closer to her than he'd ever been to any woman, even his deceased wife, to whom he'd been wed for years.

Did Mrs. Smythe feel the same? Was she sharing his sense of a heightened connection? Had she lain awake nights, pondering their strange and exciting association?

He had no idea.

With his ardor spent, he was embarrassed by his animalistic display. He pulled away, showing her his back as he straightened his clothes. When he spun toward her, she'd stood and done the same.

There were a myriad of remarks he could have made, but what emerged was, "Lord Romsey is marrying Penelope."

"That can't be right. Are you positive?"

"Mrs. Gray informed me personally—just a few moments ago."

"Poor Jordan," she muttered. "He's about to discover how little happiness money actually buys. He'll be sorry."

"I'm sure he will be. Will Kettering leave now?"

"I haven't the foggiest."

"When will you know?"

"I'll talk to him immediately."

When he'd inquired about Kettering, he'd presumed he raised the issue because he wanted some hint as to the Earl's intentions regarding Lavinia. Yet suddenly, it dawned on him that he had a totally different reason for prying.

If Kettering left, Mrs. Smythe would go, too. Robert would never see her again.

He couldn't deduce how he felt about that, and in light of their peculiar relationship, he wasn't certain what he was trying to learn.

Was he hoping she'd remain at Gray's Manor? For how long? To do what?

The answers were too difficult to decipher, and he couldn't figure out what to do but create more distance between them than there already seemed to be.

"I'm curious as to his plans," he blandly claimed. "Let me know his reply, will you?"

"I will."

Like the cad he was, he went to the door and peeked into the hall. Espying no one, he crept out and sneaked away.

CHAPTER SIXTEEN

"W here is your bag?" Lavinia demanded. "I asked you to bring it with you."

"I didn't pack it yet," Margaret said.

"Why not? Did you think I wasn't serious?"

"I know you were."

Margaret pulled up a chair and seated herself. They were separated by the library's large desk, the polished oak glimmering with their reflections. She tried to read Lavinia's mind, which she'd never been able to do. The woman's machinations were—and always had been—a mystery.

Lavinia hated her, and Margaret had never understood why. She was about to be evicted from the only home she remembered, and the notion terrified her. She couldn't fathom living anywhere else. Without Gray's Manor as her foundation, she'd be a nomadic wanderer, with no roots or ties. How would she survive?

"I'm curious," Lavinia started, "where you came by the gall to immerse yourself in a sexual affair with Lord Romsey."

Margaret blushed with mortification. She'd led such a sheltered life, had been such an innocent before the relationship had commenced, and she had no idea how to have such a disturbing, frank discussion.

"Well?" Lavinia pressed. "I'm waiting."

"He . . . he . . ."

"Spit it out! I would hear an explanation for this treachery from your own perfidious lips."

"He was in the room next to mine, and he . . . just . . ."

"Are you claiming he seduced you? How quaint."

Margaret couldn't have Lavinia assuming the worst of Jordan. Margaret was an adult, and she'd willingly chosen to philander with him.

"He didn't seduce me."

"Then how did he come to be in your bed?"

"I invited him."

"So . . . you're naught but a whore, after all. I've often wondered what sort of person you are deep down."

"I didn't mean for it to happen."

"Shut up. I won't listen to any excuses."

Lavinia seethed, her malice washing over Margaret. Any pretense of family that might have once bound them together was finally stripped away.

"I can't bear to leave Gray's Manor." Margaret sounded as if she was begging, and she was desperate to keep the panic out of her voice.

"Your remaining here is not an option."

"No one saw us but you, so no one else need ever know."

"Is that what you suppose?" Lavinia scoffed. "You've deceived me and betrayed your cousin, yet you have the audacity to assert that we should sweep it under the rug? If that's your hope, then you have more nerve than anyone I've ever met."

"If you wished it, I'm positive we could keep it a secret."

"What if you're pregnant? What then?"

Margaret's hands trembled, and she tucked them under the folds of her skirt so that they were out of sight.

"Lord Romsey said I couldn't be."

The moment she uttered the statement, she realized how idiotic it was. Girls were forced into matrimony all the time after a single tumble with the wrong boy. Why should Margaret presume herself to be free from danger?

"Lord Romsey said . . . Lord Romsey said . . ." Lavinia imitated in a mocking singsong. "Isn't it interesting how he can predict the future? Do you really imagine I will allow you to linger in my house, while your belly swells out to here with his bastard?"

She made a crude gesture over her stomach, and Margaret winced with shame and glanced down at her lap.

"No, I wouldn't expect it of you."

"Jordan is marrying Penelope."

Confused by the announcement, Margaret frowned. "What did you say?"

"You heard me: Jordan is marrying Penelope, tonight or tomorrow, as soon as the footman returns from London with the Special License."

Margaret shook her head. "That can't be right."

"Can't it? He jumped out of your bed, pranced back to his room, and advised me that he was ready to proceed. I accepted his offer. It's all been arranged."

"No . . . no . . ."

"You stupid fool! Did you believe he was in love with you? Is that how he convinced you to spread your legs?

My God, but you're naïve! Aren't you aware that a man will spew any falsehood to stick his cock in a hole?"

"It wasn't like that between us."

"Wasn't it?" Lavinia laughed shrilly; then she reached down and retrieved some documents from a drawer in the desk. "Here is your only alternative: You shall depart Gray's Manor immediately."

"Please don't make me."

Lavinia continued as if Margaret hadn't spoken. "Because your uncle was fond of you, I will provide you with fifty pounds to see you on your way, but I caution you to spend it wisely, for you shall never receive another farthing from me."

"Fifty!" It was a pittance, but at least she'd have funds for a few weeks while she figured out what to do. But when it was gone, what would become of her?

"You're lucky I'm giving you a penny," Lavinia fumed. "You will sign these papers, whereby you admit what you've done; then you'll go."

"And if I refuse?"

"I'll toss your belongings out on the road, have some burly servants throw you out bodily, then bar the doors so that you can't slither back in. If you loiter on the property, I'll send for the sheriff and have you hauled off as a common vagrant."

"He'd never let you abuse me so hideously."

"Wouldn't he? After I notify him of how you've disgraced yourself, you'll get no sympathy. The story of your downfall will race through the neighborhood. You'll be shunned by everyone; there won't be a family who will assist you. So you can take your fifty and leave quietly, with your pride intact, or you can go with nothing but scandal and infamy, but you're going."

"Why are you doing this to me?"

"Because I won't risk Penelope's learning that you were fucking her fiancé while she waited down the hall for his proposal. By being Romsey's wife, she'll have to endure much, but she shouldn't have to endure that!"

Margaret peered at her lap again, struggling to deduce how her marvelous affection for Jordan had brought her to such a despicable spot. From the first, she'd been so attracted to him, and when she'd been with him, her conduct hadn't seemed wrong.

She'd never considered the harm to Penelope or the horrid consequences once the illicit liaison was discovered. She'd been so happy knowing him, when she'd never been happy before, so it had seemed that any behavior was permitted.

A bit earlier, when he'd still been snuggled in her arms, he'd sworn that if there was a way for them to be together, he would find it. She simply couldn't accept that he'd made love to her, then waltzed out and offered marriage to Penelope.

The tale was too cruel to be true, and she had to look him in the eye and ask him if he'd hurt her as Lavinia was claiming.

"What is your decision?" Lavinia badgered.

"I want to talk to Lord Romsey."

"But he doesn't want to talk to you!"

"He owes me an accounting. He should have to tell me himself that he's picking Penelope over me."

"Why torture yourself? He doesn't love you! He never cared about you! You're acting as if you're the only female in history to be ruined after a handsome rogue whispered a few pretty words."

"You're making it sound so tawdry, but it wasn't!"

"It's always been about the money and naught else! He came to get it from Penelope, and he's leaving with his pockets full. As an added benefit, his cock was regularly sated—by you!—while he was here. I'm sure he's grateful for the entertainment you provided, especially since he didn't have to shell out any cash for whores at the tavern in the village."

"I must speak with him," Margaret insisted.

"Fine."

Lavinia bellowed for a servant, and momentarily a maid was dispatched to locate Jordan and fetch him to the library. Lavinia sat behind the desk, and they glared in silence until he marched down the hall. He entered without being announced, and as he walked in, he distanced himself from Margaret, several feet separating them.

He could have positioned himself right next to her—in a show of support—so she couldn't help but notice the slight, and she recognized what it indicated.

"You wanted to see me, Lavinia?" he inquired.

"Yes. Thank you for joining us. Have a seat."

"I prefer to stand."

"As you wish."

Since he chose to stand, she and Lavinia had to, too, but Margaret's knees were so rubbery that she worried her legs wouldn't hold her. She rose, white-knuckled and gripping her chair for balance.

He greeted her indifferently. "Hello, Margaret."

"Lord Romsey."

"I've been searching everywhere for you," he alleged.

"Really?" Not bothering to glance at him, Margaret imbued her tone with as much boredom as she could muster.

"I thought we should discuss what transpired and . . . maybe . . . we could . . ."

He stumbled to a halt. There was nothing he could say that would be appropriate, nothing he could share that ought to be voiced with Lavinia listening.

He scowled at Lavinia. "What is it you wanted?"

"I've informed Margaret of your pending nuptials with Penelope, but she refuses to believe me. Would you please apprise her of what has occurred?"

A painful interval ensued, as he shifted his weight from foot to foot, then mumbled, "It's true, Margaret."

She found the courage necessary to peer directly at him. In the past hour, he'd bathed and shaved. He was impeccably attired in a dark blue coat, a dazzling white shirt and cravat, and why shouldn't he be dressed to the nines?

Apparently, it was his wedding day. What man wouldn't like to be at his best?

He was too cowardly to return her gaze, but instead, stared at a point somewhere over Lavinia's shoulder, and Margaret snapped, "At least have the decency to look at me as you break my heart."

His cheeks reddened, and slowly, he spun toward her. The aloof aristocrat he'd initially been had reappeared with a vengeance. His expression mocked her, and there was no sign of the funny, wild, and charming man whom she'd adored beyond reason.

"How could I *break* your heart?" he coldly replied. "I made you no promises—as you made none to me."

"You said we could try to be together."

A hint of regret swept across his beautiful face. "When in the throes of passion, emotions can become jumbled."

"So you're claiming it was all lies? All of it? Did you ever care for me? Or was it just the sex?"

"Honestly, Margaret, I can't—"

"Answer me!" she demanded in a near shout.

He was unable to respond, and Lavinia interjected herself into the humiliating conversation.

"I merely explained to her," Lavinia said, "that a man will say many things when he's in the pursuit of— shall we call it—*amusement*? Wouldn't you agree?"

"Yes, I would," Jordan concurred.

"A man might even mean what he says at the time, while having no intention of acting on it later."

"Yes," he repeated.

"Why did you visit Gray's Manor?" Lavinia queried.

"You invited me to meet Penelope."

"When you consented, was it due to the size of her dowry?"

"Yes."

"As you leave, will you be taking the money with you?"

"A good portion of it has already been transferred into my name."

"Margaret isn't the first woman you've had sex with, is she?"

"Lavinia!" he scolded.

"You're hardly a virgin. Don't pretend otherwise. There's scarcely a female in the kingdom who hasn't copulated with you."

"I won't discuss this in front of her," he said, the two of them talking about Margaret as if she weren't there.

"You won't?" Lavinia hissed. "And why not? She assumes she was special to you! She assumes she mattered."

"She did," he tepidly insisted.

"Did she? Tell her how many paramours there have been over the years. Tell her how you will fuck anything in a gown. Tell her about the weekend orgies, and the soldiers' whores, and the three London mistresses, and the numerous opera dancers, and the—"

"Stop it!" Margaret cried. "Stop it, I say!"

They whipped around to gawk at her, and she detested how tears flooded her eyes, but she couldn't hold them back.

She'd never reflected on Jordan's life outside the confines of her small bedchamber, had never imagined the other women whom he'd sought for companionship. Though it was torture to learn of it, she was glad she had.

She'd been so foolishly in love that she'd been too afraid to see the stark reality of her situation. From the start, she'd understood that he could never be hers, yet she'd sacrificed everything she cherished in the entire world. For him.

Why had she succumbed to his advances? How could she have given herself to him without asking anything in exchange? Had she no self-respect remaining?

Struggling for control, she drew in a deep breath, her shaky voice belying her attempt at composure. "I've heard enough."

Lavinia nodded and glared at Jordan. "Is there any closing remark you'd like to make?"

"I'm sorry, Margaret," he contended. "I never meant to hurt you."

"I disagree. I think you meant to hurt me as much as you could. Don't try to assuage your conscience."

She gazed at him for the very last time, and in a thrice,

her enormous affection evaporated as if it had never been. The void was filled with a burning, strident hatred.

He appeared as if he might plead his case, or defend his bad behavior, but Lavinia saved her by butting in again, and for once, Margaret was relieved by her interruption.

"That will be all," Lavinia advised Jordan. "Now, I'd like some privacy while I finish speaking with my niece. If you'll excuse us . . . ?"

"There are some other things I'd like to tell her."

"She's listened to plenty of your drivel." She scowled at Margaret. "What say you, Margaret? Could you bear to have him continue?"

"No. I'd like it if he would go."

"There you have it." Lavinia stared him down, daring him to defy her.

He turned to Margaret, silently begging her to look at him. His concentration was like a silky caress, but she held firm, her eyes locked on Lavinia's.

Ultimately, he shrugged and left, shutting the door behind, and as his strides faded, Lavinia taunted, "Do you believe me, Margaret?"

"Yes, I believe you."

"He wanted to lift your skirt, and he did. You seem like such a smart individual. How could you have been so stupid?"

There were a thousand responses Margaret could have uttered to explain why she'd fallen for Romsey's flattery. She could have told Lavinia how lonely she was, how Romsey had paid attention to her, how he'd treated her as if she was pretty and interesting.

Instead, she inquired, "Why do you hate me?"

"Me? Hate you? I'd have to care about you to hate

you. Now head to your room and pack your belongings. I'll have the carriage outside in fifteen minutes. The driver will take you into the village."

The prospect of being deposited in the village, with her portmanteau in her hand, was too humiliating to contemplate. She'd have to go somewhere else, somewhere far away, where no one knew her, where no one would ever guess how she'd disgraced herself.

"Where should I go from there?"

"Wherever you want. You destination is no concern of mine. Good-bye."

The entire episode was like a dream. Margaret couldn't move, and Lavinia grew impatient. She went to the servants' bell and yanked on the cord. Shortly, the housekeeper arrived.

"Escort Miss Gray upstairs." At Lavinia's odd instruction, the housekeeper frowned, so Lavinia clarified, "She's decided to permanently leave Gray's Manor. I need you to help her with her bags so she can depart immediately."

Without another word, Margaret spun and walked out.

⸙

C ome with me."

"To where?"

Jordan studied Lavinia over the rim of his brandy. Since he'd fled the despicable encounter with Margaret in the library, he'd had several, though he expected it would take many more before he was numb.

Oblivion was his goal.

"We're off to Penelope's bedchamber," Lavinia informed him.

"Why? Are you hoping I'll finally rape her for you?"

"You've had your chance, so you'll just have to wait for your wedding night."

"Then why are we going?"

"You're about to propose—as any decent fiancé would do."

"Oh, God, isn't it enough that you've agreed to the match? Must I speak with her, too?"

"I'm sure you'll find this hard to fathom, but she's not overly keen on having you as a husband."

"You assume this is news to me?"

"I want her to view us as a united front. I want her to realize she can't fight both of us."

He sighed. The meeting with Margaret had been too distressing. She'd looked so young and defenseless. He'd felt as if he'd been kicking a puppy, and he couldn't tolerate more discord. He was too raw, too overwrought.

He filled his glass and drank it down. Filled it again and gulped it, too. "Where is Margaret?"

"She's left."

"For where?"

"After your contemptible behavior, it's really none of your business. She has no wish to see you ever again, and even if she did, I wouldn't allow it."

A sudden rage washed over him, one he hadn't experienced since he was in the army, and it was so powerful that he could murder her without hesitating. He reached out and clutched her by the neck, his broad palm circling her narrow throat tightly enough to frighten, to cut off her air.

"What have you done to her?"

"You lunatic! She's staying with an aunt of mine"—

Lavinia clawed at his fingers—"while we learn if there's a babe."

At the reminder of how he'd dishonored Margaret, he dropped his hand and stepped away.

"There is no babe," he insisted as if his declaring it could make it so.

"How can you be positive? Can you peek into her belly?" She snorted with derision. "Can you actually suppose that she'd remain here, gadding about pregnant and unwed, while the rumors crucify us? You're marrying her cousin today! Have you no shame?"

He had a great deal of shame, as well as remorse and regret and no small amount of sorrow. Events had brought their affair to such an abrupt end that he couldn't absorb all that had transpired.

The notion—that he'd never see Margaret again—was starting to sink in, and he couldn't bear how swiftly they'd been separated. One minute, he'd been holding her in his arms, and the next, there'd been only rancor and accusation.

Lavinia was correct that he shouldn't be permitted to converse with Margaret. Still, there'd been so many things he should have said to her, so many apologies he'd needed to render, when none would have been appropriate or sufficient.

He swilled another brandy. "Swear to me that she's safe, that you've provided for her welfare."

"I realize I can be a bitch," Lavinia admitted, "but she *is* my niece. Of course, I've provided for her. She'll be in seclusion till we know whether she's pregnant; then I'll make permanent arrangements for her. She can't return here. The possibility is too real that the scandal would leak out and wreck her future."

As if he hadn't felt low enough, he now felt even lower. How could he have done this to Margaret? She had no father or brother to demand reparation for his atrocious trespass. There was only Lavinia, who was focused on Penelope and who—despite her protestations to the contrary—couldn't care less about Margaret.

"You can't be certain that there'd be a scandal," he tried to maintain.

"Where have you been living? On the moon?"

"If . . . if there's a child, will you let me know?"

"Let you *know*? Are you mad? You're about to wed my daughter! I suggest you develop some respect for her and your new situation!"

"But if there's a child, I'll need to support it. I can at least do that much for her."

"Support it with what?" Lavinia chided. "Penelope's money? I think not." She grabbed his arm and pulled him toward the door. "Come. Let's get this over with."

"I have no desire to chat with Penelope."

"Have I asked what you wanted?"

She was practically dragging him down the hall, and he wondered why he was letting her. Why had he meekly consented to marry Penelope? He didn't have to do anything he didn't want to do. Why didn't he call a halt?

He could cry off, could forsake Penelope's fortune, and go to Margaret. He could beg her forgiveness and spend the rest of his life in poverty, repairing the damage he'd done.

He imagined kneeling before her, pleading for a second chance that she'd never give. He'd hurt her too deeply, had acted as the worst, most ignominious sort of man, and he didn't deserve her pardon.

Lavinia had stopped and was using a key to enter Penelope's room. Was the bloody girl being locked in? Was she that opposed to having him as a husband?

What good could evolve from such a hideous beginning?

Lavinia strutted into the frilly chamber and yanked him in after her. Penelope was lounged on the bed. When she saw them, she climbed to the floor, her insolence and disgust evident and infuriating.

"What is it, Mother?"

"Lord Romsey has something to say to you."

"What?"

He stared from mother to daughter. He must have had a dozen glasses of brandy, and he was definitely feeling the effects. Had he something to say? If so, he couldn't remember what it was.

"He's here to propose," Lavinia said. She glared at him. "Aren't you?"

"No," he replied. "You're her parent, and you've agreed, so I can't fathom why her opinion would matter in the slightest."

At his rudeness Penelope gasped. "You're insufferable, and you're drunk."

"Yes, I am, but as you're about to be my wife, you will soon learn that it is not your place to comment on my personal failings."

"And if I choose to disobey, what will you do to me? Send me to bed without my supper?"

"No, I'm much more likely to beat you on a daily basis," he boasted, enjoying how she shrunk away. "If you *really* annoy me, I'll order you to a nunnery, or better yet, I'll commit you to an insane asylum. Or I'll simply

divorce you—after I have your dowry—and for the remainder of your days, you will be poverty-stricken and
abandoned."

"You horrid, horrid man!" Penelope wailed.

"Be silent!" he shouted so loudly that both women
cringed. "I'm sick to death of your juvenile ways and
your snotty attitude. You are sixteen years old, and your
mother has decided you are to wed. She's selected me as
your husband. You will be happy about it, or you will keep
your obnoxious mouth shut. Do I make myself clear?"

Brimming with hatred, she muttered, "Yes, you've
made yourself very clear."

"Then it appears we finally understand one another."

He stormed out, Lavinia tagging along behind.

"I'm impressed," she said once they were alone in
the corridor.

"By what?"

"You're even more of an ass than I'd suspected."

"Yes, I am."

"She's biddable, if you seize control—which you certainly have. I believe the two of you will get on fine."

"I'm so glad to hear it." He kept on down the hall.

"Where are you going?"

"I'm off to my room. Have a footman deliver several
more bottles of brandy. I intend to drink myself into a
stupor, then pass out. You may wake me when it's time
for the ceremony to start."

Perhaps if he was very lucky, he'd overindulge to the
point of mortality and would never be roused. He walked
on without glancing back.

CHAPTER SEVENTEEN

As Anne approached the parlor, she heard a man and a woman speaking, so she halted and peeked inside. It was Charles and Mrs. Gray huddled in the corner, and Charles had his hand on her bottom. Anne had suspected they were lovers, and now, she had her answer.

She should have been outraged, but all she could think was that he was making a fool of himself, sniffing after the beautiful but lethal Mrs. Gray.

Anne had been sure that he was focused on the daughter and the dowry, but Mrs. Gray probably had a fortune of her own. Maybe with Jordan having become affianced to Penelope, Charles had set his sights on Lavinia.

Well, Mrs. Gray could have him, but if Charles assumed Anne would linger through another of his marriages, he was in for a surprise. She'd rather seek employment as a scullery maid.

Mrs. Gray glanced over and espied Anne in the hall. She pulled Charles into a deep, searing kiss, which she obviously wanted Anne to witness, and Anne couldn't believe how unmoved she was. The old feelings of jealousy had fled, replaced by a cool disinterest.

Mrs. Gray ended the embrace and flashed a saucy smile. "I'll see you later, Charles. In your room, after everyone is abed."

"I can hardly wait," Charles said.

She waltzed out, and Anne had stepped back to let her pass when Mrs. Gray gestured toward the next parlor. Anne followed her in and shut the door.

"You were watching Charles and me," Mrs. Gray started without preamble.

"I was."

"I'll be blunt."

"Please do."

"In light of your *friendship* with Charles, I've been very gracious in having you as a guest in my home."

"Yes, you have been."

"But you've overstayed your welcome."

"If you force me to leave, Charles will come with me. Are you certain that's what you want?"

"I wouldn't count on Charles going with you." Mrs. Gray smirked as if she had a secret she couldn't share. "Charles and I have gotten very close, and you should be aware that a wedding is imminent."

"He's proposed to you?"

Her simpering grin faded. "No, but we've thoroughly discussed it, and at any moment, I'm expecting to make an announcement."

"Congratulations."

"Thank you."

Anne was being sarcastic, but Mrs. Gray didn't realize it. She preened and continued. "While his previous wives were accommodating of his many peccadilloes, I shan't be. I intend to supply him with all the feminine entertainment he needs, so there'll be no place for you in his life. I suggest you find a new situation—if you can, given your advanced age."

"I'll begin looking right away."

"You do that." She went to the door and opened it, signifying that the conversation was over. "I'd appreciate it if you'd go first thing in the morning. Don't bother to keep in touch."

"I won't. Don't worry."

Anne walked past her, calming her breathing, willing her temper to recede; then she proceeded into the parlor, where Charles was relaxed on a sofa by the fire.

"Anne! There you are. I feel like I haven't talked to you in days."

He held out an arm, indicating she should sit and snuggle under it, but she chose the chair across from him instead, and he couldn't help but recognize that something had changed between them.

They stared and stared, and finally, she asked, "What are you doing with Mrs. Gray?"

"What do you mean?" he replied, when he very well knew.

"I thought you were planning to marry Penelope."

"I can't. Jordan snatched her away from me."

"So now what? Will it be Mrs. Gray instead?"

He studied her, and Anne could practically see the wheels spinning in his head as he pondered how much he should reveal of his various schemes.

"What if I have been considering her?"

"You were going to marry me. You promised!"

"But Anne," he said gently, "you don't have any money. You've never had any money."

"I've given you more important things, like loyalty and companionship."

"Yes, you have, and you've been an absolute blessing, too."

"Mrs. Gray has demanded that I vacate the premises."

"What? Why . . . that's preposterous. What would I do without you?"

"She claims I'm interfering in her relationship with you."

"She's jealous, is she?" He chuckled. "Don't fret about it. I'll speak with her."

She tarried, the silence settling. This was where she was supposed to back down and placate him with ingratiating remarks, but she couldn't mollify him. "I don't want you to speak with her. I've decided she's correct: It's time for me to go."

"You're being absurd." He went to the sideboard and filled a glass with whiskey, and when he turned toward her, he was all smiles, all sweet, cajoling Charles. "I'm just toying with her, Anne."

"Are you? She thinks you're serious."

"She's mistaken. You know how fleeting these dalliances are for me."

"Yes, I do."

She'd been one of them once, but for some reason, she'd kept his interest when others couldn't. She'd never understood why, had never questioned what she'd viewed as a stroke of fortune, but in reality, it was all so tawdry.

"I believe I'll retire for the evening," she said. "You won't be needing me, will you?"

"No."

"Good night, then."

"Good night," he echoed. "We're clear about Mrs. Gray, aren't we?"

"Very clear."

"You're staying, and I won't hear any argument."

"I wouldn't dream of it."

She strolled out, and as soon as she was far enough away, she broke into a run, feeling as if she was fleeing for her very life.

🍃

"Here are your records," Robert snapped.

"Fine." Lavinia glared as if he were vermin. "Leave them on the chair. I'll have a maid put them away."

With much loud, dramatic huffing, Robert deposited the huge, messy stack while struggling not to bellow at her. He was amazed that he'd actually returned the stupid documents, that he wouldn't keep on in his efforts to aid her with her financial quandary. It was so unlike him to remain angry, but it seemed as if they were embroiled in a permanent spat, and he had to calm himself, had to locate the equanimity required to deal with her.

They often quarreled, and tensions only eased because *he* came crawling back and apologized. As he was rarely the one in the wrong, his willingness to pacify her was galling, but it was too late to alter the tenor of their association. If he didn't grovel, how would they carry on?

He still wanted to marry her. Didn't he?

It had been so long since he'd wished for anything else that he couldn't fathom another ending.

The pile started to wobble, then fall, and he jumped

to brace it as numerous items toppled to the floor. Lavinia watched, bored, as he scrambled about like a servant, scooping up ledgers and stuffing them in what he hoped were the appropriate spots.

A piece of paper—one he hadn't noticed prior—fluttered to the floor, and he frowned. It was a note, in Lavinia's handwriting, and across the top, she'd jotted three columns, labeled, *My Trust, Penelope's Trust,* and *Margaret's Trust.* There was a large sum of money indicated beneath each heading, followed by arrows, additions, and subtractions.

"What's this?" He held it out to her.

She studied it, blanched; then she leapt over and snatched it away.

"It's nothing. Just some scribbling."

"But it says *Margaret's Trust,* and it shows an amount equal to yours and Penelope's."

Hastily, she crammed the odd document into the drawer of her dressing table. "I told you: It's nothing."

From her frantic reaction, it was apparent she was lying, and he was forced to ask the unthinkable. "Did Horatio leave Margaret an inheritance?"

"Don't be absurd. Why would he? He couldn't abide her."

Although he hadn't spent much time with Horatio and Margaret, he recalled that they'd had a cordial and affectionate relationship and Horatio had seemed fond of his niece. Could he have provided for her?

He shook away the disloyal notion. With how Margaret had been abused by Lavinia over the years, the prospect didn't bear contemplating, yet Lavinia had too much money. Had she stolen it from Margaret? Could she have done something that despicable?

If Lavinia had perpetrated such a terrible deed and Robert still loved her, what did that say about his judgment and character? How could they go on?

What he'd conjectured couldn't be true. He wouldn't let it be.

"Are you going out?" he inquired, desperate to change the subject.

"No, why?"

Robert dawdled behind her as she primped in the mirror. It seemed all he did anymore was observe her from the fringes of a world that no longer included him.

"You're being awfully meticulous with your preparations."

"Can't a woman be beautiful at her own supper table?"

"Has the footman arrived with the Special License?"

"No, so we have something to anticipate on the morrow."

"How did you convince Lord Romsey to propose?"

"I simply told him to make up his bloody mind or I'd find someone else who wanted her money more than he obviously did."

"Have you signed over the dowry to him? All of it—as I instructed you?"

"Of course, I did. I couldn't lie. When I initially dangled it in front of him, I apprised him of the full amount. If I'd suddenly declared the sum to be less, he'd have been suspicious."

"Yes, I imagine he would have been." Robert tamped down a sigh of relief. He'd always hoped that some of the pot might end up in their hands, but with it transferred to Romsey, the strife it had caused would vanish.

"So . . . it's all gone."

"Yes."

"Penelope will be wed shortly."

"I can't wait."

"What about Margaret?"

"What about her?" Lavinia sneered.

"I haven't seen her lately. I was just curious."

"I informed her that she wasn't welcome here any longer, and she left."

At the news, he was aghast. "Where is she?"

"I haven't the foggiest."

His level of outrage was further evidence that the spell Lavinia had woven around him was unraveling. She had a toxic side to her personality that had previously amused and intrigued him, and he couldn't figure out why he'd ever tolerated it.

"I've always felt badly about how you treated her," he admitted.

"Why?"

"She was nice to me."

"So? She wasn't *nice* to me."

"She was too," he insisted, "and now, you've sent her away."

She glared over her shoulder. "You don't know all the facts, darling, so don't criticize."

"I'm worried about her."

"Why would you be? She leeched off me for decades, and I've merely plugged the hemorrhage her presence created. She can take care of herself for a change."

She fussed with her dress, lowering the bodice, her nipples nearly visible. Once, he would have considered it a breathtaking sight, but with her lips reddened by cosmetics, and with so much bare skin exposed, he thought she looked like a trollop.

"When will Lord Kettering be leaving?" he asked.

"He's not. Not yet anyway."

"Why would he remain after the wedding?"

She wrinkled her nose and giggled. "He's having too much fun to go."

"What kind of . . . *fun?*"

A deadly silence descended, and she froze; then she laughed gaily, as if she'd intimated nothing untoward. "He likes it here, because it's so quiet and rural. He claims he's had enough of the city, and he's fond of the solitude."

"Is that right?"

"Yes."

He scrutinized her, trying to garner some hint of what was going on in her devious head. What was her game? Was she planning to seduce Kettering? Had she already?

If Kettering was her paramour, what was Robert prepared to do about it? In the past, he'd loved her beyond folly or sanity. Did he still?

He didn't know, but after everything he'd been through with her, the prospect—that she might have changed her mind and decided on Kettering—was more than he could abide.

A wave of ire swept over him, and he crudely growled, "I want to fuck you."

"What?" She whirled on her stool and scowled up at him.

"You heard me: I want to fuck you—this very second—and I won't listen to any complaints."

"Honestly, Robert, it's time to go down to supper. I'll muss my hair."

"I don't give a rat's ass about your hair. You're supposed to be my mistress, and you'd better start acting like it. Unless you're supplying to someone else what is mine, and if that's the case, I swear I'll kill you." He paused and leaned in, eager to do violence. "Is Kettering worth the price? You tell me."

The threat hung in the air, and for a moment, alarm flickered in her eyes; then she calmed and scoffed.

"How on earth did Lord Kettering fall into the middle of this discussion? And why are we quarreling?"

"Fuck me! Show me that I still mean something to you."

"You're being a boor."

"I don't give a shit."

"I won't lie down on the bed and wrinkle my clothes, but if you're determined, I'll suck you off."

"Be my guest."

He stood before her, observing indifferently, as she unbuttoned his trousers. She was in a hurry, so there was no dawdling. She licked him, then took him in her mouth. Since she hated performing fellatio, he kept on and on, but with all he'd endured, he would damn well enjoy himself.

Eventually, she grew impatient with his restraint, and she cupped his balls. The extra sensation pushed him over the edge, and his seed spewed down her throat, but there was no satisfaction in the release.

He was weary of her and disgusted with himself. He pulled away and fastened his trousers and, as if nothing had happened, she returned to admiring herself in the mirror.

"Are you staying for supper?" she blandly inquired.

"No."

"Pity," she cooed, her relief impossible to hide. "We'll miss you."

"I'll be round in the morning."

"Marvelous," she said, but she looked as if she'd swallowed a toad.

"I'm tired of your treating me like a leper. I'll expect fellatio from you more often. I'll expect it every day."

Her temper flared. "You can't be serious! I'm not about to become your sexual slave."

"Do you know what I think, Lavinia? I *think* you stole money from Margaret, and if you did, then I've uncovered your secret." He rested his palms on her shoulders, squeezing tightly enough to bruise. "Isn't my continued discretion worth a few blow jobs now and again?"

He was so close to beating her, to simply grabbing a belt and lashing at her till she was a bloody pulp on the floor, so he spun away and stomped out without another word. He stormed down the hall, ready to commit mayhem, feeling as if a stranger had taken over his body.

At the landing, he faltered, Mrs. Smythe's door beckoning to him. He had no doubt that she could soothe the beast rampaging within, but instead, he raced for the stairs and proceeded down to Lavinia's library, where he searched every drawer, every nook and cranny. Finally, stuffed behind some books on the highest shelf, he found for what he was hunting, and he traced a trembling finger across the heading, *Last Will and Testament of Horatio Gray.*

His heart pounding with apprehension, he slid the thick document into his jacket and left for home, certain that whatever the terms contained inside, his life would never be the same once he learned what they were.

I realize it's very late, but might I speak with Mr. Mason?"

"And you are . . . ?" the butler asked.

"Tell him it's Mrs. Smythe, and that I apologize for stopping by at such a discourteous hour, but it's terribly important."

"Please wait here," the butler intoned.

He studied her bedraggled condition, her wet hair and muddy clothes. After her frantic trip through the woods, she was a sight, and he was kind enough to take pity on a scared and desperate woman. He escorted her into the vestibule and gestured to a chair, then he went to find Mr. Mason, and she was grateful that he hadn't had her stand outside in the dark and the rain.

Though only minutes passed, it seemed an eternity before footsteps sounded. She glanced up to see Mr. Mason coming alone, no servant in attendance, and she was grateful again. She didn't want his staff eavesdropping, didn't want rumors wafting over to Gray's Manor.

She rose as he approached, but he assessed her wearily. There were fatigue lines clearly discernable around his eyes and mouth, and she suffered a wave of panic. Obviously, he was distraught and carrying a weighty burden, so she'd come at a bad time.

What if he sent her away? What if he refused her request for a brief sanctuary?

He'd previously invited her to visit, but she hadn't dared till now. With her having resolved to cut her ties to Charles, she was sailing into uncharted waters and careening between dread and joy. For reasons she couldn't comprehend, Mr. Mason had seemed like an anchor in the storm.

"Are your children at home?" she queried.

"No, they're still with their grandparents."

"May I stay for a bit?"

"Are you all right?"

"No. Are you?"

"No." He slipped his hand into hers. "You're freezing! Come with me."

He led her up two flights of stairs and down a lengthy hall to the master suite. It was a masculine room, with maroon drapes, and heavy mahogany furniture. A fire blazed in the hearth, and she tarried as he tossed several logs onto the flames.

When he finished with the chore, he stared at her, confused and somewhat alarmed by her arrival.

"I'm leaving Lord Kettering in the morning," she explained. "I just decided."

"Is he having an affair with Mrs. Gray?"

"Yes, but . . . but . . . he promised me that he was . . . was . . ."

She couldn't confide how hurt she was. Nor could she confess that she had nowhere to go, and she was petrified that she was about to become invisible, that soon, no one would be able to see her or hear her.

He urged her closer to the fire so the heat would warm her.

"You're soaked through," he scolded. "You didn't even wear a shawl."

"I was suffocating, and I had to get out of that house. I didn't remember . . ."

She drifted off again, content to dawdle as he unbuttoned her dress. He must have assumed she was there to have sex, and she had to admit that a mindless bout of intercourse would suit her fine. For the period they were together, she wouldn't have to think or plan; she could just *be*.

He tugged off her gown so that it pooled around her ankles. Then, he made swift work of her undergarments, and she was naked. He yanked the combs from her hair, then he snuggled himself to her backside, and she could feel that he'd removed his shirt.

Their prior encounters had been so anonymous and so detached that she hadn't viewed his chest yet, and she was delighted to note that it was coated with a thick matting of hair. She nestled herself to him, and the sensation was so electrifying that her knees nearly buckled.

"Is this what you wanted?" he whispered in her ear. "Is this what you needed?"

"Yes . . . yes . . ."

"As do I. You couldn't have picked a more opportune time to interrupt me."

"I can see that you're troubled. What's the matter?"

He was silent, pensive; then he asked, "If you'd suddenly discovered that someone you loved—someone you'd always loved—had committed a terrible wrong that needed to be righted, what would you do?"

"I suppose it would depend on how *terrible* the wrong."

"It's a crime," he said very quietly, "a contemptible felony. The person ought to go to prison and never be let out."

"I don't know what I'd do."

"Neither do I, and at the moment, I don't care to discuss it. I want to focus on something else. You, for instance." He reached around and pinched her nipples. "You have the most magnificent breasts."

"Harder," she begged. "Do it harder."

"I love fucking you."

"Show me how much."

She was numb, and she wanted him to be very rough. If he wasn't, she was afraid she would not feel anything, at all.

His fingers drifted down, sliding into her sheath to probe and play. She moaned, arching against him, seeking more of what he was offering.

With a few flicks of his thumb, she came, the agitation so potent that she had to grab onto a chair to keep from falling to the floor. While she was still in the throes of her orgasm, he eased her forward, spread her thighs, and entered her in a smooth thrust.

Clutching at her flanks, he pounded into her, but he was as aroused as she had been, and he came, too, then collapsed onto her, both of them pinned to the chair. Chests heaving, pulses slowing, he drew away and stood, and she stood, too, and as always happened when their ardor cooled, she was embarrassed.

They had nothing to say to one another, and she wished she could snap her fingers and magically be dressed, then snap them again and be gone without a farewell.

"Turn around," he commanded, and she was suddenly shy, not eager to have him observe her forty-year-old body.

She didn't budge, and he repeated, "Turn around! Let me look at you."

Grudgingly, she did, and she held her head high, determined to survive his scrutiny without worry or shame. After this tryst, she'd never see him again anyway. Why care about his opinion?

He evaluated her, his gaze keen and perceptive; then

he traced down across her breasts, the tuck of her waist, the curve of her hip.

"Kneel down for me."

"Like this?"

"Yes. Remove the rest of my clothes."

She started with his shoes and stockings, then his trousers, jerking them down and off. It was the first time she'd seen him naked, and as she peered up his torso, she was thrilled with his manly form. He had strong legs, a flat stomach, wide shoulders, and muscled arms. His cock was long and thick, already swelling with lust.

She held him, stroking him, licking him; then she sucked him inside. He inhaled in a sharp breath, stunned and excited by the pleasure she generated, and he fisted his hand in her hair, guiding her, forcing her to take more, but she didn't mind.

From the minute she'd met him, riotous emotions had been driving her, and they were growing more powerful and more decadent. She couldn't ignore them or tamp them down; she could only revel and enjoy.

He flexed for an eternity, ravaging her mouth, and she was happy to let him, elated that his climax was approaching, but abruptly, he pulled away and scowled down at her.

"Why are you here?"

"I couldn't stand to be alone just now," she admitted.

"Why do you keep having sex with me?"

"Because I'm attracted to you, and I've never previously felt anything like it."

"But what do you want?"

"I want to stay for the night. That's all."

"That's not very much. Why don't you ask for more?"

"I doubt you'd give it."

"You might be surprised."

"Would I?"

He was hinting that he'd allow her to remain. Would he like an arrangement that was more permanent than a few fast and lewd tumbles?

She hadn't even left Charles yet. Not really. Dare she contemplate a relationship with Mr. Mason? She scarcely knew him, but then, she'd known Charles forever and their association was in its death throes.

Who could predict what might transpire?

He helped her to her feet.

"Get into my bed," he advised. "I want to see you lying on my pillows."

She went over and clambered up, and she reclined on her side, so she could watch him as he walked over to join her. She caressed his erection, liking the proof of how much he desired her.

"You're very handsome, Mr. Mason. I'm glad I finally stripped off your trousers."

"I want to try everything with you." He frowned at her as if braced for a refusal.

"Fine." She clasped his wrist and dragged him to her. "Just swear to me that you won't stop—even if I beg."

He rolled her onto her stomach and ordered, "Climb up on your knees."

She complied, and he centered himself and pushed in from behind, both of them gasping as he filled her.

"You make this all so easy," he said, and she chuckled.

"Do I?"

"Yes, you do, but I don't understand you."

"Good. I like being a mystery."

"But it means that I can't let you go till I've figured you out."

"All right."

"It may take me days or weeks or months."

"I hope so."

She shut her eyes and offered a prayer that her visit wound up on the long end of his estimation.

"You can't return to Charles Prescott. I won't permit it."

"I won't. I can't."

"Promise me."

"I promise."

At her vow, he began thrusting, penetrating to the hilt, then retreating, keeping on and on with the wild abandon she craved. Eventually, he came again, and they both fell onto the mattress, his large body pleasantly crushing hers.

He was snuggled to her, their passion ebbing, and she was amazed to feel him kiss her ear, her hair. She didn't think he'd kissed her before, or if he had, she couldn't remember.

She smiled, ecstatic that she'd taken a chance on him.

"By the way," he started.

"What?"

"My Christian name is Robert. What's yours?"

"Anne," she said. "My name is Anne."

CHAPTER EIGHTEEN

W ho's there?"
Penelope sat up in her bed, squinting
through the darkness. A man had sneaked in,
and she panicked.

What if it was Lord Romsey? Was he about to rape
her? If that was his intent, she'd have to marry him.

"Who is it!" she repeated more forcefully.

"Hush!" Lord Kettering replied. "If you continue
with your carping, you'll wake the dead."

She sagged with relief as he walked over and lit a
candle. Dressed in a flannel nightshirt, a robe pulled
over top, he was ready to proceed with her ruination.

"How did you get in?"

"I used a key. How would you suppose?"

Penelope smirked. Lavinia was so stupid. She'd
locked Penelope *in,* but she hadn't fathomed that her
more important goal should have been to keep the Earl
out.

"Why have you come? What do you want?"

"If you have to ask, perhaps I should go." He didn't

move to depart, though. Instead, he ordered, "Take your hair down."

"Not until we establish a few rules."

"Rules?" He chortled. "I'm agog to hear what they might be."

"You will afford me the deference I'm due as your future wife, and you will exhibit the utmost courtesy at all times." She glared, daring him to rebuff her. "If you can't be civil, then I don't want you here."

He scoffed. "I don't know why your mother doesn't have you whipped on a regular basis."

"Whipped! I won't brook any insolence from you! Now get out or I'll scream bloody murder."

"Go ahead. Bring your mother running. I'm eager for her to see us, although I'm hoping we'll be a tad farther along when she arrives."

His flip retort kept her silent, and she scowled. There was no way to take charge of the encounter or make him behave appropriately. He wanted every bad thing she wanted, only he had a firmer grasp of how to achieve it—and with the least amount of scruples.

"I changed my mind," she petulantly said.

"About what?"

"I've decided to marry Romsey as planned."

"I don't think so."

"I am! So you might as well leave."

He ignored her and lit another candle; then he went to the hearth and stoked the embers, throwing on kindling so the fire was roaring.

Once he'd finished, he rose and dusted off his hands. "There, that's better. I hate to fuck in a cold room."

"I don't know what that word means."

"You don't need to know the definition to be able to do it."

He came to the bed and sat on the edge.

"Take your hair down," he said again.

"No."

He grabbed her braid and yanked at the ribbon, fluffing the blond strands so that they floated around her shoulders.

"Remove your nightgown."

"I won't. Go away, I tell you. Go!"

"Don't you want to be my countess?"

She was still desperately willing, but if he thought she was about to refuse him, maybe he'd be nicer. "You're too loathsome, so the title of viscountess will suit me just fine."

"You greedy wench. We both know that's a lie." He gestured to her nightgown. "Take it off."

"No."

He clutched the front and ripped it in half. "You have to learn that it's pointless to argue with me."

"Why, you . . . you . . . you . . ."

She clasped at the destroyed garment, trying to hold it together, and while she was distracted, he rolled over and stretched out on top of her. She could feel him all the way down, especially the foul rod between his legs. She had a vague notion of what he'd do with it, and at realizing what was about to happen, she shuddered with dread.

"Let me explain how it's going to go," he said.

"I won't listen."

Like the spoiled child he always accused her of being, she clamped her hands over her ears, but he gripped her wrists and pinned them over her head. The new position was even more intimate, their anatomies more closely aligned, and his passions further inflamed. She squirmed and fought, but the only thing she accomplished was to rub the torn pieces of her nightgown so that they fell away and her entire nude form was rasping against his.

He looked down at her breasts, and he grinned in a manner she didn't like; then he dipped down and put his mouth on her nipple. It was rough and disgusting, and she detested that the marital act had to be so physical. She didn't like being groped and mauled, and though Lavinia insisted she'd get used to it, she couldn't see how she ever would.

"I will spend the night," he advised, "relieving you of your chastity."

"Then what?"

"We will keep at it, until you're good and truly ruined, so that your mother can't dump you on Jordan."

"That's it?"

"Believe me, it's more than enough. What time does the maid deliver your breakfast?"

"Mother has ordered me awakened at six. I'm to be ready when her messenger returns with the Special License."

He glanced over at the clock. "Which gives us three hours of fucking before we're *discovered*. Let's see how you take to it."

He started in on her breast again, and she'd presumed she was prepared for the onslaught, but when his fingers drifted down her belly to the juncture of her thighs, she threatened, "If you touch me there, I'll cut off your hand."

As if she hadn't spoken, he slithered through her womanly hair and poked around inside her. He stroked in and out, in and out, the sensation odd and vile.

"Oh, what a tight little puss you have. My cock will be ecstatic."

"Stop it!"

She batted at him, striking him about the shoulders, and he ignored her until she landed a fairly solid blow; then he sat on his haunches and tugged the belt from his robe. Before she grasped what he planned, he tied one end around her wrists and the other to the headboard so that she was fettered.

"Do I have your attention?" he asked.

"Yes."

"If you raise a fuss, I'll gag you, too."

"You wouldn't dare!"

"Wouldn't I? There's one thing you should know about me."

"What's that?"

"I like to copulate in peace. If you can't be pleasant and amenable, then you are to be submissive and silent."

"If you suppose I'll blithely obey your commands without a peep, you've picked the wrong girl."

"Have I? Over the years, I've trained many virgins to their marital duties, and I'm an expert at it. I don't imagine I'll have much trouble with you."

She pulled hard, trying to free herself but to no avail. "Let me go!"

"No, I'm enjoying myself too much."

"I'll do whatever you demand! Release me!"

"No."

There was a plaintive note in her voice that made her

sound as if she was begging, but she couldn't help it. Events had escalated too rapidly, and she hated not having control over what was about to transpire.

"You can't keep me tied up forever. If you don't let me loose—this very second—I'll kill you. Maybe not right away, but someday when you least expect it, you'll be dead."

"Penny, Penny, Penny," he scolded, using the nickname she detested. "You don't appreciate the consequences of what you've set in motion, do you?"

"What do you mean?"

"From the moment I arrived, you've thrown yourself at me. I've finally decided to give you what you crave, but everything comes with a price. The cost of sharing my title is very high, and you'll have to pay it in whatever fashion I require."

"You talk as if I'm to be your slave."

"Not my slave, no, but you will be a biddable and respectful wife."

"And if I decline to be led like a lamb to the slaughter?"

"You do so at your peril. You see, once I breach your maidenhead, no other man will have you—except me. Then your fortune will be transferred to me, and you will no longer be an heiress. The money will be mine—not yours—so you will have no value to me. If you persist with your juvenile, annoying habits, why would I keep you around?"

She received his message loud and clear: She could aggravate and exasperate him, or she could shut her mouth and do as he asked. She could spread her legs and obtain all the boons that went with being a countess, or she could complain and wind up with nothing.

She struggled to appear meek, which she intended to be temporarily. But in the future—oh, in the future!—there was no telling how she'd strike back.

Her false capitulation tricked him, and he mused, "Good, we're beginning to understand one another."

"Yes, we are."

"I believe we've established some of the ground rules that had you in such a dither. I trust they're acceptable to you?"

She nodded, and he smirked.

With great courtesy, he inquired, "Would you like to be my next bride, Miss Gray?"

"Yes, I would, Lord Kettering."

"Fine, then. Let's proceed."

"Would you . . . would you . . . untie me? I promise I'll behave."

"No. Your bondage makes it seem more like rape, which I enjoy very much and don't get to indulge in nearly enough. I'll release you once we're finished."

"Please?"

"No."

She bit down on the diatribe she was yearning to hurl. He thought he'd won the game, and she'd let him have his illusions, but she was smug with the certainty that, ultimately, he would be so sorry.

He stood and shrugged out of his robe; then, with no concern for her virginal state, he drew off his night-gown, too, so that he was naked.

She hadn't had the foresight to glance away, so she saw every inch of him. For such an elderly fellow, he was actually quite fit, but he was hairy all over, much of it gray in color, which sickened her and reminded her of the disparity in their ages.

She'd convinced herself that she wanted an apathetic marriage to an aristocrat, but now, with him about to take the steps that would permanently bind them, she was rethinking her ploy.

Perhaps, she should have held out for love, or at least a few crumbs of affection, and it occurred to her that she had chosen Kettering for all the wrong reasons.

At his crotch, his phallus jutted out, and it seemed to be pointed directly at her. It was a huge, ugly thing, covered with reddened skin and ropey veins. As she watched in horror, he wrapped his fist around it and squeezed. She squealed with affront and crunched her eyes closed, but she could feel the mattress shift with his weight as he joined her again.

"Open your eyes, little girl," he coaxed. "Observe the instrument that will bring about your ruination."

He eased forward and brushed something against her mouth, and she clamped her lips together.

"Now, now," he reprimanded, "we have an agreement, remember? You must do as I say."

She whimpered with fright, and he pinched her nipple so hard that she winced and peeked over at him. His rod was there! In her face!

She jerked away as he chuckled.

"This is my cock," he proudly proclaimed. "Why shy away? You insist that your mother told you all about it."

"Yes, she has." Suddenly, she abhorred Lavinia's attempts at enlightenment. Penelope would much rather have been completely in the dark.

"I like to have sex several times a day," he bragged, "and I take my pleasure any way it suits me. Some men are more polite with their spouses and have their mistresses do all the dirty work, but not me. I make every lover—be she wife or whore—perform the same deeds."

He stroked the filthy appendage across her lips. "Lick the end, Penelope."

She was in matrimonial hell, and the vows hadn't even been spoken yet! "I can't; I can't."

"You can and you will. You'll do as I've requested—at once—or I shall beat you, and then you'll have to do it anyway. Isn't it better to simply comply?"

He would beat her? With her being trussed like a Christmas goose, how could she prevent him?

She relented and dabbed at the tip with her tongue.

"There now," he soothed, "that wasn't so bad, was it?"

"I feel like I'm going to retch!"

"No retching will ever be permitted. Any display of repugnance will result in the whipping I promised."

"I can't help it if I'm disgusted by you."

"I don't mind if you're disgusted. I only demand that you learn to hide it." He touched her with his phallus again. "Lick me again, and keep at it until I tell you to stop."

She heaved a frustrated sigh, but did as he'd ordered, continuing on as moisture oozed from the end, which she couldn't abide.

"Enough!" she declared. "Do something else. Put me out of my misery."

He drew away and slid down her body, and after widening her thighs, he centered himself at her sheath, then wedged into the folds. He started pushing in, and he wasn't even looking at her. He couldn't care less that it was she. His partner could have been any anonymous female, and it dawned on her that, deep down, she'd wanted a husband who adored her, but the insight came much too late.

"You're hurting me," she complained.

"I couldn't possibly be. I haven't done anything."

"It will never fit."

"It'll fit fine, but it will be very tight, which is just how I like it."

He increased the pressure, cramming in another inch, and another.

"Jesus," he nagged, "you're dry as an old hag."

"I am not!"

"You are, but it's all right. It extends the moment for me."

Sweat popped out on his brow, his shoulders and arms quaking with the effort, when abruptly, he burst through the barrier. She arched up and cried out, but he clapped a hand over her mouth, stifling her distress.

He thrust into her as if she'd had sex a thousand times prior, and as she endured the deluge, she could almost see the money from her dowry flowing into his bank account—until he had everything and she had nothing.

After an eternity, he concluded the indecent business. With a loud grunt of satisfaction, his seed flooded her womb, and she imagined it taking root, planting a babe that would make her grow ugly and fat. She shivered with dread, praying that it would never happen— or if it did that she could find a competent, ruthless barber.

Eventually, the torture ceased, and he rolled off her and smugly gazed at the ceiling. When he finally glanced over at her, he seemed surprised, as if he'd forgotten she was present.

"Untie me," she commanded.

"Certainly."

He reached over and tugged at the knots. The belt fell away, and she curled into a ball, rubbing her abused wrists.

She was stunned and revolted. Was this to be her future? Was she to spend the rest of her days trapped in a bedchamber with this selfish, cruel oaf?

The prospect didn't bear contemplating.

"I love fucking virgins," he crudely said.

"Shut up."

"Your mother won't be able to keep us apart."

"No, she won't," she glumly concurred. Belatedly, she wished Lavinia had been a tad more strict, that she had heeded her mother's admonitions.

He slapped her on the bottom. "Get up, and fetch a towel."

"Why?"

"Because I'm covered with your maiden's blood, and I want you to clean it up."

"I'm not your servant. Get it yourself."

He slapped her bottom again, more forcefully. "Do as you're told—or I'll be very angry."

She climbed out of bed and teetered over to the dressing room. As she peered at herself in the mirror, a huge wave of disappointment swamped her, and she was crushed by the recognition that she'd made a hideous error in judgment, that none of her dreams would ever come true.

"What's taking you so long?" he barked.

She hurried to the washbasin, dipped a cloth, and scampered back to him.

Her nose wrinkled in revulsion; she wiped him down, not touching him more than she had to. When she was finished, she dropped the cloth on the floor and glared.

"Now what?" she asked.

"Now you get back into bed with me."

"I don't want to."

"So?" He patted the mattress, indicating that she didn't have a choice.

"I'm too sore."

"I don't care."

He dragged her to him, refusing to let her disobey, and she conceded the fight. He was so much older, so much more confident and assured, and she had no idea how to best him. But she'd learn how—and soon!

She lay there, stiff as a board, and as he snuggled himself on top of her, tears leaked from her eyes.

"Why are you bawling?"

"Because I'm sad."

"Why would you be sad? You're about to receive your heart's desire—which is marriage to me!"

"But you don't love me."

"Of course, I don't love you," he bluntly replied. "This is a business transaction. Nothing more."

"I thought it would be different," she sniffed.

"Well, it's not. This isn't some juvenile fantasy. This is real life."

He yanked at her legs, his cock hard and eager.

"I can't possibly do it again," she protested.

"Yes, you can. You have to. In fact, we're going to do it over and over, until you start to get the hang of it."

He entered her and began to flex.

CHAPTER NINETEEN

M rs. Prescott, you say?"

"Yes."

Margaret kept her face carefully blank, not reacting to the fake surname she'd adopted as her own. In the period since she'd left Gray's Manor, it had occurred to her that she'd get on much better as a widow than she would as a single woman.

When she'd initially been asked, she could have assumed any identity in the kingdom, but for some perverse reason she'd selected *Prescott* without hesitation. She couldn't figure out why she'd chosen Lord Romsey's family name, but Mrs. Prescott she'd picked, and Mrs. Prescott it would be from this moment on.

The proprietress of the boardinghouse pushed open the door to a dingy room, and Margaret stepped in. Foul odors assailed her, as if the rubbish from the prior tenant hadn't been cleaned out.

She looked around, too distraught to fret over how low she'd fallen, or to wonder if her fortunes could plummet even further.

"What do you think?" the proprietress inquired.

There was a rickety cot in the corner, a dilapidated dresser along the wall, and a narrow slit of a window. It was tiny and dirty and pitiful.

"I'll take it."

The woman nodded. "Rent is due on the first."

"That's fine." Margaret handed over the appropriate amount, shielding a wince at how rapidly her cash was disappearing.

"If you don't pay on that day, I'll set your things out on the street. So don't forget."

"I won't."

"Meals are at six and six. I can't abide slackers, so don't be late or you'll go hungry."

"I understand."

"I'll expect you to work, too. I won't tolerate sloth, so widow or no, you'll have to get a job straightaway."

"I intend to be gainfully employed," Margaret boasted.

"At what? What could you possibly know how to do?"

"I'm a teacher."

"A teacher! My lands! What next?"

"I'm positive there will be students in the area."

"People are poor as church mice. Who could afford such an extravagance?"

"You'd be surprised," Margaret bravely contended. "Everyone wants to improve their children. I'm certain I won't have any trouble."

The woman departed, and Margaret put her satchel on the dresser and went to the window, rubbing at the grime till she could peer outside. Off in the distance, she could see the hills through which she'd just traveled. She'd come such a long way, had caught rides with farmers, with teamsters, had walked and walked.

She'd wanted to keep moving, to the ends of the earth and beyond, but she'd grown too weary to continue.

She'd changed directions, had gone left, then right, then left again. She was determined to vanish, to never be found by anyone who might search—not that anyone ever would.

Previously, she'd been a good person, had tried her best to be kind and helpful, to be friendly and cooperative, but where had it gotten her? She'd lost everything, so she'd decided that the spinster from Sussex, Miss Margaret Gray, would cease to exist. In her place, a new woman had emerged, a tougher, wiser woman, the very private widow, Mrs. Margaret Prescott.

She sat on the lumpy mattress and pulled out a crust of bread, a remnant from her supper the night before. As she nibbled on it, the quiet pressed down on her, and she could hear her pulse pounding in her ears, each beat reverberating his name—Jordan—through skin and bone.

"How could you leave me like this?" she murmured. "How could you do this to me?"

But it was fruitless to ponder why, pointless to question Fate.

She opened her purse and counted the last of her coins. The small pile panicked her, but she tamped down any anxiety. This was to be her life now—this silent, terrible world where there was only struggle and deprivation—and it was futile to brood over her plight.

The owner of the boardinghouse hated indolence, and so did Margaret. She had to establish herself in the village, had to find a way to make do, but the notion of expending any energy was too much to contemplate.

I'll survive this, she told herself. *I will.*

She lay down, her head burrowed in her hands. Her

empty stomach rumbled, and she stared at the grubby wall, a single tear dripping down her cheek.

❧

"Here it is!" Lavinia crowed in triumph.

"What?" Jordan moaned groggily and rolled over to glare at her through bloodshot eyes.

"The Special License! The Special License!" She waved it like a flag of surrender. "My footman rode all night so I'd have it this morning. The vicar is on his way, so haul your ass out of bed. You're about to be married."

With great relish, she yanked at the drapes, sunlight flooding in, and he howled in anguish and hid under the covers.

"Lavinia!" he snarled. "Have mercy! Please!"

"Get up! Get up!" she nagged. "Time's wasting!"

"I have the worst hangover in history," he grouched. "If you don't go away—at once—you're putting yourself in mortal danger."

She marched to the dressing room and located a shirt and trousers; then she rushed back and tossed the clothes at him, which caused him to stir and sit up. His hair was standing on end, his skin pasty, his brow sweating, and he looked about to keel over.

"What will it take to get you moving?" she demanded.

"There's nothing you can do. Just drag me out to the woods and shoot me."

There was a decanter of brandy on the floor, and she poured a tall glass and gave it to him.

"What's this?" he asked.

"Hair of the dog. Drink it down. You'll feel better."

He scowled at it, his pallor increasing, but ultimately, he chugged it in one gulp. Then he shuddered and collapsed onto the pillow.

"I'll expect you downstairs in thirty minutes," she warned, "to say your vows. I don't care if you bathe. I don't care if you shave. I don't care if you have to be carried in on a stretcher. Just be there."

She whirled away to hurry out.

"Where are you going?" he managed.

"I have to make sure Penelope is up." His eyes started to close, and she barked, "Don't you dare fall back to sleep, or I swear I'll bring the vicar up here, and we'll hold the ceremony with you lying there naked."

She stomped out and down to the front parlor, issuing commands about hasty flower bouquets, chairs, and food. Begrudgingly, she'd decided on a blasé attempt at having a real celebration, but it was for the minister's benefit, so that he wouldn't deem the event odd.

With preparations proceeding, she gestured for two maids to follow her to Penelope's bedchamber, and her glee was so immense that she could barely keep from skipping down the hall.

At Penelope's door, she paused and frowned, stunned to note that it wasn't locked. Had the horrid child sneaked out? Had she run away?

Lavinia spun the knob and entered, the two maids hot on her heels, when she stopped in her tracks. She blinked and blinked, her mind working furiously, but she couldn't make sense of the scene before her.

Penelope was nude and on her knees, clutching the headboard, as Charles thrust into her from behind. Lavinia tried to tell herself that she'd stumbled on a rape, that Charles had crept in and taken what couldn't be his, but they both glanced over and grinned.

Charles halted, chuckling with feigned embarrassment. He drew away from Penelope and slid onto the mattress, snuggling her down with him. They lay on their sides, facing Lavinia.

Time seemed suspended as the pair froze, letting her have a good look at what they'd done; then Charles grabbed a blanket, tugging it over their privates as if they were posed in a shocking painting.

"Oh, my dear Lord," one of the maids mumbled, which prodded Lavinia to react.

She whipped around, desperate to keep them from seeing, but it was too late. Both women gawked at the spectacle.

"Get out of here!" Lavinia hissed. "And if you breathe a word of this to anyone, you'll answer to me. The least of your problems will be your immediate termination. Do I make myself clear?"

They curtsied and fled, but Lavinia was aghast to find a footman staring in, too. How would she keep the scandal quiet? How would she prevent the spread of gossip?

She'd never marry an earl, would never become a countess. She'd spend the remainder of her life as the poor relative, tagging after Penelope. Her only other choice would be to wed Robert, to live out her days in pathetic, rural obscurity.

Her dreams had crumbled to ashes, and she was insane with rage. Anger raced through her, the likes of which she'd never experienced. She slammed the door and advanced on them, fully capable of committing murder, and she wondered which one would be first.

"Lavinia, old girl"—Charles tried to appear contrite

but failed—"can you believe what's happened? I've been swept away by passion."

"Passion? Is that what you call it?"

"I couldn't wait. I beg you to accept my humblest apologies."

"You think you can offer a tepid apology and make this all right? How could you do this to me?"

"To *you*? I didn't do anything to you."

"You've had sex with my daughter!"

"So? You've been trying to snag her a husband. Now you have—and with very little effort. You should be happy."

"Happy? Happy?" She was screeching like a banshee, but she couldn't stop.

"I informed you of how badly I desired her. Did you assume I was joking?" He patted the mattress in invitation. "Why don't you join us? We can still have the *ménage à trois* you promised me."

Quaking with wrath, she glared at Penelope. "Get out of that bed."

"No."

"I am your mother, and I'm not going to tell you again. Get out!"

"No! I've been ruined and the whole world's witnessed it, so Lord Kettering and I have to marry. There's nothing you can do about it, and I don't have to listen to you anymore." Her triumphant gaze was cruel and hard. "I'm about to be a countess. Me! Not you! Couldn't you just die of envy?"

"I wanted him for myself!" Lavinia seethed. "You knew I did!"

"Well, he didn't want you back, did he? I told you: You're too old for him."

"Ladies, ladies," Charles chimed in, "let's not quarrel. There's plenty for everyone." He patted the mattress again. "Come, Lavinia. I was about to teach your daughter how to perform fellatio—which I'm sure she'll hate—so you can hold her down while I proceed."

Lavinia studied Penelope, and a loud buzzing rattled in her ears, and it grew and grew till it drowned out every other sound. Her vision clouded over, a red haze enveloping her.

Like an automaton, she lurched forward, her arms outstretched, a roar gurgling from her mouth. She leapt onto the bed, seized Penelope by the throat, and began to squeeze with all her might.

❧

Jordan stood at the window, watching for the vicar to ride up the lane. His head was pounding, his hands shaking, and his stomach roiled from his hangover, but despite his physical misery, his mind was incredibly sharp. How could he have known that his night of overindulgence could lead to a morning of such clarity?

He thought about Margaret. Where was she? What was she doing? Did she miss him? Was she thinking of him and pining away—as was he?

He couldn't believe she was gone, that he couldn't march down the hall, stroll into her bedchamber, and see her waiting for him. Her absence in the house was like a tangible wound, the space she'd occupied seeming to pulsate with the dreadful reminder of how she'd been wronged.

How could he have spurned her over something as

frivolous as money? How could he have let her go without a fight? She was the only person who'd ever cared about him, the only person who'd ever loved him, and he'd let her walk away.

He had to find her! At once! Had to track her down and beg her to take him back, to build the life she'd been positive they could create.

To hell with Lavinia, and Penelope, and her fat dowry, and their wedding!

If anyone had ever deserved to be left at the altar, wasn't it Penelope?

Margaret had insisted that he could choose happiness over money, that he could choose contentment over duty, and she was correct. He could. So why not do it? Why not grab for the sole thing he ever truly wanted? What was stopping him?

A frantic excitement beating in his breast, he pulled on his jacket and raced for the stairs. Someone had to know where she was, and he intended to bully and nag and sweet-talk until he learned of her location. Then he'd go to her, would plead and grovel until he was forgiven.

He ran out onto the stoop, awhirl with plans, when he noticed a teamster's delivery wagon in front of the barn. Three bedraggled children—who looked lost and frightened—were standing next to it, and he lurched to a halt, his elevated disposition dashed in an instant.

It was his twin half brothers, ten-year-old Johnny and Tim, plus a tiny girl he'd never seen before. She was sucking her thumb and clutching a ragged doll, observing him with wide, poignant eyes. Tim pointed to Jordan and whispered something to an aged, grizzled driver who leapt down from the box and stalked over.

"These young 'uns," he started without preamble, "say as how they're kin to you."

"They are," Jordan answered. Jordan knew the boys were related, but he wasn't certain about the girl, though he wasn't about to deny her to this stranger.

"I found 'em alone, on the road."

"On the road?"

"Yes, so I went four days out of my way to see 'em here safe and sound."

"Thank you."

The man was extremely angry, his furious glare condemning.

"What?" Jordan asked. "What is it?"

"You may be a high-and-mighty *lord*," the driver accused, "but I have no tolerance for the abuse of children. You ought to be ashamed."

"What do you mean?"

"The little lassie's in an awful state. See to her."

He turned and stomped to his wagon, muttered something to the twins, patted the girl on the shoulder, then climbed up and clicked the reins. As he lumbered off, Jordan walked to the trio, and they scrutinized him warily, obviously terrified over what he might say or do.

"Hello, sir," Tim said, stepping forward.

"Hello, Tim."

"I'm sorry we've arrived like this, but we hadn't anywhere to go."

"We didn't know what to do," Johnny added.

Jordan was mortified. He'd been so busy with lusting after Margaret that he'd never responded to the housekeeper who'd written, inquiring about them, and this was the result. His brothers—children of an earl, siblings of a viscount—had been tossed out to wander

England's back roads, hoping someone would take them in.

"It's quite all right." He struggled to keep his emotions in check. "I'm glad you came to me." He gazed down at the girl. "And who's this?"

"Our sister, Mary."

He squatted down so that they were eye-to-eye. "Hello, Mary. I'm your older brother Jordan."

She didn't reply but stared and stared in a vacant, unnerving way. He glanced up at the boys.

"She doesn't talk anymore," Tim explained.

"Why not?" Jordan asked.

"We don't know," Johnny offered. "She's never lived with us, but someone dropped her off the morning before we were sent away, so we brought her along."

Gently, Johnny lifted her wrist, pushed at the sleeve of her tattered dress, and showed Jordan her arm. There were round, festering scab marks that made it appear she'd been burned with a lit cheroot. Jordan's stomach churned, his temper flared.

"We couldn't leave her behind," Tim said.

"No, you couldn't."

"Can we stay with you, sir?" Johnny entreated. "Just for a bit till we can figure out where to go next? I promise we won't eat very much."

"And we'll watch over Mary," Tim vowed. "She won't be any trouble. I swear it."

Jordan rose and peered down the road to where Margaret had to have traveled when she'd departed Gray's Manor. Would there ever come a day when she'd understand the pressures that were motivating him? Would she ever comprehend the burdens that weighed him down?

Happiness and contentment were for idiots and fools. He had to care for these children, as well as the rest who were scattered across the country, had to see to their welfare and ensure their safety and security. They couldn't continue on, cast to the vagaries of fate.

"Of course, you can stay," he murmured. "For as long as necessary."

"Thank you, sir," both boys chimed soberly, though Mary had no reaction.

"You've come at the very best time, too," he said, trying to lighten the solemn moment. "I'm getting married! In a few minutes. You can help me celebrate." He herded them toward the kitchens. "Have you had breakfast?"

"No."

"Well then, let's feed you; then we'll get you settled."

He ushered them inside and deposited them with an older, matronly housemaid; then he proceeded to the front parlor and sat, morose and stunned, his head in his hands, his mood at its lowest ebb.

What had he ever done to deserve a better ending? He wished the vicar would hurry, that the entire, sordid affair could be wrapped up as quickly as possible. Why delay the inevitable?

He peeked up, looking for a clock to see the hour, when he noticed Anne loitering in the threshold.

"May I interrupt?" she inquired.

In his vile condition, he didn't want to speak with anyone, but he said, "Certainly."

She turned to someone in the hall and urged, "Don't be afraid."

"I'm not," a man answered. "I should have stopped this years ago."

"I've known Jordan forever," she explained. "He's very fair, and he'll give you good advice."

"I just hope I don't lose my boys over this." The man's voice was tremulous, as if he was on the verge of tears.

"Why would you?" Anne responded. "It was none of your doing."

"I should have guessed, though. How could anyone assume I didn't know what was happening?"

"But you didn't. Now come."

Jordan's curiosity was piqued as Anne entered, followed by Mr. Mason, Lavinia's handsome neighbor. Mason had seemed smitten by Lavinia—poor fellow!— but with how he was regarding Anne, Jordan was no longer sure of anything.

"Jordan, I believe you've met Mr. Mason."

"Yes, I have." He was too miserable to stand as courtesy required, so he merely gestured to the opposite sofa. "What is it? What's wrong?"

"Mr. Mason has something to tell you, something you must know before you marry Miss Gray."

"You'd better make it fast," Jordan said. "The vicar should be here any second."

"To start the ceremony?"

"Yes."

Anne rested a reassuring hand on Mason's shoulder. "It will be all right."

"I doubt that."

"You two should talk alone. I'll be outside if you need me."

She exited and shut the door, and as an awkward silence ensued, Jordan's annoyance boiled to rage.

Obviously, Mason had a horrid story to share about Penelope. It would prove to Jordan that he shouldn't marry her, and Jordan couldn't bear to listen. He didn't need Mason supplying him with reasons not to proceed—he had too many of his own—but with the arrival of his half siblings, no other conclusion was possible.

"Well?" he snapped. "Get on with it."

"Lavinia's done a terrible thing."

"Why am I not surprised?"

Mason reached into a satchel he'd brought and retrieved some papers. "Anne—that is, Mrs. Smythe— felt I should confide in you."

"You're awfully friendly with Anne all of a sudden."

Mason glared, but didn't jump to fill the opening Jordan had furnished. If the pair had sexual secrets, Mason wasn't about to divulge them, and he instantly rose in Jordan's esteem.

"I take full responsibility for my failure to act," Mason declared, "and I'll accept any punishment that is leveled."

"A very gallant speech, Mr. Mason, but what have you *failed* to do?"

"Did you know Lavinia's husband, Horatio Gray?"

"No."

"When he died, he was incredibly wealthy. He left the women of this family very well-off."

"I'm aware of that fact. That's why I'm here."

"What you don't know is that he arranged three trust funds. One for Lavinia. One for Penelope." He paused, gathering his courage. "And one for Margaret Gray, whom Mr. Gray loved as his own daughter."

Jordan wasn't sure he'd heard correctly. "He created a trust for Margaret Gray?"

"Yes."

"Then why has she been living like a pauper all these years?"

"Because Lavinia hid it from her. Margaret was never informed."

Jordan went very still. "I hope to hell you're lying."

"I'm not. Lavinia is a dreadful spendthrift. In a matter of months, she'd squandered her own money, then she began using Penelope's, and soon, it was gone, too."

"So . . . the money that remains, it's Margaret Gray's?"

"Every penny of it."

"Penelope has none, at all?"

"Not a single farthing."

"Penelope knows this to be true?"

"Most likely."

"And Lavinia?"

"Set the plot in motion and implemented it with cool precision."

There was a table between them, and he piled some legal documents on it, urging Jordan to read them, but Jordan couldn't. He thought of Margaret, shipped off in disgrace because of his reckless conduct.

Since their appalling encounter in the library, he'd been uneasy, feeling as if he'd missed an important detail or hadn't noted what was in plain sight.

She'd been such a tragic figure, so wronged, so mistreated and alone. He'd blithely renounced her, as if she'd meant nothing to him, as if he'd never cared. He'd let her go. For money! For Penelope Gray's money, but Penelope didn't have any!

Was there ever a more cruel twist of fate? Could there possibly be a more hideous ending? Were the gods conspiring against him?

"Let me ask you a question, Mr. Mason."

"Anything."

"Mrs. Gray mentioned that Margaret has departed Gray's Manor."

"Yes, she has."

"Do you know where she is?"

"I'm guessing she could be anywhere by now. I'm not positive how we'll ever locate her."

Jordan's heart nearly stopped. "Why couldn't we? Lavinia said she went to stay with an aunt."

"Lavinia told you that?" Mason chuckled, but without mirth. "You seem to be well acquainted with Mrs. Gray. Could you actually presume she'd have bothered with Margaret?"

"No."

Since his last conversation with Margaret, he'd been so disordered that he wasn't reasoning clearly. Of course, she wasn't all right! The worst sensation of alarm swept over him. Lavinia might have done anything to her.

"I noticed Margaret was gone," Mason was saying. "When I asked Lavinia about her, she advised me that she was weary of supporting Margaret and had tossed her out."

"Is there anyone who might have offered her shelter?"

"No. Margaret only had this place and no other."

Jordan winced as if Mason had delivered a blow. In his effort to forget how offensively he'd behaved, Jordan had soothed his guilty conscience by picturing Margaret tucked away with kindly, sympathetic kin.

How could he have been such an idiot? Why had he been so willing to believe Lavinia? When had he grown to be so gullible?

He was tormented by distressing images of Margaret. With no coins in her purse, and no contacts away from Gray's Manor, she'd be scared and forlorn— might even be cold and hungry—and he was revolted by the disaster he'd wrought.

He rose and scooped up the papers Mason had brought, stuffing them into the satchel and tucking it under his arm.

"Did you know I loved her?" he said, facing the awful, wonderful fact for the first time.

"Margaret? Really? I didn't think anyone ever had."

"I loved her, yet I stood there and let Lavinia send her away. I did nothing."

"Neither did I," Mason admitted. "Not once in all these years. I'm sick about it."

"We'll hammer out a solution to this mess, Mr. Mason, and I'll expect us both to atone. Even if it takes the rest of our lives."

"I understand," Mason agreed.

"I must speak with Lavinia. Do you—"

Just then, the strangest sound wafted by. It was a keening wail, or maybe a shriek of agony, but whatever it was, it made the hairs rise on the back of his neck.

"What is that?" Jordan queried.

"I don't know," Mason replied.

Jordan walked into the hall, Mason trailing after him. On observing them, Anne shrugged, indicating that she'd heard it, too, and didn't know what it was. Jordan headed toward the stairs where a group of servants was whispering.

"What is it?" Jordan demanded.

"It's Lord Kettering and Miss Gray, milord," a maid explained.

"And Mrs. Gray, too," another added.

A footman cast them a warning glance, then said, "Perhaps you should see for yourself, Lord Romsey."

The wail turned into a scream, and Jordan took off at a dead run, bolting up the stairs, with Mason and Anne racing behind him. He followed the clamor to Penelope's bedchamber, the commotion becoming louder as he approached. He burst in and skidded to a halt.

A very naked Penelope was brawling on the floor with her mother. Lavinia had her fingers wrapped around Penelope's throat, and they were caterwauling like geese pecking in the barnyard.

Charles was lounging on the bed, naked, too, sipping on a brandy and watching the altercation. He tipped his glass at Jordan, appearing smug and thrilled to have two females fighting over him.

"For pity's sake," Jordan grumbled with disgust.

"Holy shit!" Mason exclaimed, as Anne glared at Charles and muttered, "You son of a bitch!"

Charles sheepishly grinned at her as if to say he hadn't been able to behave any better, but Anne spun and stomped out.

"Sorry, Jordan," Charles contended, once she was gone, "but I guess you won't be marrying Penelope."

"I guess not," Jordan concurred.

"We're desperately in love," Charles lied, continuing to chat as if there weren't a major fracas occurring directly in front of him. "We couldn't help ourselves."

"Oh, spare me."

"There will have to be a wedding, but unfortunately, it won't be yours."

Jordan peered over at his father, flashing such a powerful smile that Charles was actually flustered. He realized that something had transpired to change the stakes and that a new hand of cards had been dealt to everybody.

"Yes, we'll have a wedding," Jordan echoed, "and it *will* be yours. I intend to see it happen if it's the last thing I do. It will serve you right!"

He stepped into the fray to pull the combatants apart, and he struggled to subdue Lavinia, but it was like wrestling with a slippery eel. He managed to jerk her to her feet, as Mason clasped hold of Penelope and did the same.

Both women were scratched and bruised, Penelope's neck sporting purple marks where Lavinia had throttled her.

"Let me go!" Lavinia insisted. "Let me at her."

"No," Jordan responded. "Calm down and tell me what this is about."

"I wanted him for myself!" Lavinia screeched.

"My father?" Jordan shuddered with revulsion.

"She knew I did, and she took him anyway."

"You jealous hag!" Penelope taunted. "He wanted me because I'm young and pretty—not old and used up like you—and now, he's all mine, and you can't do anything about it!"

Assuming the battle over, Jordan had relaxed his grip, as had Mr. Mason, but Penelope's hurled gibe was too much for Lavinia. She dove for Penelope, and before either he or Mason could intervene again, Penelope raised a fist, reared back, and punched Lavinia in the face. Blood squirted everywhere, flesh cracked against bone, and Lavinia dropped like a rock, an unconscious, ignored heap on the rug.

Penelope stood, flaunting her nudity, rubbing her

knuckles, as she glowered at all three men and announced, "Now then, if you gentlemen will excuse me, I must dress for my wedding." She leveled her hateful gaze on Charles. "The vicar will be here any minute, so I'll see you downstairs. Don't even *think* about being late."

CHAPTER TWENTY

"Good-bye, Lavinia."

"Good-bye? What are you saying?"

She was a mess from her skirmish with Penelope. An eye was blackened and puffy, her nose swollen. There were claw marks on her face, bruises on her body. She was extremely bedraggled, her hair ratted and clumped, her skin mottled from rage and weeping.

She clasped Robert's arm, and it was all he could do not to shudder in distaste. How had he ever presumed himself in love with her? Why had he fallen for her deadly charms?

He had to have been bewitched. It was the sole explanation he could abide, for he refused to admit that he'd been a besotted fool.

He grabbed her hand and removed it from his person.

"I can't do this with you anymore," he apprised her.

"Do what?"

"I can't continue on in this web of lies and deceit. I have to forge a new path."

"But Robert, you can't abandon me now, not in my

hour of need!" Pretty tears dripped down her cheeks, and she dropped to her knees in supplication. "Penelope has wed. The last of my money will go to Kettering. I'm all alone in the entire world!"

He was in no mood for her theatrics. "Why don't you talk to Kettering? Perhaps he'll let you reside with them; then he can crawl into Penelope's bed one night and yours the next."

"Oh, how could you be so horrid to me?" Crying and keening, she clutched at his coat. "I love you! I've always loved you! Don't forsake me!"

"Please, Lavinia, you're embarrassing yourself."

"You mean everything to me. If I must grovel to keep you, then I shall!"

Rolling his eyes, he drew away, then went to the door. "I stopped by to inform you that I'm getting married."

"What?" Immediately, her clamor ceased, and she rose to her feet.

"As opposed to you and your tepid regard, I've met someone who truly cares for me."

"Who would want *you*?"

He ignored the jibe and happily pronounced, "Mrs. Smythe."

"Kettering's whore?"

"Yes, she's been a whore—as you have been, yourself. The main difference between the two of you is that she regrets her decision."

He marched out, and there was a loud thumping on the wall as she threw an object after him. He rushed to the stairs and raced down—toward home and Anne—glad and relieved that he'd never have to see Lavinia again.

ere is your one and only option."

Lavinia glared at Jordan. He was seated behind her desk in her library, acting as if the place were his, and she yearned to reach over and slap him.

She was in a frantic condition, her thoughts careening through various stages of dread, each image pitching her further and further into a despairing void. She'd lost Kettering, then Robert, too, and she was most rattled by Robert's departure. He'd been her rock, her foundation. Without his fawning adulation and annoying loyalty, how would she ever regroup?

"My only option?" she snarled. "After the day I've had, if you think to dictate to me, you're mad."

Jordan patted some documents that were piled on the desktop. "Mr. Mason has been here and left."

"What of it?"

"The jig is up, Vinnie."

"You're babbling in riddles; I can't understand you."

"This is Horatio's Last Will and Testament. Mr. Mason gave me a copy."

"I've never been particularly interested in legal folderol."

"Really? Mr. Mason claims that you're riveted by it, that you're an expert at detail and nuance."

Surely, Robert hadn't said anything incriminating! Yes, he was angry with her, but what could he possibly know? She'd been too shrewd in her calculations.

She flashed a nasty smile. "I'm completely in the dark about Horatio's will. When he died, I was in a state of shock. Robert handled everything."

"Even the transfer of funds between the accounts?"

"There were transfers? My goodness, I had no idea."

"So any signatures bearing your name would have been forged?"

"Forged? What are you implying?" She kept her expression blank, providing no hint of the terror churning inside.

"Where is Margaret?"

"I told you: She's in seclusion. We're waiting to see if there's a babe."

He rose slowly, hands braced on the desk, and he leaned toward her.

"Where is she?"

"She's staying with family."

At her response he was furious, and she nearly laughed. Did he suppose he could intimidate her? Did he think he could scare her? There wasn't a man in the world who could frighten her into doing anything, and Lavinia calmly watched him as he watched her, and finally, he eased down in his chair.

"Here's what will happen," he said. "I'll only say it once, so pay attention."

"I will not be harassed. Not by you, and most certainly, not when you are a guest in my home."

All bravado and umbrage, she stood to go, when he barked, "Sit down!"

"You will not—"

"Sit!" he shouted with such wrath that she plopped down.

He appeared crazed, as if he might swagger over and assault her, and after Penelope's attack, Lavinia was too wretched to endure another. She struggled to seem cowed.

"Margaret will be found and informed of her fortune,"

he declared. "The trust will be vested in her. I've already written to my London solicitor, Mr. Thumberton, to have the arrangements made, with himself installed as the new trustee."

"Why would I care?"

"Penelope and Charles can wallow in the poverty they deserve."

"What do you mean? Your father is an earl."

"Yes, he is—an earl who is flat broke and being chased across the country by creditors. The sole chattel he still owns is his carriage—which he will keep so long as he's not caught, so your daughter can join him in it as they flee from one village to the next."

She wanted to groan in disbelief. While she was humored to hear of Penelope's predicament, she was reeling at her own bad luck. If she couldn't reside at any of Kettering's properties, what would she do?

Gad! She should have been nicer to Jordan! Was there any chance he might take her in? How could she convince him?

"As to you . . ." His voice trailed off.

The phrase sounded ominous, and she shifted uncomfortably, swamped by the knowledge that she'd made every stupid choice. She cursed Horatio for dying, Kettering for his penury, Robert for leaving, Penelope for marrying above her station, and Margaret for being richer than all of them combined.

"What about me?" she sneered.

"I am determined to find Margaret and bestow what is lawfully hers, so you have one minute to tell me where she is."

A paltry minute? Why . . . the bastard was using the

same tactic she'd utilized in coercing him to settle on Penelope! Well, the joke was on him! She was made of sterner stuff, so his ploy wouldn't succeed.

"She was staying with my aunt, but they had an argument, and Margaret left without a word as to her destination. I don't know where she is."

"If you apprise me of her whereabouts, I shall intervene with your banker and ask him to give you six months to vacate the premises before he forecloses."

"My banker? Why speak with my banker?"

"Mr. Mason tattled, Vinnie, so don't pretend with me. I'm fully cognizant of your dire straits."

"I'm perfectly fine," she blustered.

"If you refuse to cooperate," he continued, "I shall advise him to immediately proceed with the eviction, and you'll be tossed out in a matter of days, with only the clothes on your back."

"You wouldn't!"

"I would. You should also be aware that serious criminal charges can be leveled—or not. If you assist me, I will work to see that the scandal is private and the penalty small. But if you decline . . ."

His voice trailed off again, but his warning was clear. She could be prosecuted! Oh, the repercussions were too terrifying to contemplate!

"I can't help you!" she insisted.

"Have you ever toured a British prison, Vinnie? Can you imagine yourself incarcerated in one? Your sixty seconds start now."

His gaze shifted to the clock, and she could hear it ticking, each click seeming to nip away at her life. Her mind screamed at her to make up a credible lie that might buy her a few weeks or months, but then what?

This was all Margaret's fault, and Lavinia would get even if it was the last thing she ever did!

The minute ended, and Jordan steepled his fingers over his chest. "Well?"

Lavinia gnawed on her lip, feeling like a rat in a trap. "She went to Brighton."

"Are you certain that should be your answer?"

"Yes."

Years earlier, she'd visited the town, and she remembered the names of the major thoroughfares. She grabbed a quill and jotted down a fabricated address.

"She's there."

"You realize that I'll investigate, don't you?"

"She's there! I swear it."

"We'll see."

"You'll find her," Lavinia asserted with such confidence that she almost believed it herself.

"Will I? I doubt it, and when I learn that she's not in Brighton, I will return to Gray's Manor, and I will personally throw you out and lock the doors behind you."

Lavinia trembled with a rage that she dare not vent; then, regal as any queen, she swept out.

Margaret! she seethed. Would she never be shed of her bothersome niece?

Eventually, Jordan would locate Margaret, and when he did, Margaret would receive what remained of Lavinia's money. But Margaret wouldn't have it for long. Lavinia would follow him and recover it, so Margaret had better hope that Jordan's search was a lengthy one, because once he found her, there was no telling what might happen.

࿐

A nne, wait!"
        Charles frowned as Anne walked by, headed toward the foyer. When he caught up with her, she was standing next to her packed bags. He hadn't seen her since his coup in Penelope's bedchamber, and with the wedding having just concluded, they ought to be sipping champagne and celebrating his stroke of fortune, but she'd been markedly absent.

He supposed she was upset that he'd wed again when he'd specifically promised he wouldn't, but money didn't grow on trees. He wasn't a magician who could pull cash out of his hat. His marriage to Penelope had rescued them both. Why wasn't she smiling?

"Darling," he said, "what are you doing?"

"I'm leaving you."

"You're joking."

"No, I'm not."

"But . . . but . . . how will you get on without me?" His confident façade slipped for a moment.

"I imagine I'll *get on* just fine."

"Where will you go? What will you do?"

"Actually, I'm about to marry, too," she claimed.

"You are not."

"Yes, Charles, I am. I figured if you can do it, so can I."

"You're being absurd."

"I'm not. For once, I'm being totally rational. The blinders are off, and I'm doing what I should have done years ago."

"Which is?"

"Run away from you as fast as I can."

"There's no need for insults," he huffed.

"No, there's not. Good-bye."

She turned as if she planned to go that very second, and he grabbed her arm. "What's the matter with you?"

"Nothing. I'm better than I've ever been."

He gazed into her beautiful brown eyes and felt as if he was staring at a stranger.

"I married the girl for us, Anne. For us! So that we could get back on our feet." He clasped her hands in his and linked their fingers. "I'm so wealthy now! It will be just like the old days. There'll be no more traipsing about the countryside, no living in cheap hovels, or sneaking out of town in the middle of the night. I've secured our future."

She sighed. "I take it you haven't spoken to Jordan."

"Why should I? He'll only nag."

"You must talk to him. Ask him about Penelope's trust fund."

"What could he possibly have to say that would be of any significance?"

She drew away and flashed a pitying look. "Good luck to you, Charles. I honestly mean it."

She started out, and he snapped, "Hold it right there! I don't give you permission to depart."

"I'm not your servant, and I'm not your property. If I choose to go, it's none of your affair."

It finally dawned on him that she was serious, and he was stunned. She was the only one who'd stayed, the only one who'd been loyal, and now, after he'd wed Penelope to fix their problems, she was ready to call it quits.

He'd never understand women!

"You can't expect me to believe you have somewhere to go."

"I don't care what you believe."

"What's this nonsense about your marrying?"

"It's true. All this time, while you were trifling with Penelope and Mrs. Gray, I was fucking somebody, too. And he's mad about me."

Her admission was so outrageous that if she'd aimed a pistol and shot him, he couldn't have been more shocked. "You . . . you . . . had a lover? While you were my mistress?"

"Isn't it wild? Isn't it grand?"

She marched outside, her bags abandoned, and she kept on down the drive, nearly skipping with delight at the prospect of being away.

He went out on the stoop, and he hollered after her, "I won't ever take you back."

"Don't worry. I won't be back." She didn't bother to glance around at him.

"When you new . . . new . . . lover tosses you out, and you come crawling to me, I'll shut the door in your face. Even if you beg, it's over!"

"Yes, Charles, it's definitely over."

Shortly, she veered off into the woods, and he watched till he could no longer see her. In all the years they'd been together, they'd never quarreled, and he was shaken by the encounter. She'd always been there for him, like a comfortable pair of shoes or an old robe. Yes, he'd taken her for granted, but that was hardly unusual. She was female and a lowborn one at that.

He studied her luggage and scoffed. She was in a temporary snit, but it would pass.

A maid strolled by, and he directed her to haul Anne's

things upstairs, but before the woman could move, his bride rushed down the hall.

"What did you just say?" Penelope demanded.

"Mrs. Smythe had considered leaving us, but I've persuaded her to change her mind. I've advised the maid to carry her belongings to her room and unpack them."

"That . . . that . . . hussy will not remain here," Penelope insisted, and she glared at the maid. "Have these bags set out on the road."

A muscle ticked in his cheek as he said to the maid, "Would you excuse us?" She vanished like smoke, and he whirled on Penelope, his temper sparking. "I have no idea why you would presume to countermand my orders."

"I will not have your mistress residing under my roof."

"I can see that you have miscalculated the terms of our relationship, so let me be very clear: What I do—or don't do—will never be any of your business."

"If you allow her to stay, I'll kill you in your sleep."

He laughed and laughed. "You are the most horrid, spoiled child I've ever met. Now be off—or I'll take a belt to you."

"I will not be dismissed like a common servant!"

She stamped her foot, and he reached out and yanked her close to whisper a threat in her ear.

"Have you forgotten the things I made you do last night?"

"Let me go!"

"I showed you a bit of what I'll expect. It can be much worse, or it can be much easier for you. The choice is yours, but whenever you disobey me, I shall drag you into the bedchamber and force you to do something you loathe." He shoved her toward the stairs.

"Proceed to my room and wait for me. I'll be up soon to consummate the union."

"I hate you!" she seethed.

"The feeling, my dear, is entirely mutual."

She bristled, about to explode; then she spun and stormed off, which was just as well. It had been a trying day, and he had no patience left for dealing with her. He still had to endure the ordeal of the marital joining, and he was sincerely pondering whether to have someone observe it so that there was a witness. With so much at stake, he couldn't give Lavinia any opportunity to cry foul.

He went to find Jordan, who was located in a rear parlor, staring into an empty hearth. Charles sauntered over and sat next to him.

"Look who's finally slinked in," Jordan said. "Did you say hello to your children?"

"What children?"

"Three of them arrived this morning."

"Why would they come here?"

"They didn't have anywhere else to go."

"I take it you've seen to them?"

"Don't I always clean up your messes? I realize it's your wedding day, but I really hope you rot in hell."

"Is that any way to congratulate me on my nuptials?"

"You want me to congratulate you?"

"Of course. All's fair in love and war. You know that. It was a vast sum. You can't assume that I'd permit you to have it without a fight."

"I didn't."

"It was a game; you lost. So . . . don't be surly. It's beneath you."

Jordan shook his head in derision. "My God, but you're a piece of work."

"I merely wed an heiress—as any sane insolvent man would."

"Do you ever feel remorse about anything?"

"No. Why would I?"

"I have to tell you, Charles, you deserve Penelope."

"I agree. You could have raped her at any time, but you didn't. It's hardly my fault that you were timid in your pursuit."

Abruptly, Jordan stood. "Let's go."

"To where?"

"To your bedchamber. I intend to watch the consummation."

Charles had been thinking to request the very same, but still, Jordan's offer surprised him. "Why would you want to?"

"I plan to ensure that you never wiggle out of this."

"Be my guest." They walked out, when Charles pulled Jordan to a halt. "By the way, I spoke with Anne, and she made an odd comment about Penelope's trust. She said I should ask you about it."

"It's nothing," Jordan insisted. "We can discuss it later."

Jordan kept on, and Charles accompanied him, eager—in a thoroughly vain and masculine fashion— for Jordan to jealously view what Charles had stolen from him.

❧

What is Lord Romsey doing here?"

"He's a witness."

Penelope   frowned.   "He . . . he's . . . a what?"

"It's an ancient custom," Lord Kettering explained. "When there's a chance that others might question the validity of the marriage, witnesses are brought in to verify the consummation."

"You mean he's going to . . . to . . ."

"Yes, he is," Kettering said.

"But that's . . . that's . . . positively medieval."

"Isn't it, though?"

"Don't you care if he sees you . . . if he sees me . . ." She wailed. "You can't intend for him to ogle me as you thrust away!"

"Actually, that's precisely what I intend."

"I can't let him see me without my clothes."

"Don't worry. With how homely you are, I don't think he'll notice."

"Could we cease with the chatter?" Romsey interjected. "This will be extremely unpleasant, and I want it concluded as rapidly as possible."

"You can't stay!" Penelope declared. "Go. At once!"

"Sorry, but I can't oblige you." Romsey pulled up a chair and sat a few feet from the bed.

"You're doing this to humiliate me," she hissed at her husband.

"No," Kettering said, "I'm doing it so that you can't trot off with your fortune."

"And I'm doing it," Romsey chimed in, "for your protection."

"*My* protection?"

"Yes. My father is a scoundrel. He's landed himself in this sort of predicament before, but he always worms his way out of it. My presence will guarantee that he can't evade your matrimonial noose."

The statement should have made her feel more secure,

but the notion of never being able to escape Charles was so disheartening.

If she divorced him or murdered him in his sleep, would she still be a countess? Or would she lose the title when she lost the man? Why did life have to be so complicated? Why couldn't a girl buy a title and leave the man out of it altogether?

"Could we get on with it?" Romsey pestered. "I'm in a hurry."

"What's the rush?" Kettering said. "It's my wedding night. I plan to enjoy it."

"You can *enjoy* it after I go. I have no desire to hang around and drool over your alleged prowess."

"I could teach you a few things, my boy," Kettering boasted.

"I'm sure you could," Romsey agreed. "Now get moving!"

"How can I make you go away?" she inquired of Romsey.

"Climb up on the bed and spread your legs," he crudely advised.

"And after that, how can I make your father go?"

"You can't," Romsey claimed. "You wanted him, and he's yours forever."

The word *forever* reverberated around the room, and she shuddered, frantic to delay the inevitable.

"Could we talk about this?" she asked.

"No," they responded in unison.

"I've changed my mind, though. I don't care to be a countess, after all."

"Fickle brat!" Kettering scolded. "Do you see why I need a witness, Jordan?"

"You have to proceed," Romsey asserted. "That's

the price for what you've done. Refusal isn't an option."

"But I don't have to do anything I don't wish to do. My mother said so."

"Shall we fetch her?" Kettering interrupted, and he chuckled spitefully. "No doubt she'll be happy to discuss your behavior—if she's regained consciousness."

"What if he's planted a babe?" Romsey mentioned.

"He hasn't."

"You don't know that. He's disgustingly virile, and he seems to sire offspring wherever he goes."

She blanched. "He what?"

"He has many, many children—both legitimate and illegitimate. This very second, some of them are napping down the hall. Didn't he tell you?"

"Gad no!"

She scowled at Kettering, but he preened, delighted to have his potency revealed.

"You can't assume," Romsey continued, "that you're immune to pregnancy simply because you're against it occurring."

"If I'm with child, I'll kill myself." She paused. "I take that back. If I'm pregnant, I'll kill *him*."

"It's definitely something to consider," Romsey concurred. "Remember: You don't have to remain with him. You can live with your mother. You can seek refuge with friends. But for now, you *do* have to complete the marriage. You'll never survive the scandal if you don't."

She stared at Romsey, then Kettering, then Romsey again.

An image flashed—of herself in London, parading into a grand ballroom and being introduced as the Countess of Kettering. She could practically hear the mothers gasp with shock, could almost see the other girls turn green with envy.

Wasn't such a moment worth any price?

"Fine," she stated. "Have it your way."

"I always do," Kettering replied, automatically presuming that she'd been speaking to him.

"Shut up." She climbed onto the bed and gazed at the ceiling as Kettering fussed about, apparently unbuttoning his trousers.

"Don't you dare undress," she snapped.

"I agree with your bride," Romsey said to his father. "The less I see of you, the better."

"What's the fun of having you watch," Kettering queried, "if I can't really go at it?"

"Just get it over with! Please!" Romsey sounded as if he was begging.

Kettering laughed, then climbed up, too. With no wooing or finesse, he lifted her skirt, entered her, and sawed away.

Her virginal membranes were tender from the prior evening, so she was very sore. She winced, but tamped down any display of agony.

I'm a countess now. . . I'm a countess now. . .

The refrain rang in her head, chiming in a rhythm with Kettering's bouncing on the mattress. For such an elderly fellow, he had an enormous amount of stamina, but his filthy groping didn't bother her in the slightest. She felt nothing and was thoroughly bored.

"Would you finish?" Romsey demanded.

"Certainly." Kettering consented as if they were discussing the weather.

He tensed, his seed shooting into her, and she decided that she needed to find a competent midwife.

Supposedly, there were potions and charms to avert pregnancy, and she had to learn what they were.

Kettering grunted with satisfaction and rolled off her.

Penelope peered over at Romsey and asked, "Have you seen enough?"

"Yes, plenty."

Kettering smirked. "This could have been yours, Jordan."

"I'm elated to let you have her. The two of you make a wonderful couple." He stood and looked at Penelope. "I'll leave it to you to break the bad news about your trust fund."

There was an awkward silence, and Penelope glowered. "What are you talking about?"

"Don't pretend not to know," Romsey responded. "While your mother may ultimately end up in jail, your age will probably save you. But you might as well have the pleasure of explaining things to him."

Kettering scrambled to his feet. "What are you saying?"

"There is no money," Romsey said. "There is no trust fund. She's not an heiress."

"That's a lie!" Penelope maintained. "I'm rich! I've always been rich!"

"Give it up, Penelope," Romsey admonished. "Mr. Mason showed me the papers that detail the thefts committed by your mother. Even as we speak, a search has begun for Margaret so that the pilfered bequest can be returned to her."

Kettering gaped at Penelope in horror.

"No money?" he wheezed.

"Not a single farthing," Romsey added.

"You tricked me!" Kettering charged. "You knew, and you didn't apprise me till it was too late."

"You're correct," Romsey affirmed. "I deliberately kept it a secret."

"It's . . . fraud! It's . . . duplicity! It's . . . it's . . ."

"It's a sixteen-year-old maiden who you ruined," Romsey hurled back.

"You trapped me! You swindled me!"

"You trapped yourself," Romsey argued. "I merely ensured that you gave her your name and the scant protection it will provide—though why she'd want to be a Prescott is beyond me."

Kettering was so furious that he was shaking, and Penelope was tickled by his level of upset. Perhaps he wasn't as omnipotent as he seemed. Perhaps there'd be some chances to best him, after all.

"I'm still a countess, right?" she inquired of Romsey.

"Yes, Penelope, you're still a countess," Romsey said. "Consider it my parting gift to you. I hope you're happy, and that it brings you the status and recognition you seek, though with him as your spouse, I wouldn't count on it."

"I am happy," she declared. "I absolutely am."

Romsey stared at his stunned father. "Lavinia wants the two of you gone—today. So I suggest that you pack your bags, load your carriage, and slither out the same way you slithered in."

He walked out, and Penelope grinned, already planning her triumphant entrance into London society.

CHAPTER TWENTY-ONE

C ongratulations, Mrs. Mason."

"Thank you, Mr. Mason."

Anne smiled at Robert, still stunned by events. "I can't believe you married me."

"And why wouldn't I? I love you."

"But I can't figure out why you do."

She stared at her hand, and even in the dark confines of the carriage that had whisked them to Scotland and back, she could see the simple gold band he'd slipped on her finger during their hasty wedding. Once prior, she'd settled for so little, had shredded every ounce of self-respect in her quest to keep Charles Prescott happy. Yet Robert didn't care about her past. He was looking to the future.

Of course, in light of his relationship with Lavinia Gray, he was in a glass house and in no position to throw stones. He'd made some terrible choices, but so had Anne, and both hoped that after their experiences with folly and disaster they would be a tad wiser.

The carriage rattled to a stop, and she sucked in an

anxious breath. Their elopement had transpired so rapidly, the trip north carried out in such a fleet, unplanned manner, that she wasn't prepared for this moment.

Robert sensed her distress and hugged her. "Don't be nervous."

"I'm not. Well, maybe I am. Just a bit."

"It will be fine."

"I know."

"I'm so glad you're with me."

"So am I."

It was very quiet, and as the driver calmed the horses, she peeked out the curtain. A footman emerged from the house to lower the step.

Finally, the door was opened, and Robert rushed out to running feet and boyish whoops of welcome. Then he leaned in and extended his arm to her.

"Come, Anne," he said, "and meet my sons. Come and meet your family."

Ready for anything, she climbed out to begin her new life.

❧

"How long will you be gone?"

"I don't know."

"When will you return?"

"I don't know that, either."

Jordan peered into the worried faces of Johnny and Tim, a still-silent Mary loitering discreetly behind them, and he wished he could provide them with more satisfying answers. He was aware—better than anyone—how awful it was to have the Earl of Kettering as a father. After suffering through so many upheavals in their young lives, they viewed Jordan as a safe port in their personal storm, and it had to be terrifying to watch him prepare to depart, but he had to go.

If it took the rest of his days, he would find Margaret Gray and see her established in the style her fortune mandated. It was his fault that she was missing, that she could be in any dire situation. If it was the last thing he ever did, he would ensure that she was apprised of the peculiar twist of fate that had propelled her from an anonymous, penniless woman to one of great wealth and position.

As Attorney Thumberton worked in the London courts to have the mess with the trust resolved, Jordan had teams of men scouring the countryside, looking for her, but they'd had no luck. She had vanished, leaving no trace as to where she might be.

"When you locate Miss Gray," Tim asked, "will you marry her?"

"Me?" Jordan adjusted the strap on his saddle and smiled. "Marry Miss Gray? Why would you think I would?"

"Mr. Mason says that she's an heiress. If you married her, you'd have plenty of money, so we could stay with you forever."

At the boy's hopeful tone Jordan chuckled, but he shook his head. "No matter what happens, you can stay with me, but no, I would never wed Miss Gray."

"But why?" Johnny pressed. "I heard she's quite pretty."

"She's very pretty," Jordan agreed, "but we would never suit."

The children regarded him as some sort of hero, and he wouldn't diminish their esteem by confessing how he'd actually treated Margaret. He could imagine nothing more wonderful than to have her as his bride, but a marriage between them could never be.

He'd refused her when she was poor, so he could never have her when she was rich. It would be the height of hypocrisy, the pinnacle of pretension, to dream of such an absurd ending. Should he so much as suggest a union to her, she'd laugh herself silly, and he'd never embarrass her—or himself—in such a despicable and pathetic fashion.

He assumed full responsibility for her plight, so duty and honor demanded that he find her for Thumberton, that he guarantee she was informed of her surprising circumstance, that he assist in having her brought to London so she could revel in her elevated condition. But after seeing her arranged in her new life, he'd tactfully disappear.

If he secretly yearned for a different result, his recent actions had proven that he neither deserved nor had he earned a happy resolution.

Struggling to seem calm and unmoved, which was difficult, he turned to the children. Against his will, he'd grown too attached to the three of them, and it was agony tearing himself away.

"Take care of Mary for me," he said, "and behave yourselves for Mr. and Mrs. Mason." Anne and Robert had volunteered to let the children remain with them until Jordan was settled.

"We will," both boys replied.

Jordan knew there was little need to discuss their conduct. They'd been through so much, yet they were extremely reserved and respectful. "Keep yourselves out of trouble."

"We will," they repeated.

There was an awkward hesitation; then Tim tentatively probed, "When you're finished with your search, you will come for us, won't you, sir?"

"I promise I will." They were so dubious, Mary's gaze sharp and distressing, and he added, "I swear it."

He mounted his horse and, with a curt wave, he trotted off, three tiny pairs of eyes boring into his back.

✌

You have a caller."

"A caller?" Margaret frowned at her landlady.

"A gentleman!" the surly woman announced. "Rode up—bold as brass—on a fancy horse that would have cost a normal person a lifetime's wages."

In the eight months Margaret had resided in the boardinghouse, the woman's mood hadn't improved.

"Did he say who he is or what he wants?"

"No, but you know you're not allowed to have male visitors. Learn his purpose, then get rid of him. He's awaiting you down in the parlor."

She stomped out, leaving Margaret to fuss in the quiet. Since she'd left Gray's Manor, it was the first instance where someone had sought her out, and she had no idea who the man could be. The only adults she ever saw were the other female tenants in the house and the parents of her students.

She'd started a small school, where she earned enough money to pay her rent and buy a bit of food, but the fathers of her pupils were laborers and farmers, and none of them would ever be described as a *gentleman*.

Trudging to the stairs, she felt exposed and notorious in a way she hadn't in a very long while. Her sordid history had been successfully buried, her humiliating affair with Lord Romsey naught but a faint memory. Luckily, there'd been no child as a result of the liaison, so no hint of scandal had trailed after her.

She'd never been questioned about her status as a widow, had never felt uncomfortable with the lie or required to explain herself. As she'd quickly discovered after departing Sussex, there were many poverty-stricken females in the country, all of them attempting to eke out a spot in a world where being alone and adrift was almost viewed as a sin.

In the foyer, she paused. There was a cracked mirror on the wall, and she took stock of her appearance, which she tried not to do too often.

With bathing a luxury that was rarely indulged, she'd cut her beautiful hair. The auburn locks now curled around her shoulders, but they were listless and dull, the sheen having vanished. Her eyes weren't green, but had faded to hazel, as if the emerald shade they'd once been was too vibrant for her reduced situation.

As food was an extravagance, she was much thinner, too, but she refused to feel sorry for herself. Many others were in dire straits much worse than her own. In comparison, she lived like a queen.

At least I have a roof over my head, she mused, even as she realized it was a miserable standard by which to measure her condition.

Sighing, she walked on. It was futile to rue or regret, foolish to gaze into the mirror and yearn to glimpse the woman she used to be.

Ready for anything, she stepped into the parlor, and

she nearly collapsed in astonishment. Lord Romsey was standing over by the window, peering out the torn curtain at the muddy street, and at seeing him she couldn't believe the ridiculous spurt of delight she suffered.

Suddenly, she was so happy. She felt as if the sun had popped out from behind a cloud, or that a rain shower had moved on and there was a rainbow in its place.

He was still the tall, dynamic individual he'd been, but he seemed to have lost weight, too, as if the past few months had been hard on him as well, though she couldn't imagine why they would have been. With his garnering Penelope's fortune, he should have been ecstatic. Then again, marrying Penelope would make any man wretched.

At remembering how money had swayed him, at how he'd coveted it above all else, her spurt of elation was easy to tamp down. She was reminded of how little she'd meant to him, how little he'd cared.

She couldn't figure out why he'd come, and she wanted him gone before his male company got her evicted.

"Hello, Lord Romsey," she murmured.

He spun slowly, and his expression was so strange. She couldn't decide if it was relief, or surprise, or consternation at how she looked—which was vastly changed and much more unkempt than when he'd known her prior.

Although she'd never been wealthy when she was at Gray's Manor, she recollected that earlier period as a time of enormous leisure and affluence. She'd always been washed, groomed, and meticulously attired, even if her clothes hadn't been the highest state of fashion. Now, she just had to make do, and the alterations were blatant and discouraging, but her current predicament couldn't be helped, and if he didn't like it, he could leave.

She wouldn't be ashamed or embarrassed.

"Hello, Margaret." Then, "You've cut your hair."

"Yes."

"You're so . . . different."

He faltered, the moment awkward, as he struggled with whether he should cross to her or stay where he was. Ultimately, he stayed away, and she knew she should have been thankful for the imposed distance, but an idiotic part of her wished he'd come closer and at least pretended to be glad to see her.

"I was wondering if I'd finally found you," he said.

It was a peculiar comment, one that indicated he'd been searching, when she couldn't conjure a single reason why he might have been.

"You've been looking for me?"

"For months now. Ever since you left."

"I can't fathom why you were."

"I have some news."

"From Sussex?"

"Yes."

The only topic he could have to discuss was Lavinia or Penelope, and the very idea of talking about either of them was so distressing that she wouldn't consider it.

"I don't need to hear any." She gestured toward the door. "So if that's all you came to say, you might as well go."

She hated how the remark sounded. It seemed to imply that she'd been hoping he had a personal motive for the meeting, that he had something special and intimate to communicate, which hadn't been her intent.

He could fall to his knees and pledge his undying devotion, and she wouldn't believe a word he said.

"It's important," he insisted, so he'd probably badger her until she agreed to listen.

"Won't you sit?"

She motioned to the filthy, rickety sofa, and he hesitated, his aversion plain, but he possessed a modicum of courtesy and wouldn't insult her by declining. He perched on the edge of the cushion, while she sat in the chair opposite.

They were silent, and he studied her oddly, unable to tell her what had brought him, and she was frantic for him to get on with it.

Each second in his presence was torture. She had many precious memories, but they'd been doused with doses of cruel reality, and she wouldn't have any of them bubbling to the surface.

She was tired of waiting for him to begin, so she probed, "How is married life treating you?"

"Married life?" He was confused. "Oh, you mean to your cousin."

"Yes." Her smile was so cold that she was amazed her face didn't crack.

"I didn't marry her."

"You didn't?"

"No."

A thousand questions swarmed into her head. Why hadn't he? What had transpired? What had become of Penelope? What was he doing instead? Had he landed himself another heiress?

She crammed the questions—and any possible answers—into a vault in her mind and locked the lid.

She would not ask any of them, for she was truly disinterested as to his replies.

"She married my father," he explained.

"Your father? She chose him over you?"

"Yes. She was eager to be a countess immediately, rather than a mere viscountess."

"I'm not surprised. She was such an impatient child."

She bit down on the urge to giggle, finding it incredibly satisfying that he hadn't gotten what he'd craved, after all.

"What happened to all her money?" she queried. "Is your father spending it as fast as he can?"

"She didn't have any money."

"Of course, she did. She bragged about it constantly."

"Lavinia frittered it away."

"Really?"

"Yes, and that's why I must confer with you."

She could barely keep from scoffing aloud. She wouldn't chat about Lavinia and Penelope, didn't want to be apprised of how Lavinia was a squanderer or Penelope a financial drain. Margaret had severed her ties so completely that it was like reading about strangers in the gossip columns.

She didn't care!

"None of this is any of my concern, Lord Romsey."

"You used to call me Jordan."

"That was a long time ago."

She stared into those blue eyes that had once held her so rapt, and she was astonished to note that he seemed hurt, as if she'd slighted him, and his dismay baffled her.

Had he anticipated a warm welcome? Had he

presumed she still had fond feelings? In light of all that had occurred, after how he'd spurned her, how could he assume any affection remained?

He sighed and nodded, accepting the detachment she was determined to maintain.

"Yes," he concurred, "it was a long time ago."

She couldn't abide how he was focused on her, and she was desperate to hurry him along. She rose and went to the window where he'd been when she'd initially entered.

"Why are you here?"

"As I was untangling the farce between my father and Penelope, I learned something that you should have been told."

"What is that?" She glanced over her shoulder.

"Your uncle Horatio provided for you in his Will."

"How nice. I never knew."

"I know you didn't."

Her expectations were so lowered that she couldn't conceive of anyone thinking of her, and at the realization that her uncle had remembered her in his last hours, her eyes flooded with tears. She hoped it was an amount sufficient to buy a new dress or perhaps some books for her school.

"In fact," Romsey kept on, "I've had people traveling the countryside, making inquiries, so that I could be sure you were informed."

"Well, it seems you've found me. You may leave my stipend and go. Thank you for bringing it."

There was a portfolio on the table, and he reached into it, but rather than pulling out the few pound notes she'd foreseen, he retrieved a thick stack of papers.

"Come here." He patted the spot next to him on the sofa. "Let me show you what's happened."

The couch wasn't very large, and he simply took up too much of it. She didn't want to be so close to him. Though she hated to admit it, she was disturbed by him, and apparently—despite his disavowal, his treachery, his proven lack of regard—she wasn't immune to his significant charm.

She could scarcely keep from rushing over, from throwing herself at his feet and weeping with joy that he'd finally arrived.

In those first terrible days after she'd fled Sussex, she'd been positive he would follow her. She'd prayed and fantasized, persuading herself that he hadn't meant the awful things he'd said, that he would relent and track her down.

She'd created dozens of scenarios where he'd been repentant, where he'd pleaded for forgiveness and had instantly received it. She'd visualized them together and deliriously happy, but as days had turned to weeks, then weeks to months, the dreams had faded, replaced by the stark reality of her predicament, the certainty that he wasn't coming and she would always be alone.

His appearance had shaken loose those hungry thoughts, and it was growing harder and harder to keep them at bay.

"Just tell me what it is," she said, refusing to move nearer to him.

"All right." He was obviously disappointed by her response, but he forged on, making the best of a difficult situation. "Your uncle left the bulk of his estate in three trust funds: one for Lavinia, one for Penelope, and one for you."

"For me?"

"Yes, they were equal shares."

"That can't be correct."

"It is, Margaret. After Horatio died, Lavinia spent her share very quickly. Then she spent Penelope's, too. The one remaining—that was supposedly Penelope's dowry—was yours, and I've managed to reclaim it before they could spend it, as well." He gestured to the documents. "It's all here. I merely need your signature to finalize everything."

"Finalize it how?"

"I've had an acquaintance of mine, a Mr. Thumberton, go into court and have the entire debacle rearranged. He's an honorable and reliable London solicitor, and he's your new trustee. He's written you a letter of introduction and explanation."

He held it out so she could cross over and read it, but still, she didn't budge.

"Do you know what it says?" she inquired.

"Yes. He's sent money with me—in case I located you—and he begs that you use it to hire a companion and travel to London to meet with him. He has employees who will help you get settled in the style to which you're due. They'll assist you in buying a house and hiring servants, and they'll purchase whatever else you need."

"Buy a . . . a . . . house? Are you mad?"

"You're very wealthy now, Margaret. You'll never have to struggle again." His voice cracked, charged with emotion he could barely contain. "For the rest of your life, you'll live in ease and harmony."

There was a chair next to her, and she sank into it. She must have looked as if she was about to swoon, and she definitely felt like it, for he grew alarmed and hurried over.

He reached out to take her hand, but in the end, he didn't, and she was relieved. She was anxious for solace and empathy, for guidance and counsel, but the time when she might have turned to him for support had vanished in the fog of their bitter past.

"What can I get you?" he asked. "What do you need?"

There were so many things she *needed* that she couldn't begin to list them all. First and foremost, she had to review the papers he'd brought, while she decided what to do next.

"I'm fine," she insisted. "Just surprised—and a tad overwhelmed."

"Understandable."

When he was hovering, she couldn't concentrate, and she pushed herself to her feet and walked across the room so that the sofa was between them. He was assessing her intently, as if he was about to reveal something she couldn't bear to hear, and a hideous notion dawned on her: If what he asserted was true, that she really had inherited a fortune, then she'd suddenly become an heiress.

Is that why he'd sought her out? Is that why he'd volunteered to chase around the country, picking through every village and hovel till he stumbled on her? Why else would he have been so determined to find her?

She'd once loved him beyond imagining, but he'd forsaken her because she was poor. Would he have the gall—now that she was allegedly rich—to declare himself infatuated? Could he be that crass? That tactless?

Her heart broke all over again, and she forced a smile and indicated the door, wanting to be very clear that their appointment was over.

"I appreciate your coming," she said very calmly, "but you'll have to excuse me. You've given me so much to contemplate, and I must have some privacy while I consider my options."

"Certainly." He bowed, but didn't depart. Instead, he peered around the dilapidated space, his astute gaze missing no detail of how appalling it had been.

"I'm sorry," he murmured, and he approached till he was directly in front of her.

"For what?"

"I didn't know that Lavinia had sent you away. She claimed you'd gone into seclusion, lest there was a babe, and she said that—"

She held up a hand, halting his tirade. He might feel the urge to confess his sins, but she was hardly the person who had to listen.

"Please, Lord Romsey, it's all in the past."

"I was about to come after you. I wanted to be with you, but then—"

"Please!"

"I've been searching for you ever since, to be positive you were all right. I'm . . . I'm . . . so glad that you are."

He appeared so lost and forlorn, and he seemed to need something from her, something she couldn't give him.

"Leave it be," she quietly implored.

"Would you like me to stay on? I'd be happy to help you interview for a companion, or to pack your things. If you wished, I could escort you to London."

"It's kind of you to offer, but not necessary. I'm an adult woman, and I've learned that I'm fully capable of making my own way."

He scrutinized her, taking in her features as if memorizing them. "If you ever need anything from me—anything at all—promise me that you'll notify Mr. Thumberton."

"I won't ever need anything from you."

"You just never know," he mused. "I'll come straightaway."

She kept her expression blank, furnishing no hint of the spark of hope he'd ignited. Evidently, she was still smitten and foolishly ready to leap to folly and ruin, once again, when she truly didn't think she could survive another go-round with him.

Finally, his evaluation complete, he stepped away and went to the foyer. At the last second, he glanced over.

"Do you ever wonder what might have happened if we had—" He stopped. Waiting . . . waiting . . .

"No, I never do," she lied.

He nodded, then left, and she sagged down onto a chair. She perched there till his horse's hooves clopped away; then she staggered to the window, watching till he was a tiny speck on the horizon. She returned to the sofa and picked up the papers he'd conveyed.

She clutched them to her chest, praying they were genuine, and knowing that—whatever else he might be—Romsey wasn't the sort of man to have perpetrated a hoax. Very likely, she was now incredibly wealthy.

She stood in the dingy, silent chamber—just her and her trust documents and the envelope of cash he'd delivered.

Eventually, the landlady came in to light a lamp and kindle the fire.

Without a word, Margaret headed for the stairs, climbed to her room, and shut the door.

CHAPTER TWENTY-TWO

Jordan gazed up at the decrepit boardinghouse where Margaret had ended her flight from Gray's Manor. He tried to imagine what the passing months had been like for her, but he couldn't wrap his mind around the reality of her repugnant situation.

If he lived to be a hundred years old, he would never forgive himself. At least he'd found her! At least he'd had the temerity to keep searching.

What if he'd given up? What if he'd decided she couldn't be located? The notion—that a lack of persistence on his part would have sentenced her to squalor for the rest of her days—was too shocking to ponder.

He couldn't blame her for being cold and distant, but oh, how it hurt to learn that her prior affection had vanished. She'd once held him in such high esteem, but none of her strong emotions remained. How could he have expected them to endure? What had he ever done to sustain an attachment?

Their lengthy separation had galvanized his feelings, but obviously not hers. Finally, he had the courage to admit how much he loved her, how much he would love her forever, but she despised him.

He'd let her go—for money! It was a great and terrible shame, and in spite of how fervently he wished it were otherwise, he didn't deserve any kindness or even simple courtesy from her.

When he reflected on events, he could only assume that the entire sordid affair had been a celestial test, which he'd failed. She'd been plopped in front of him as a sign of what mattered, of what was important, but he'd been too obtuse to note what was right before his eyes.

With a sigh, he mounted his horse and galloped away, headed back to London and the shambles of his life. He'd rented rooms in a seedy section of town. Mary and the twins resided there with him, as well as several other half siblings who'd shown up unannounced. In hopes of enticing another bride, he concealed the exact location from High Society, but his furtiveness hadn't helped. As his father's fortunes fell, Jordan's plight had worsened, too.

Girls who might once have been interested were openly hostile and bluntly rude. His difficulties were enough to make him consider leaving England altogether, just hopping on a ship and sailing away. Of course, booking passage would require funds—which he didn't have.

He raced round a curve in the road, lurching to the side to avoid a carriage rushing in the opposite direction. The curtain fluttered in the wind, and he was so distracted by gloomy thoughts that he was quite a distance away before he realized that he'd seen the lone occupant and that he knew her all too well.

Lavinia Gray! He was sure of it!

He reined in and stopped. What was she doing traveling toward Margaret's lodging? Her arrival couldn't be a coincidence.

She'd disappeared from Gray's Manor, slipping away after she'd sent him on his fruitless trip to Brighton. By the time he'd returned—without Margaret—she'd fled, having been aware that he'd be bent on revenge.

Since then, he'd been so busy hunting for Margaret that he hadn't chased after Lavinia. He kept telling himself that he'd deal with her later, after Margaret was safe, yet here she was, like a bad toothache, prancing along behind him.

Had she been following him? Why would she?

There was only one reason: She was hunting for Margaret, too, and he understood Lavinia well enough to know that whatever her motives, they couldn't be good ones.

"Damnation!" he cursed. He pulled his horse around and cantered after her.

§

"Hello, Margaret."

Margaret whipped around. "Lavinia? What are you doing here?"

"Looking for you. What would you suppose?"

"Looking . . . for me?"

"Yes."

Lavinia shut the door as she hastily assessed the pitiful room. The small space seemed even smaller with two adult women sequestered in it, and though her own fortunes had plummeted to nothing, she couldn't resist taunting, "You've certainly come down a few pegs since last I saw you."

"We can't all be as lucky as you, I guess."

"Are you making fun of me? Are you? Are you?"

There was a note of hysteria in her voice that she hadn't intended, but she was on edge, having been shoved beyond normal banter or behavior. Her clothes were worn and disheveled, her hair ratted and unwashed, and—as circumstances prevented regular bathing—she smelled.

In the endless period that she'd been hiding and scraping by, she'd had ample opportunity to ruminate over her downfall, and after a significant interval spent trying to leech off friends, she'd been stunned to discover that she didn't have any.

She was on her own, having forfeited all, and she blamed everyone for her adversities: Horatio, Robert, Penelope, Kettering, Romsey, and Margaret. Mostly, she blamed Margaret.

If Jordan accomplished what Lavinia suspected he had, then Margaret had wound up with everything, while Lavinia had wound up with nothing. How could the universe have conspired against her so completely?

"Are you feeling all right?" Margaret asked. "You seem a bit . . . distraught."

"Why wouldn't I be? I've lost my home, all my worldly possessions, and what remained of my money. My ungrateful daughter married the man I wanted for myself, my lover left me, the law is probably after me, and I've been living off the charity of strangers."

"You have?"

"Yes, and I must tell you, Margaret, that I haven't cared for any of it."

"I don't imagine you have, but why come to me? I must admit that I'm surprised."

"Lord Romsey just visited you," Lavinia accused.

"Well . . . yes, he did. How did you know?"

"I've been hot on his trail for months."

"For months?"

"Yes."

"Have you gone mad?"

Occasionally, Lavinia felt as if she had, but then, with what she'd endured, who wouldn't be agitated?

"What did he want?" she demanded.

Margaret had no knack for deceit, and Lavinia was positive that whatever her reply, it would be false. Lavinia was past the point when patience or cajoling would suffice. She walked to the bed and deposited the box she'd brought; then she opened it and retrieved one of the two pistols she'd been hauling around for this very confrontation.

At seeing that Lavinia clutched a gun, Margaret blanched and stepped back.

"What are you thinking?" Margaret snapped. "Have you tipped off your rocker?"

"What did Romsey want?" Lavinia repeated.

"He came to check on me," Margaret fibbed. "After I departed Gray's Manor so abruptly, he was worried."

"Really?"

"Yes, really."

"As I recall, he was overly fond of you. Was there no lovers' tryst? No secrets shared?"

"No. Now put that thing away before you hurt yourself."

Margaret's gaze furtively shifted to the bed, where

there was a large stack of what appeared to be legal documents. Lavinia gestured to them.

"I suppose those are kindling for the stove."

"They're essays my students wrote. I've started a new school."

"You always were the worst liar." She gestured again. "Place the papers in that satchel, then hand it to me."

Margaret hesitated, calculating the odds. Should she rush Lavinia and wrestle for the weapon? Should she race into the hall and scream for help?

"I won't do it," she ultimately protested. "I don't understand what you want, but I no longer have to—"

Lavinia straightened her arm and fired a shot into the mattress, which absorbed some of the loud bang, but not nearly enough. Feathers flew, and smoke filled the air as she grabbed the other gun.

"I can see that I have your attention," she jeered. "I have one more round, and it's primed and ready. If you don't do as I've commanded—at once!—I shall use it to kill you. Now give me those papers!"

Trembling with terror, Margaret hustled over and scooped up the documents, stuffing them willy-nilly into the satchel. She held it out. "Here! Take it."

"Have you a pen and ink?"

"Yes." Margaret hastened to a rickety table in the corner.

"Draft a letter that says you don't want the money, that you're transferring it all to me."

"Who would believe something so idiotic?"

"Just do it!" Lavinia shouted, sounding more deranged by the second.

Margaret sat down and picked up a quill. With shaky

fingers, she dipped it in the ink, then paused. "To whom should I address it?"

"I don't know! I don't know. Just write the blasted letter!"

"I will. Calm down."

Margaret was moving slow as molasses, and Lavinia paced in frustration. She couldn't tolerate any delay, and as a better notion dawned, she smiled grimly.

"I've changed my mind," she explained.

"Fine."

Margaret's pen was poised over the empty page, and Lavinia instructed, "Write this across the top: *Last Will and Testament of Margaret Gray.*"

"I most certainly will not."

"You will, and you'll name me as your sole heir."

"You're being absurd."

"Trust me: I've never been more lucid."

"But you can't inherit from me unless I die."

"Precisely." Lavinia nodded. "This should have occurred to me ages ago."

Margaret stared, but composed no words, and Lavinia threatened, "Would you rather I kill you and forge the document myself?"

"I'm not about to be the author of my own demise."

"Then allow me to orchestrate your finale for you."

Margaret rose and sidled away from the table. "I'm not afraid of you."

"You should be."

Suddenly, Margaret whipped out, and too late, Lavinia realized that she was clasping the bottle of ink. She hurled it, and though Lavinia tried to duck, the black contents splattered her face and hair, dripping off her chin and down her chest.

She glanced down, horrified by the spreading stain. "You've ruined my dress! My only one!"

"I'm so sorry!" Margaret taunted.

Lavinia was momentarily blinded, the dark liquid dribbling into her eyes and stinging them, and as she swiped at the mess, Margaret lunged. Lavinia raised the pistol, her finger on the trigger, and Margaret was so close that it wasn't necessary to aim.

The jarring blast rang out, just as someone burst in the door and pounced on her. More smoke clouded the air, choking her with its pungent smell, as she was tackled, powerful arms smacking her down to the floor with a painful thump.

She'd discharged both her weapons, and in the hazy confusion she couldn't see if Margaret was dead or not. Had Lavinia wasted her opportunity? Wouldn't it be just her luck to fire at point-blank range and miss?

She had to learn the answer, and she fought with all her might, trying to stand and finish the job. Wanting justice, wanting vengeance against the entire world, she was in an uncontrollable frenzy. She seemed to have the strength of ten men, but whoever held her was even stronger, and she couldn't wiggle free.

"Desist!" a male voice ordered.

"No! I'm going to kill her!" Lavinia insisted. "I'm going to kill everyone! Everyone, I tell you!"

"You are out of your bloody mind!"

She lashed out wildly, the heel of her hand clouting the man's nose, and he growled with rage.

"I was taught never to strike a female," he said, "but in your case, I think I'll make an exception."

He punched her so hard that she was stunned, and she slumped to the floor in a rubbery heap. She'd ended up in the exact same humiliating position the morning Penelope had assaulted her in front of Lord Kettering.

Was this to be how the rest of her despicable life was to play out? Was she to spend it scrapping and brawling and being knocked unconscious?

A renewed torrent of fury surged through her, and she roared and bucked with her hips, but the man simply punched her again, and she whimpered and gave up.

Her arms were yanked behind her back, a cord securing her wrists. A gag was stuffed in her mouth.

The man left her side, saying, "Margaret! Margaret! Are you all right?"

"I'm fine. Shaken, but fine."

"Were you hit?" he frantically inquired, as Lavinia recognized that it was Romsey, that he'd returned unexpectedly to foil her scheme.

"No," Margaret said. "You pushed her away. The ball went into the plaster."

"Oh, my God! I thought you were dead. Sit down! Sit down—before you fall down!"

Another voice sounded, a belligerent woman in the hall. "What is happening in here? Sir!" she barked at Romsey. "Male guests are not permitted in the rooms!"

"Get out!" Romsey snarled.

"Aah!" the woman shrieked. "There's a hole in my wall! Who will pay to have it repaired?"

"I will," Margaret grumbled. "Don't worry about it."

"Don't worry? You have visitors who are scuffling and shooting guns and you tell me not to worry?"

"The excitement is over," Margaret declared. "They were just leaving."

"I'm afraid you'll have to go with them," the woman carped. "I can't have such outrageous behavior in my establishment."

"I'm delighted to oblige you," Margaret calmly said. "I was about to come down and notify you that I'm off to London."

"To London? Well . . ." The news temporarily silenced the annoying woman; then she complained, "What should I do about losing your rent money? Am I to pull another tenant out of my hat? You can't tot off without notice and without—"

The smoke was beginning to dissipate, and Lavinia could see Romsey walk over, physically pick up the woman, and set her out in the corridor.

"Go downstairs and wait for me," he commanded.

"I most certainly will not! I—"

"Go!" he hissed with such vehemence that she skittered off.

He slammed the door, then proceeded to where Margaret was huddled in a chair. Ninny that she was, she started to weep.

"Oh, my darling," Romsey soothed, "it's over now. Don't cry. I can't bear it when you're sad."

He reached out to hug her, but to his amazement, Margaret eased him away.

"Please," Margaret wailed. "I can't take any more."

"I know it's been dreadful for you."

"Just get her out of here. Lock her away somewhere so I can be sure she won't ever come back."

Romsey was stricken by her rejection, and he dawdled, then reached out again. Margaret glanced away, overtly declining the solace he was desperate to offer.

"Please," she murmured again.

He stared at her, the moment growing awkward; then he sighed and mumbled, "As you wish."

He spun and grabbed Lavinia, hauling her to her feet with a sturdy yank. At his rough handling she yowled with anguish, but her mouth was muffled, so neither of them could hear how passionately she cursed.

"I had decided," he seethed as he dragged her into the hall, "to ignore your contemptible presence on the face of the earth, but after this stunt, I'll see you prosecuted to the fullest extent of the law."

Bastard! she hurled with her eyes.

He had no trouble deciphering her message, and he replied, "I hope you hang."

Gripping her by the waist, he lugged her down the stairs, through the foyer, and outside to his horse. As if she were a sack of flour, he tossed her across the saddle on her stomach, so that her head flopped down, her legs dangling in the other direction.

"Let's go find the nearest gaol," he said.

He leapt up behind her and kicked the animal into a trot.

CHAPTER TWENTY-THREE

G et me out of here!" Lavinia demanded. "Let me live with you."

"With me?" Penelope laughed. "You must be joking."

Disdainful and smug, Penelope glanced around and wrinkled her nose at the dreadful odors. For some reason, Lavinia had been lodged in a solitary cell, rather than in the main section of the prison with the common prisoners, but despite the privacy, the place was disgusting, the atmosphere bleak.

She'd invited Penelope to sit, but Penelope had refused, saying she didn't want to soil her dress. At being confronted by her daughter's contempt, Lavinia could barely keep from leaping off the cot and strangling her.

"I'm your mother! You must help me!"

"Is that a rule that's been posted somewhere?"

"Any dutiful child would comprehend that it's expected."

"I've never been *dutiful*, and at this late date, why would I start behaving any differently?"

"You wretched girl!" Lavinia seethed. "Everything I did, I did for you. So you could flourish in Society. Yet you repay me with scorn and ridicule."

"I *am* thriving, and I did it all on my own, without any of your tepid assistance."

"You dastardly ingrate!"

"Oh . . . I'm so ashamed of how you tormented my dear cousin, Margaret." Penelope pressed a dramatic wrist to her forehead. "The poor woman! All those years! How she suffered under your roof! How was I to know that my mother was naught but a petty thief?"

"You spent every penny I stole! You were complicit in every act!"

"Was I? I can't remember."

Penelope grinned, relishing Lavinia's downfall, and Lavinia was close to committing murder. How could Penelope have landed on her feet while Lavinia rotted in a hellhole? How could Fate be so cruel?

Penelope was attired in a fashionable gown and a stylish hat that had a jaunty feather trailing behind. Her cunning eyes were merry, her cheeks rosy. She looked affluent and beautiful and chubby with good health. In comparison, Lavinia was unkempt, unclean, and hungry most of the time.

"I thought Romsey might intercede on my behalf," Lavinia complained, "but he's washed his hands of me."

"The members of the aristocracy can be so fickle."

"He claims I'm to be transported."

"Yes, so sorry to hear it."

"Sorry?" Lavinia shrieked with outrage. "Is that all you have to say?"

"I'll be so sad to see you go. You'll write, won't you?" She paused, then chuckled. "I take that back.

Don't bother corresponding. I really don't care to be contacted by you ever again."

Lavinia rippled with malice, but tamped it down. Throughout her lengthy imprisonment, Romsey had been her sole caller, but his visits had ceased after she was convicted.

Penelope was her only hope, so Lavinia didn't dare antagonize her. A very despicable bribe had been required to get a message to her, and this—this!—was how Penelope responded. There was no justice in the world!

"You must speak with Lord Kettering," Lavinia implored, growing frantic. "He'd help me; I'm certain he would. He's an earl. They'll listen to him."

"Kettering? You think he'd come to your aid?"

"I know it for a fact. I was one of his favorites."

"His favorite what?"

"Lover!"

"You presumed you were a . . . a . . . favorite?"

"I was!"

"That's rich, Lavinia. Absolutely rich." Penelope made a tsking sound. "He's a rutting dog. He'll fuck anything. Don't you realize that he was using you merely to win me?"

"You're lying. He was smitten by me! Smitten, I tell you!"

"No, Mother, he wanted *me*. I was the prize. Not you."

She went to the door and knocked for the jailer, and Lavinia panicked.

"Where are you going?"

"I'm off to Bath to take the waters."

"To Bath? But Romsey maintains that Kettering is destitute."

"He is."

"Then how can you afford such an extravagance?"

"I'm a countess. You can't imagine how many people want to be my friend. I don't have to pay for anything."

She rapped again, and Lavinia whined, "You can't mean to leave me here."

"Actually, I do. I have no sympathy for you. We were on a sinking boat—you always said so, and that it was every woman for herself. I swam away, while you . . ." She smirked. "Well, we can see what you did. Goodbye."

The jailer arrived, and Penelope stepped into the hall as Lavinia desperately clutched at her arm.

"Send Kettering to me," Lavinia begged. "Please!"

Penelope pushed Lavinia away, and she flashed an expressive, guileless smile at the jailer.

"My poor mother," she sighed. "She's quite mad."

"So I've been told, milady."

"What's a daughter to do, hmm?" She slipped him a coin. "Would you have her properly tended—as she waits for the ship that will spirit her away from me?"

"I will, Countess."

"I would be ever so grateful."

Penelope waltzed off, her cloying perfume the only indication that she'd been there, at all. Once she disappeared, the jailer's polite demeanor vanished. He shoved Lavinia into the cell and spun the key in the lock.

Lavinia screamed and screamed until her voice was hoarse, and her nails broken and raw from clawing at the wood, but no matter how violently she carried on, the door never opened and Penelope never returned.

O h, dear Lord!"
Penelope stumbled to a halt, her mouth dropping in shock and disgust.

"Why, Penelope"—Charles chuckled nervously—"I didn't expect you back so soon."

"Obviously."

He was on the bed in the hotel room where she'd left him when she'd traipsed off to chat with Lavinia. A blond maid—who wasn't even pretty!—was with him. Her skirts were rucked up, the bodice of her dress pulled down to bare her bovine breasts.

Charles was positioned between her plump thighs and had been sucking away at a large nipple. Penelope's untimely entrance had interrupted his thrusting, and he had the decency to withdraw and roll away.

The trembling maid pleaded, "I'm sorry, milady. He made me do it."

Penelope scoffed, "That's a bald-faced lie, you little slut."

"It's true, ma'am. I swear."

"I'm sure you enjoyed every second of it. What has he promised you that convinced you to spread your legs?"

"Nothing!"

"He's flat broke, so whatever he offered, you'll never see a farthing. Now get out of here, or I'll talk to your employer and have you fired."

There was a belt tossed across the end of the mattress, and Penelope grabbed it and lashed out, whipping the girl across the head and shoulders as she raced out.

Penelope chased her to the stairs, landing blow after blow, until the maid started down and moved out of range.

"Don't come sniffing after my husband again," Penelope shouted, just because she supposed it was the sort of thing a wronged wife ought to say.

She stomped off, but she wasn't really upset by Charles's philandering. She didn't care what he did. The more he sought out whores for his pleasure, the less she had to provide.

His continued presence as her spouse was insupportable, and she avoided him as much as possible, but still, she was glad she'd married him. It was amazing, the boons a woman could acquire with the title of countess next to her name. By observing Charles, who was a veritable master at cunning and deceit, she'd learned how to take full advantage of every circumstance. With her being so young and so beautiful, others were loathe to refuse her anything, so she foresaw only profit and comfort in her future.

As to Charles? He was on his own, and she wasn't about to wallow in his penury. He had dug the hole he was in, and she wouldn't hoist him out of it.

When she entered the room again, he was standing, his clothes straightened, every hair in place. He was calm and collected and completely unrepentant, as if he hadn't just been fucking a hussy before her very eyes.

"Lie down on the bed," he had the gall to insist.

"No."

"I command that you perform your marital duty. Your intrusion kept me from finishing, and I'm hard as a rock. You will satisfy me at once."

"Considering where your rod has been"—she yanked out a knife she'd begun to carry everywhere and gestured to his cock—"if you wag it at me, I'll slice it off."

"If I am in need of wifely tending, you will render it without complaint."

She laughed. "Your tricks and threats don't work on me anymore, Charles. Can you actually assume to order me about and get away with it?"

"I am your husband. You will do as I say, or I will beat you to within an inch of your life."

"If you touch me, I'll stab you to death when you're done."

He frowned, ready to kill. "You are entirely too disobedient, so evidently, I haven't been sufficiently instructive during my lessons."

"Your *lessons*—as you like to refer to them—are over."

"What do you mean?"

"I'm leaving you."

"Leaving me? Hah! I don't give you permission to go."

"Your opinion is irrelevant. From now on, you can fornicate with every trollop in the world, you can defraud every innkeeper, you can cheat every acquaintance, but I don't have to stay and watch."

She went to the dressing room and retrieved the satchel she'd packed earlier, and she peeked inside to ensure that her secret stockpile was hidden there. Charles had stupidly informed her that he kept a tiny hoard of gems that he was slowly converting to cash so his creditors wouldn't realize his ploy.

She'd pilfered the jewels before visiting Lavinia, and she was delighted to note that Charles hadn't noticed they were missing. She closed the flap on the bag, then sauntered out.

"Farewell, Charles."

"What?"

"I'm off to Bath with friends. I'll relax for a few months. Then . . . ? I can't decide, but from this point on, my whereabouts are none of your concern."

"Listen to me, you spoiled little fiend—"

"Sod off, you old drunkard."

She marched out and fled the hotel, hurrying down the block and around the corner. The ruffian she'd hired was waiting for her, and she walked over to him. They spoke in low tones.

"Were you able to steal his coach?" she asked.

"Yes."

"Did you locate a buyer?"

"Of course."

"For the horses, too?"

"They fetched a pretty penny."

Charles prided himself on his continuing to possess the fancy conveyance with the sleek matched bays. He liked to brag how the fleet animals kept him one step ahead of debtor's prison.

The ruffian handed over an envelope of cash, and at seeing the large amount generated by the sale she grinned. She'd always detested the cumbersome, pretentious vehicle and was relieved to be rid of it—though she doubted Charles would feel the same.

"Marvelous!" she gushed. "Thank you."

"You're welcome, milady. Is he in the hotel?"

"Third floor, first door on the right. If you go immediately, you'll catch him. Will I get the reward for turning him in?"

He submitted another envelope. "Half now, and the other half when he's in chains."

"Have you my address in Bath?"

"Indeed, I do, Lady Kettering. Indeed, I do. I'll send the rest of the money as soon as everything's finalized."

"He'll never know it was me who betrayed him, will he?"

"No. I guarantee it." He tipped his hat. "I'm glad we're on the same side. I'd hate to have you as an enemy."

"Yes, you would."

"It's been a pleasure doing business with you."

"And with you, as well."

She proceeded farther down the block, to the hansom cab she'd previously arranged. She climbed in, the driver cracked the whip, and she dashed off without a backward glance.

🦢

U nhand me, you wretch!"

"No."

Charles struggled with the restraints on his wrists and ankles, but couldn't loosen them. "You obviously don't realize who I am."

"Don't I?" The smug villain chuckled.

"I'll see you hanged for this outrage."

"For a fellow who's completely bound, and about to be gagged, you're awfully bossy."

"For a fellow who's completely insane," Charles retorted, "and has committed a deranged act against a personal friend of the King, you're awfully brave."

"Let's go, Your Majesty."

"To where?"

"Debtor's prison. Where would you suppose? There are plenty of folks eager for me to escort you there."

"Prison! I say, you can't just waltz into a man's hotel room and cart him off to the gaol."

"I can, and I have." The criminal reached for Charles's arm, yanked him off the bed, and steadied him on his feet. "Now let's go."

"I demand to see a magistrate! I demand to contact my solicitor!"

"So sorry, but I can't oblige you."

"I'm an earl. A peer of the realm. Only my equals can sit in judgment of me."

"Well, they'll have to find you first, won't they? Though somehow, I suspect they won't bother to look."

The thug started toward the door, dragging Charles with him, and Charles bellowed, "Help! Help! I'm being kidn—"

A wad of cloth was crammed in his mouth, his protests silenced. The brute peeked into the hall and, espying no one, he pulled Charles out, lugged him down the rear stairs, and tossed him into a waiting carriage. As his head banged painfully and his body landed with an undignified thump, the driver clicked the reins, and the horses whisked him away at a fast trot.

In a matter of seconds, he disappeared as if he'd never been.

❧

Margaret sat on the verandah of the elaborate house she'd purchased near London. With a small farm and stable as part of the property, it was a bucolic location. The grass was so green, the summer sky so blue. With the breeze that was blowing, there were sailboats out on the Thames, their sails fluttering in the wind, and as she watched them, she suffered the worst wave of melancholy.

She gaped around at her monstrosity of a residence, wondering what had possessed her to think she needed so much. She'd heeded Attorney Thumberton's counsel as to how she should live according to her elevated station, but in this she'd been foolish to follow his well-meaning advice.

The lengthy corridors and high ceilings echoed with how alone she was, and she couldn't stand to walk across the marble floors. Her heels clicked so loudly that she'd bought dozens of rugs merely so that her strides would be quieter.

She'd attempted to make friends in the neighborhood, but had quickly learned that she was notorious. People were still talking about Lavinia, about Penelope and Lord Kettering, and with Margaret being a blood relative, she'd been painted with the same scandalous brush.

Out of boredom, she'd tried to establish another school, but hadn't had any luck attracting students. The local gentry deemed her too infamous to teach their progeny, and the common citizens was unnerved to see such a wealthy lady working, so she had nothing to do, and the monotony was driving her mad.

She riffled through the morning's mail, surprised to discover a letter from Lavinia that must have been posted just before her ship departed for Australia. Margaret crumpled it into a ball, knowing she'd never read it. Over the past few months, she'd received several others, and they'd been filled with such vitriol and malice that she was positive it wasn't worth breaking the wax seal.

Despite how Lavinia had almost murdered her, she pitied her aunt. Margaret understood desperation and despair, how they could make a woman do things she'd never dreamed, so she hadn't wanted to be vengeful. At the same time, Lavinia wasn't exactly sane, and she'd proven she could be extremely dangerous. Margaret had been terrified at the thought of her being freed.

She supposed she could have aided Lavinia with her legal troubles, or at the least, begged for mercy on Lavinia's behalf, but she hadn't intervened, and she couldn't decide if it had been the appropriate choice or not. Though Lavinia had never been apprised, Margaret had paid to have her lodged in a private cell as she'd awaited trial and deportation.

It wasn't much, but it was something, and she tried not to regret that she hadn't provided more assistance.

Kettering's name sporadically popped up in the gossip columns, and there'd been claims of his being in debtor's prison—which she didn't believe. Penelope was often mentioned as attending house parties and fancy soirees. Apparently, she had become a belle of High Society, but Margaret scarcely noted the stories. She truly didn't wish to know how her cousin was faring.

At the bottom of the stack of mail, she was delighted to see a letter from Mr. Thumberton that contained the report he'd prepared at her request. She couldn't figure out what had spurred her to solicit the information. She'd been strolling in the yard, on a warm evening in May, and the most riveting deluge of loneliness had washed over her as she'd caught herself remembering Jordan Prescott.

It had been the same kind of day precisely a year earlier when she'd initially met him. Though she hated to be maudlin, she vividly recalled every detail of the occasion when he'd wrongly barged into her dressing room at Gray's Manor, thinking her to be the heiress he'd needed.

Images floated through her mind, and for once, she didn't chase them away. She reflected on how handsome he'd been, how strong and confident. He'd seen a passion and hunger in her that no other person had ever observed, and she missed being the woman he'd known.

He'd rejected her because of money, and she couldn't ignore the months of trauma she'd endured after Lavinia had tossed her out. Yet, during that last violent afternoon, when Lavinia had tried to kill her, Jordan had saved her life.

She'd never forget the look in his eye as he'd knelt before her in the clearing smoke of Lavinia's assault. He'd gazed at her as if he'd still cherished her, as if the affection she'd once sensed was still rolling around somewhere inside him.

She'd been distraught and bewildered by the attack, so she'd pushed him away, and afterward, she'd been too proud to contact him and ask him to come back. But where had her pride gotten her?

When she'd been in love with him, she'd felt so alive, brimming with joy and hope, and since she'd left Gray's Manor, everything seemed so tepid and dreary. She yearned for those heady days of lust and ardor, when she'd been so eager to cast caution to the wind.

Did he ever fondly recollect that period? Did he ever miss her?

She studied Mr. Thumberton's blunt account, committing the words to memory: *Lord Romsey has intensified*

his search for a bride . . . due to family history, having no
success . . . residing in London with younger siblings . . .
quite destitute . . .

As she reached the final paragraph, she frowned and
sat up in her chair. Jordan had an appointment with a
sixteen-year-old American whose parents were keen to
buy her a British title. Thumberton described her as
pretty, sweet, and biddable, and with her parents being
foreigners, they hadn't been privy to many of the rumors, so they were more inclined toward Jordan than
others had been.

Margaret struggled to picture Jordan with a fetching,
docile bride, but she couldn't get the vision to gel.
Whenever she dared to ponder, it was always herself
she saw standing next to him. How could an impres-
sionable debutante presume to be his partner? When he
was so virile and exceptional, how could a child be a
viable match for him?

Disturbed by the tidings, she stood and paced, but
she couldn't find any comfort on the terrace. She entered the quiet mansion and glanced toward the grand
staircase that led up to so many empty bedrooms. Jordan had never confided how many half siblings he had,
and she speculated about them. Where were they? Who
were they? How old were they?

She visualized rowdy boys running and shouting
down the corridors, and cute girls twirling through the
parlors in frilly party dresses. Their presence would
create noise and commotion, chaos and bustle.

She walked out to the verandah and penned a note to
Mr. Thumberton, explaining her plan; then she went in
to speak with the housekeeper.

"Would you have a footman deliver this letter right away?" she inquired, handing over the sealed missive. "Then instruct the maids to pack my bags. I'm going to town for a while." For the first time in ages, she smiled. "If I'm very lucky, I'll be bringing someone home with me."

CHAPTER TWENTY-FOUR

I n here, sir."

A courteous butler escorted Jordan into a frilly salon decorated in feminine shades of pink and gold that made him uncomfortable.

"I was told," the butler confided, "that you enjoy a brandy now and again, so I fetched several varieties. Would you like me to pour you one?"

"Yes, thank you."

The casual remark was disconcerting. Who was his hostess, and how did she know that he preferred a brandy in the afternoon?

He didn't suppose he should have a drink, but he was suffering from the worst case of nerves. Mr. Thumberton's note regarding an heiress's sudden request for a meeting had been enigmatic and brief, but too tempting to ignore. Jordan had washed, dressed, and rushed over.

The butler gestured to a table in the corner, where there were numerous decanters of liquor.

"Have you a preference?" he asked.

"Any of them is fine."

The man filled a glass and handed it to him. "May I get you anything else?"

"No."

"Then my mistress bids you make yourself at home. She'll be with you shortly."

He bowed and exited, closing the drawing room doors, and Jordan sat in a chair by the window, sipping his beverage as the silence settled around him.

On a second table, there were trays of cheeses, meats, and pastries—enough to feed an army. He enviously studied the victuals, ashamed to realize that he'd steal some of the food when he left. He had several boys living with him, and they were always hungry, so pride and scandal be damned. He'd take it for his siblings and to hell with what others thought of the deed.

He sighed, reflecting miserably on his low circumstances—he'd been reduced to thievery from a rich stranger!—but his ruminations were too perturbing. He rose and wandered about, snooping at the books on the shelves, the paintings on the walls, trying to form an impression of the affluent owner.

Across the room, a door opened to an inner chamber, and it was slightly ajar. He peeked through the crack, when he noticed that someone was inside. It was a woman, humming to herself and . . . and . . . bathing!

He paused, aware that he should shift away, but something masculine and ferocious kept him locked in place.

Was it the heiress who had summoned him? It had to be, and she had to know he was in the adjoining chamber. Did she want him to see her? Discovery had to be her intent, but why?

He leaned in, and he could make out the large silver tub in which she reclined, naked, her back to him. Her

hair was a rich auburn—very much like Margaret
Gray's had been—and it was piled high on her head, a
few delectable strands tumbling down in an adorable
way that tantalized him.

Without warning, she stood, the water sluicing down
her rump and thighs. She let him look his fill—on purpose, it seemed—then she bent over and grabbed for a
towel that was just out of reach. He was afforded a
shocking and erotic view of her bottom and privates,
and he was jolted with a stab of desire that was so
painful it almost doubled him over.

Clearly, she was displaying her numerous charms,
and there were many. She had broad shoulders, a tiny
waist, curved hips, and long, slender legs. He felt as if
he were at a fair and had stumbled into a strange bazaar
of fleshly delights. She was obviously schooled in the
sexual arts and wanted to demonstrate that she was. To
what end? Was she hunting for some sort of male stud?
Was he to be groomed and trotted out to show what
she'd been able to purchase with all her money?

Very slowly, very deliberately, she glanced around,
and he nearly fainted with astonishment. If the Queen,
herself, had been there, he couldn't have been more
surprised.

"Hello, Jordan," Margaret said.

With no hint of modesty, she turned to face him. Her
fabulous body was fully exhibited, and though it was
wrong to stare, he couldn't stop.

He'd always considered her to be the most beautiful
woman he'd ever known, and nothing had occurred to
change that fact. If anything, she now had an air of ele-
gance and sophistication that made her even more al-
luring.

"Hello, Miss Gray. Or is it still Mrs. Prescott?"

When he'd found her in Cornwall after so much frantic searching, he'd been apprised that she'd adopted the false name, but he'd never learned why she had.

"It's Miss Gray"—she flashed a sly smile—"for now."

"Was it you who sent for me?"

"Yes."

"Why would you?"

"Don't you know?"

"I haven't the vaguest idea."

"Really?"

"No."

Her gaze meandered down his torso, evaluating him in what could only be a carnal fashion, and he was startled by her blatant assessment. When he'd first met her, she'd been a sheltered virgin and spinster. From where had this aggressive, assertive female sprung?

Her lusty confidence fascinated him, but it suggested a passionate history that he couldn't bear to ponder. In those fleeting, forlorn moments when he allowed himself to reminisce, he liked to remember her as the enticing, frank, and lonely woman she'd been, and he never permitted his memories to age or alter her.

Evidently, there were many things about her that were different. He'd seen her once in an entire year, and he hadn't a clue how she'd spent the intervening months. Since they'd last spoken, perhaps she'd had a dozen lovers.

"Would you fetch my towel for me?" she asked. "I can't seem to reach it."

"I don't think I ought." He wrenched his eyes away and forced himself toward the door. "If you'll excuse me . . ."

"Actually, I don't excuse you, and I desperately need that towel."

He whipped around, feeling like an insect trapped under a glass. "I don't understand this, and I can't assist you."

"What's to understand?"

"You're naked."

"Yes, I am."

"Why?"

"Because I'm bathing."

"But you knew I was coming! You knew I'd look in and see you!"

"I admit it." She laughed a sultry laugh. "I'm trying to seduce you, but if you can't tell, I guess I'm doing a lousy job."

She climbed out of the tub, all that wet, slippery skin just a few feet away, and his anatomy responded as he might have expected. Instantly, he was hard as stone.

She approached until they were toe-to-toe. Brazenly, she snuggled herself to him, and she couldn't help but bump into his erection.

Arrogant as sin, she cocked a brow. "Maybe I'm having more success than I realized."

He enjoyed a touch of boldness in a female, but from her, when he recollected her as being so sweet and innocent, it was too much. If she'd suddenly sprouted another head, he couldn't have been more disoriented.

He physically lifted her and set her away so that she wasn't pressed to him.

"What are you doing?" he demanded.

"I told you: I'm trying to seduce you."

"But . . . why?"

It had been so long since a woman had gazed at him

with ardor and affection that he could scarcely recall what he was supposed to do. After his prior transgressions toward her, he'd sworn to improve his conduct, and he'd made good on his vow.

His life was so boring, and so celibate, that he could have joined a monastery and fit right in with the other monks.

"I haven't seen you in ages," she said.

"No, you haven't."

"Have you missed me?"

Every minute of every day, he thought, but he was too proud to confess how wretched he'd been. He was haunted by visions of how he'd stumbled on her in that hovel, so he never let her slither into his consciousness.

He would not remember! He would not pine away over what was never meant to be! A man could drive himself crazy with that type of spurious hunger.

"No, I haven't missed you," he lied. "Not at all. Is that why you brought me here? Is that what you needed to know?"

"May I share a little secret?"

"If you feel you must."

"I've missed *you* every second."

"You couldn't possibly have."

In his quest for her cousin's money, he'd hurt and shamed her, had ruined and forsaken her, and in the end, he didn't even receive the blasted cash. It had all been for naught, another one of the universe's cruel jests. He'd lost her, he'd lost the money, and he'd lost what minimal self-respect he'd harbored.

Though he'd constantly tried to deny it, he was an exact replica of his father, an ass, a cad, an untrustworthy manipulator, and he didn't deserve any continuing fondness from her. He didn't even deserve common civility, and he couldn't fathom why she was offering it.

"From the moment I left Gray's Manor," she claimed, "I kept waiting for you to find me. I was positive you'd come to your senses and track me down."

"In light of the trouble I caused you, it's fairly clear how much *sense* I have, which I'd say is close to none, at all."

"I agree, so I decided I had to take matters into my own hands."

With each word, she was sidling nearer until she was pressed to him, once more. She was determined to torment him with her nudity, and his body reacted violently, his phallus throbbing with need, his heart pounding with excitement. He didn't think he could set her away again.

He'd always lusted after her, and apparently, neither time nor distance had quelled his desire.

She started unbuttoning his trousers, and though he realized it was wrong and he shouldn't participate, the male animal within insisted that there was no reason to stop her.

"Are you mad?" he snapped.

"Perhaps."

"If you keep on, you know what will happen."

"Here's hoping."

The last button fell away, the placard loose, and she slipped her fingers inside, gliding them around his cock and caressing the proof of how easily she could still titillate him.

She smirked. "Quit pretending you haven't missed me."

"What if I have? What of it?"

"You used to be such a randy fellow. What must I do to ignite a fire under you?"

She dropped to her knees and tugged him free, and she licked him over and over, then sucked him into her mouth. He watched her, his conscience at war with his beastly capabilities, and his basc nature won the argument.

He could no more have called a halt than he could have kept the sun from rising.

A year of suppressed rage and disgrace bubbled to the surface, and in a single motion, he lifted her and propelled her back against the wall. Her legs circled his waist as he initiated a stormy kiss, pouring out all of the anger and regret he couldn't speak of aloud.

She joined in the tempestuous embrace, meeting him with equal passion, with equal remorse for what had been forfeit due to his stupid obsession with finding a wealthy bride.

His fixation had cost him Margaret, and since he'd never loved anyone before her, he hadn't grasped how terrible it would be after she had gone. The world without her was lonely and unbearable, and he truly had no idea how he'd carried on.

He needed her as he needed air to breathe, or water to drink, yet as he ripped at his trousers, as he centered himself and plunged into her, he knew she could never be his. Despite how fervently he wished it were otherwise, his bad behavior cursed them both, and they could never move beyond it.

He thrust, again, again, his phallus demanding satiation, but he couldn't do it to her. If he spilled himself, she'd be bound to him, and he wouldn't force her into such an untenable quandary.

Plunging deep, he relished the final sensation; then he pulled away and her feet slid to the floor. He hovered next to her, his face buried at her nape, his respiration ragged, his pulse hammering in his chest, when she did the worst thing of all. She hugged him, cradling him close, her fingers riffling through his hair and stroking up and down his back.

He yearned to stay just there, to stay forever in the comfort of her arms.

"What is it, Jordan?" she quietly inquired.

"I can't do this with you."

He drew away and gazed down at her, for once letting his love shine through, letting her see it without pretense, without masks.

"I have to go." He whirled away, buttoned his trousers, and walked out.

In the fussy salon, he tarried, straightening his clothes and calming his arousal, when she came up behind him. He spun around, relieved to note that she'd covered herself with a robe, that temptation was veiled, though the wrapper did little good. He desired her more than ever.

"Why can't you do this with me?" she queried.

"You should have a husband and a family and . . . and . . ."

"Yes, I should." She smiled. "Don't you know why I summoned you?"

"No."

"You had to have received my invitation from Mr. Thumberton."

"Yes, but he claimed there was an heiress who wanted to discuss marriage."

"There is, you silly man. *I* want to discuss marriage with you."

"With me? Why would you?"

She chuckled. "Sometimes I think you are the thickest creature who ever lived."

"I'm not *thick*; I'm just so confused."

"By what?"

"Why would you ask me here?" He peered around at the ostentatious surroundings, where she now seemed so at ease and he felt so out of place. "Why would you want me?"

"Because I love you."

He snorted in disbelief. "You don't."

"I do, and I'm weary of waiting for you to figure out that we should be together."

"But I abandoned you. I renounced you. My folly nearly got you killed. How could you possibly still care about me?"

"It's simple really." She led him out into the hall, urging him to look around. "Do you see anyone out there?"

"No."

"Well, this is how I pass my days. I wander through these huge houses that I own, wishing I had someone to talk to."

"You imagine that it could be me?"

"I *know* it could be you." She hesitated. "You used to care for me, too. I was sure of it, but maybe I was wrong. Maybe, all these months, I was remembering how I'd wanted it to be, rather than how it was."

"Oh, Margaret . . ."

He went to the window to stare out at the garden. He'd convinced himself that he'd wrecked any chance with her, that he'd made a mistake he could never fix, and he didn't know how to view their relationship any other way.

The moment grew awkward, and finally, she sighed with resignation. "If you don't love me, if you never did, just tell me. I'll never bother you again."

He pictured himself as such a brave man. Why then was it so difficult to verbalize what she needed to hear? He turned to her.

"I do love you." The confession was wrenched from the pit of his soul. "I've always loved you."

"Then what is the matter?" His stubbornness had sparked her temper, and she glared, developing a fine fury. "I'm presenting you with everything you've ever wanted—practically on a silver platter!—yet you're gaping at me as if I'm speaking in a foreign language."

"I have to marry for money!" he scethed, embarrassed at having to remind her.

"And I have so much, more than I could ever want, more than I could ever spend."

"You're offering it to me?"

"Yes! Yes! Must I spell it out for you? Marry me, and it's yours. Please take it! I'm begging you! Rescue me from this prison of silence and solitude. Give me laughter. Give me friendship. Give me a family. I'm tired of being so alone."

"There must be strings attached. What are they?"

"Oh, for pity's sake." She tossed up her hands. "You were prepared to wed Penelope—the most awful, unpleasant person I've ever known—without question or thought. Yet you dicker over details with me? You were set to marry someone you loathed, for her fortune. Why is it so hard for you to consider marrying *me* for love?"

Marrying for love . . .

The phrase hung in the air between them, a tangible concept that dangled, eager to be seized. Did he dare?

The prospect was so outlandish, and so unexpected, that he couldn't quite grasp the ramifications. He'd never believed that love was real. *Love* was the stuff of storybooks, of poetry and fairy tales. Yet he was so tempted to fall headlong into the beguiling, bewildering mire.

Why shouldn't he be happy? Why **shouldn't he** reach out and grab for what he craved? To **love her,** to marry her, to be with her always, would be his secret fantasy come true.

"My siblings would need assistance," he blurted out, the initial inklings of hope stirring in his breast.

"Have **you** any idea of how many empty bedchambers I have?"

"You would welcome them?"

"Of course, I would. We can send out letters immediately, advising them all to pack their bags and come."

"I have so many employees, who've worked for my family for generations. They need salaries and pensions and . . . and . . ."

"Just say the word, and your debts are paid."

He stared out the window again, imagining himself with her, with her each and every second till he drew his last breath.

Still, he was very proud, and arrogance made him foolish, when he couldn't deduce why he would be. He was drowning, and she was throwing him a rope. Why couldn't he simply latch on?

"It's so much more than I deserve," he said. "What must I do to earn it?"

"That's the easy part. Stay with me always, and love me forever."

He gazed at her, the sun shining on her hair, her eyes

ablaze with affection. He'd discarded her once, had told himself he didn't need her, but it had been the worst blunder, and he wouldn't be so imprudent again.

He went over and clasped her hands in his.

"I could do that," he admitted. "I could love you forever."

"You could?"

"Yes."

"Then when do you intend to start? For I must tell you that I've been waiting a very long time, and I'm ready for you to get on with it!"

He laughed, then sobered, and he dropped to his knee. Humbled, happy, he announced, "I love you, Margaret. I've loved you from the first moment I met you, and I never stopped. I've been horrid to you, I've been stupid, I've been an ass—"

"Yes, you have been."

"—and I'm so sorry. I swear I'll spend the rest of my life making it up to you. Will you let me? Will you marry me?"

"Yes, I will."

"As soon as we can arrange it?"

"Yes."

"I can't live another day without you by my side."

She helped him to his feet, and as she nestled herself to him, his entire being relaxed into her. He was finally loved; he was finally home.

"Thank you," he murmured.

"For what?"

"For not letting me walk away."

"It was touch and go there for a minute. I actually thought you might leave. In the future, I shall always act to save you from yourself."

"I'll appreciate it."

She kissed his cheek, the sweet gesture inflaming the passions he'd doused a bit earlier. He bent down and caught her mouth, their lips connecting in a tender embrace that pledged and promised, that vowed and redeemed.

They'd both been so alone, but together, they could build something fine, something permanent.

"I have one last important question," he said.

"What is that?"

"Is there a bed nearby?"

"Yes, there is. It's in excellent condition, with a thick, plush mattress."

"Is it the sort where we could lounge for hours—or even days?"

"Absolutely."

"Then I think you'd best show me where it is."